THE LIBERATION OF JOHN GRUNEBURG

robert h. laudeman

Final edit by Colleen Marie Glennon

America Star Books
Frederick, Maryland

Published by
America Star Books, LLLP
P.O. Box 151
Frederick, MD 21705
www.americastarbooks.pub

First Printing

SOFTCOVER 9781683945314

ACKNOWLEDGEMENTS

The involvement of many made this book possible. From the very beginning I had the kind support of family and friends. Their encouragement made the writing and editing an enjoyable experience, and in the end, drove this book to completion.

I was blessed to have Marcia Salvatore as a friend who was willing to provide my first edit. She was tactful and sincere, when she told me, "Eliminate the first six chapters and start with Chapter Seven." Marcia's suggestions were key: "Develop a new outline before rewriting and when a draft manuscript is complete, find six people to read it, to determine if you indeed have a story. Make sure that it makes sense to your readers."

I followed her advice, and my second blessing occurred when I chose my six "willing critics" who provided both encouragement and the consistent comment, "You have a story but it does not have an ending." Those friends included: Ann Kline, Diane Wargo, Joann and Chuck Holberg, Colleen Glennon, and my sister-in-law Helen Vought. A bonus occurred when they returned my manuscript and included the added benefit of their edits and suggested improvements to the flow of the story.

Colleen, Diane, Joann and Chuck continued to patiently share their talents and expertise, editing the next two revisions. Their combined efforts, time after time, surfaced numerous corrections. Their contributions made my manuscript into a book. Colleen's reminder that "writing is 10% inspiration and 90% perspiration" reinforced the reality that it takes many hours, at least for me, to complete, edit and rewrite a story.

Early conversations with Marcia Salvatore also provided an understanding of the expectations of future readers of my story. I recall that she said they will expect a good story that is written with the best possible use of the English language. My daughter Karen also emphasized that you had to capture the attention of your reader in the first one hundred pages or they may fail to complete the story.

My friend, Colleen Glennon agreed with the opinions of Marcia and Karen, and took on the challenge of assisting me with the completion of my final edit. Colleen encouraged me to eliminate details that did not add to the main theme of my narrative and provided changes that improved and enriched the flow of the story. Her insight, vision, and gentle guidance helped me to shape my choppy manuscript into a readable book. I am truly thankful to be blessed with such a friend.

The first person whom I contacted when I started down the path to creating this story was Judy B. Wolfman. She was also the person whose advice I sought when this manuscript was complete and it was time to research potential publishers. Judy generously shared with me her publishing experiences and provided information on the numerous options that exist for publishing a book. Judy is a wealth of information, always encouraging others, a mentor to all that wish to write their story. I am fortunate to have her guidance.

My wife Barbara, daughters Karen, Jenny and Amy and her husband David Colberg offered assistance, support and fact-checking edits throughout the two years that this story has been in the making. My sincere gratitude and thanks to both family and friends for their kind, unwavering support throughout the writing process. You made it possible! Thank you! Thank you to all for making this book possible!

✴ ✴ ✴ ✴ ✴ ✴

Do not do an immoral thing for moral reasons.
Thomas Hardy (1840-1928)

✴ ✴ ✴ ✴ ✴ ✴

CHAPTER 1

Standing atop a hill overlooking a place of honor for those who have served our country, a young John Gruneburg found himself in front of a large marble tomb. John and his father, visitors to our nation's capital had crossed the Potomac River to witness the changing of the guard at the Tomb of the Unknown Soldier at Arlington National Cemetery. On a pleasant spring evening, John stood motionless as the sentinel commander faced the spectators and asked them to stand in silence as this solemn ceremony began. John had been told that each sentinel was selected from the elite Third United States Infantry Regiment. Known as *The Old Guard*, this is the Army's oldest active-duty infantry unit, serving our nation since 1784.

Watching, John counted as the sentinel marched a precise twenty-one steps and he remembered his father's explanation that this number was chosen because it symbolized the highest military honor, the twenty-one-gun salute. His father had also emphasized the discipline of the sentinels, explaining that their formality and precision continued uninterrupted throughout the night, twenty-four hours a day, three hundred and sixty-five days a year. The sentinel's dedication to guarding the Tomb of the Unknown Soldier represented our deep respect for those that have lost their lives defending our country. Withstanding all conditions: rain, sleet, snow, the cold winter winds, and the heat of the summer sun to honor all who were killed in combat.

At the conclusion of the ceremony, John moved closer to the Tomb and his father asked him to study the three figures on the side of it. As John gazed at the figures his father explained, "The figure on the left represents Peace and she is holding a dove in her left hand, while holding the right hand of the center figure, which represents Victory. The figure on the right represents Valor and he is facing Victory holding a broken sword in his hands. Remember that Valor symbolizes courage and bravery." His father paused, and then said, "Notice that Victory is holding the hand of Peace and she is extending an olive branch towards Valor."

His father now asked John to think about the words inscribed on the opposite side of the Tomb: *Here rests in honored glory an American soldier known but to God.* As John reflected on the words he felt a newfound reverence for this soldier known only to God, and then his father said, "Always remember John that we honor the devotion and sacrifice of the Unknown Soldier, and because of his courage, peace is victorious. We owe our freedom and our way of life to men and women who are willing to dedicate their lives for our country."

Years later John faced a white marble wall that honored another group of Americans. Standing taut as if at attention, and transfixed in thought, he remembered the words of his father as he read the inscription on this wall at the CIA Headquarters in Langley, Virginia: IN HONOR OF THOSE MEMBERS OF THE CENTRAL INTELLIGENCE AGENCY WHO GAVE THEIR LIVES IN THE SERVICE OF THEIR COUNTRY.

Beneath this inscription on the CIA Memorial Wall, stars are carved into the white marble. Each star represents a CIA employee who died performing a mission; many stars represent officers of the Special Activities Division, individuals who put their lives at risk to safeguard the security of our nation and protect American lives.

These men and women, fallen heroes, were members of our most secretive intelligence organization, often working in hostile regions of the world, not wearing a uniform or carrying identification that would associate them with the United States government. If their true identity or mission were exposed the government denied all knowledge of their operation. And if the ultimate price was paid, their death was honored with a star, the highest honor awarded within the CIA organization.

What motivated these individuals to risk so much and sacrifice their lives for their nation? Was it patriotism? Was it national pride? Was it an allegiance to code, a belief in honor, duty and mission, questions that so many Americans face in service to their country? When we think of patriots, we must remember that the beliefs of our forefathers were founded by societies loyal to the Church or a monarch. Loyalty to a nation is a relatively new concept. Nationalism, driven by one of our most fundamental of human motivators, is the need to belong. It started with our American Revolution, rallying the colonists around symbols of our early nation. In contrast to patriotism, which involves the social conditioning of the individual, nationalism involves national identity, the individual becoming attached to one's nation. Is it patriotism or nationalism that motivates an individual to sacrifice one's life for one's country?

In his inaugural address on January 20, 1961, John F. Kennedy said, "And so, my fellow Americans: ask not what your country can do for you – ask what you can do for your country." Do these words ring louder for some Americans? Military personnel affirm that they *will support and defend the Constitution of the United States against all enemies, foreign and domestic*. Members of Congress and all federal employees are bound by this same oath. As citizens we *pledge allegiance to the Flag of the United States of America, and to the Republic for which it stands*. Does this instill patriotism in the American citizenry? What drives men and women to serve their country honorably, working to benefit all Americans, focused on values that demonstrate integrity and honesty, being true to the people they serve?

On January 27, 1838, Abraham Lincoln delivered an Address in Springfield, Illinois titled "The Perpetuation of Our Political Institutions" in which he said, "*Let every American, every lover of liberty, every well wisher to his posterity, swear by the blood of the Revolution, never to violate in the least particular, the laws of the country; and never to tolerate their violation by others.* Was this a call to all Americans to respect the moral fiber of our nation's laws? To remain steadfast to the law as a matter of principle, to pledge to never disobey the law, having the insight that to do so would destroy our very liberty? Are these words that Lincoln so eloquently spoke echoed in the hearts of those that serve our nation without question?

John Gruneburg's innate inner core along with his upbringing implanted in him the heart of a patriot. He was raised and educated in an environment where family, friends, and mentors understood and valued the significance of service to one's country. John served his country surrounded by individuals who respected those who sacrificed their lives for our nation. Lincoln challenged Americans to pledge their lives to protect the laws of this nation and never tolerate their violation by foreign or domestic enemies. John's education at the Naval Academy instilled in him the principles of duty and honor, and prepared him morally to take on the responsibility to defend the United States of America.

John also faced the reality of being bound to disobey any order that violates the Constitution of the United States. When the enemy is known and the boundary between good and evil is obvious, moral judgment is resolved through the chain of command. What happens when the difference between good and evil is blurred, when the distinction between shadow and light is unclear, when the covert assassin is on a mission to kill without knowing the reasoning behind the order? How does one overcome the conscious struggle of knowing right from wrong, the yin and yang that justify how opposing forces are balanced, when following an order to eliminate an individual whose violation to our nation is unclear?

Like most people, life's events impacted John's moral character. September 11, 2001 was a day that sparked a renewal of John's patriotic values, an awakening of his American spirit. Was it the realization that the United States had been attacked?

Did our apparent vulnerability strengthen his resolve to defend his nation? Did the September 11th attacks trigger a major surge in his patriotism and shape his attitude, bringing new meaning to the oath to support and defend our nation?

John Gruneburg faced these questions. As a talented young man who chose a military career rather than an open door to an Ivy League education, John sought the discipline and principles that so well defined a Naval Academy education, drawn to a life of purpose, where dedication to one's country had meaning, where he could answer the call to patriotism.

Recruitment of CIA personnel is challenging, searching for professional qualities that are rare, seeking individuals who will accept the enduring principles that define the CIA's core values: "Nation first, Agency before unit, and Mission before self". John Gruneburg's background and profile presented the CIA with an uncut jewel and all the sought-after characteristics of an operative: intelligence, physical prowess, moral strength, and international exposure. Past performance confirmed the traits that indicated that John would adhere to the highest standards of lawful conduct. And once again, John accepts the call to duty. What motivates him to risk so much? Is it an allegiance to code, a belief in honor and mission, a patriotic fervor?

Strong family relationships set the tone for John Gruneburg's life, and mentors and role models formed and refined his character. John experienced the good fortune of building strong relationships with two particular members of Congress, Senator Sam McDowell and Congressman Joseph Spencer.

Senator McDowell and Congressman Spencer strived to perform their duties honorably, doing their best to protect our country, understanding the sacrifices of those asked to accomplish difficult and dangerous missions. Is it their position in Congress that drives their dedication to duty and motivates their support for those who sacrifice so much for our nation? What motivates a member of Congress to rise and defend the efforts of those engaged in covert operations and to champion those who perform the difficult and dangerous missions; thus, reinforcing their belief in honor and mission, bolstering the spirits of nameless members of our most secretive intelligence organizations, confirming an allegiance to code, a belief in honor, duty, and mission?

Our congressional duo relied on their close relationship with the National Security Agency's George Harthmann to keep them informed about new developments in intelligence gathering techniques and concerns over heightened cyber security threats. Trust was the key to George's relationship with Senator McDowell and Congressman Spencer and his trustworthiness proved to be invaluable when their need for confidential information was entwined with national security issues. They could count on George to hold fast to the highest standards of lawful conduct, committed to the protection of the nation from foreign or domestic enemies.

And so this story begins. Relations built on honor and duty play out in one of life's dramas where an exceptional navy officer who was trained to manage risk, never to shy away from it, is compelled by duty to stay focused on the operation from the moment the mission begins until his last dying breath. What happens when his dedication to country has compromised his moral judgment? What happens when deception and dishonest officials lead him to a tangled encounter with the Agency to which he is assigned? Does he lose himself completely or can he find his way homeward?

CHAPTER 2

Located on the west bank of the Chesapeake Bay, renowned for its history as well as being the hub of Maryland politics, Annapolis is a blend of tradition and innovation. Its roots go deep to the dawn of America, a Puritan settlement founded in 1649, named Annapolis in 1694 in honor of the future Queen of England, Princess Anne of Denmark and Norway, and the temporary capital of the United States in 1783. Today it is the proud capital of Maryland.

On a hill above the harbor is the Maryland State House. It has the distinction of being the oldest state capital still in continuous legislative use and the only state house to have served as our nation's capital. The original state house was built in 1695 and the current structure was started in 1772. It is a distinct two story Georgian style brick building topped by the largest wooden dome in the United States constructed without nails. The dome is topped by a lightning rod that was constructed and grounded to the specifications provided by Benjamin Franklin.

Completed in 1779, the present Maryland State House has been home to numerous historic events. In 1781, the Maryland governor signed the document that empowered the Maryland delegates to Congress to ratify the Articles of Confederation with all thirteen states initiating the final act to form the United States of America. The present State House was also the home of the Continental Congress from November 1783 to August 1784 and it was there that George Washington resigned his commission as Commander of the Continental Army and the Treaty of Paris was ratified, ending the American War of Independence. Today, the State House is home to the Maryland General Assembly for three months each year and the offices of Governor and Lieutenant Governor.

Located twenty-six miles south of Baltimore and twenty-nine miles east of the District of Columbia, Annapolis was at the center of commerce, politics and American society from the early 1700's through the American War of Independence. By 1780, the center of society was transitioning to its neighbor to the north. Baltimore had a much deeper harbor and skilled shipbuilders that constructed the infamous Baltimore clippers, and it was also home to our Continental Navy.

In 1845, the Secretary of the Navy was looking for the future home of the newly established Naval School. Annapolis was chosen as a fitting location that was away from the temptations of a large city, and by 1850, the Naval School transitioned to the United States Naval Academy.

Today's Annapolis is more like a small town than a metropolitan city. Holding onto its history, staying politically savvy, with the breezes of the Chesapeake sustaining its title as the sailing capital of the world, and of course, home to a Naval Academy that is often synonymous with Annapolis. Weekends find tourists filling narrow streets, giving a feel of a vacation destination rather than a state capital. These tourists are history buffs, lovers of the arts and crab cakes, those drawn to fresh air and Chesapeake vistas, and visitors to the Naval Academy. It was this tourist environment that an sixteen-year-old John Gruneburg was introduced to on his first visit to Annapolis.

Growing up in New York City's Upper East Side, John Gruneburg's early life was filled with the attentiveness of two highly educated parents. They provided opportunities for travel, learning languages, and to be tutored in subjects beyond his young years. Early childhood was far from ordinary, spending summers in France and Germany was the norm. Strasbourg was a second home for the Gruneburg family and what is today the University of Strasbourg was the hub for his parent's summer activities. As visiting professors, the majority of their time was spent in the classroom or leading research projects in international law, politics or diplomacy.

Located in the Alsace region of eastern France and close to the German border, Strasbourg's residents were as fluent in German as their native French. Bridging language, culture and religion, the city's universities presented an environment of learning that promoted respect for all people. During these years, John's constant companion was an au pair from the Alsace region and her language skills reinforced his fluency in French, German, Dutch and English. Responsible for John's care during the day and most evenings, au pair Gwendolyn was a trusted member of the Gruneburg family, living with them in France and New York City. In French, au pair equates to equality, or in short, another member of the family. John's parents treated au pair Gwendolyn as his older sister. She had her own room, ate meals with the family, and vacationed with the family whereever their travels took them. She was entrusted with more than John's care, she educated and nurtured him, every waking moment of his young life. In return, the Gruneburgs created a fund to meet her educational aspirations and provided her with an opportunity to experience numerous cultures and practice foreign languages. John did not find his early ability to speak, read and write in multiple languages to be unique, it was what his family did.

New York City presented a much different lifestyle than Strasbourg for the Gruneburg family. Columbia University's School of International Affairs and the European Legal Studies Center provided a world stage for the Gruneburg's study of international law. While in the city, Columbia was their focus, and their circle of friends revolved around the university. As long as John could remember, those friends included Shuk Wa Lau and her daughter Wenli. Shuk Wa was a professor in the Department of East Asian Languages and Cultures at Columbia and both a professional and trusted family friend.

Family photographs documented a childhood filled with sports - swimming as a toddler, then gymnastics, tennis, skiing on winter holidays, and golf in settings that looked more like a formal garden than a golf course. Every sport was learned properly, as his father dictated, with lessons and wearing the correct clothing. Nothing was left to chance; trial and error was not an option. John remembered Saturday mornings when everyone gathered for the short walk to the clay courts in Central Park. Clay tennis courts required special tennis shoes in addition to a proper tennis outfit. John's father would ask if he had his tennis kit which included so much more than a racquet and balls. Every sport had a unique uniform, and lessons also included learning the game's etiquette. Even when running in Central Park, there were never wild romps through the Meadows, jogging required running shoes and proper dress. Discipline, rules, and patience were part of every sport; good behavior and proper dress were just as important as your level of play.

Sundays were special. They participated in Mass at Saint Ignatius of Loyola Church and were always joined by Shuk Wa and Wenli. Attending church and celebrating holidays together, these were gatherings that left lasting memories with a young John Gruneburg. Church also required proper dress and their parish community confirmed the affluence of the city's Upper East Side. Jesuit priests greeted parishioners after Mass and Sunday regulars spent time exchanging greetings. Wenli and John were students at Saint Ignatius Elementary School and often received comments about their excellent efforts with their studies. John's father always emphasized humility and taught John to thank the priest for his kind words.

After church they descended to the Lower East Side to enjoy dim sum and fresh seafood at their favorite Chinatown restaurants. Seeking out notably smaller family run businesses that served better food than the larger dim sum establishments, they knew where to find Hong Kong style dim sum as well as special fish dishes. Fish that were swimming in restaurant seafood tanks minutes before being steamed in a spicy ginger sauce were presented by the restaurant staff with applause from their happy group. One of their favorites was the Nom Wah Tea Parlor. In business since 1920, they presented the finest Cantonese style dim sum and the friendly welcoming management were friends of Shuk Wa whom they treated with the utmost respect.

New York City is home to one of the largest and oldest ethnic Chinese societies outside of Asia with most speaking Cantonese and Mandarin. The influx of Cantonese speakers from Hong Kong and the Pearl River Delta cities of the Guangdong province dominated Manhattan's Chinese population and the Cantonese dialect was spoken in most dim sum restaurants.

Shuk Wa's conversations with Chinese speaking restaurant staff intrigued John and his curiosity grew even more intense when Shuk Wa included Wenli in discussions when ordering specialty dishes. Shuk Wa explained that the Chinese characters on the menu had the same meaning regardless if a person was speaking Cantonese or Mandarin, and yet when saying the word, the two Chinese dialects sounded very different.

Sunday afternoons were spent in the Gruneburg's living room surrounded by a sea of newspapers and exchanges of opinions on current events. Wenli and John enjoyed this time. They would point to a word in the newspaper and say it in a language other than English. John favored French and German and Wenli relied mostly on French, but tried her best to introduce John to Cantonese and Mandarin. Their game was often reinforced by the adults, who commented in French, or if John remembered a word in Cantonese or Mandarin, congratulating him in the Chinese dialect he was learning.

The transition to elementary school presented change in many ways. Au pair Gwendolyn went off to the university and Wenli and John met a new circle of friends. The biggest change came with an announcement on a Saturday afternoon in the middle of the Christmas holidays. John would soon be privileged to have a baby brother or sister. The whole idea seemed redundant to John, he already had Wenli and au pair Gwendolyn.

Classroom commitments in Strasbourg would require John's father to be in France when John's mother was giving birth to his brother or sister in New York City. So the following summer, John and his father went off to France accompanied by au pair Gwendolyn with the mission of bringing back a new au pair who would care for the newest member of the Gruneburg family. On the fourteenth of July, while celebrating the La Fête Nationale or French National Day, John's father received a phone call and announced to John that he now had a Bastille Day baby sister, baby Aimée Marie.

Returning to New York in late summer opened a new chapter in John's early life. Change surrounded him. The dominant language of their new au pair Sophia was German, using French as her backup, with English being her language of last resort. This frustrated John's mother, leading to occasional outbursts, "Please speak French and English with my baby. I specifically asked for another French speaking au pair. Why do I hear so many German conversations?"

Although change was occurring in the Gruneburg household, one steady constant remained, John's relationship with Shuk Wa and Wenli. In fact, this relationship was growing even stronger. Wenli and John enjoyed au pair Sophia and introduced her to their New York City neighborhood. They embraced her use of the German language and quickly learned words and phrases, expanding their language skills in a playful yet very effective way. They welcomed her youthfulness and joined her on walks with baby Aimée Marie, or as au pair Sophia would say, Kleine Prinzessin, German for Little Princess. John adopted to the role of big brother without hesitation and baby Aimée Marie was accepted as the new center of attention by the Gruneburg family.

Final acceptance of the new au pair was expressed when it was time to celebrate Sophia's birthday. The family ventured north on Second Avenue, just above 85th Street, to the Yorkville neighborhood and the Heidelberg Restaurant. Established in 1936, it was considered by many to be Manhattan's best German Restaurant. John's mother planned an exceptional evening for Sophia with an abundance of German food, giving Sophia the opportunity to announce each dish in German and explain what they were about to eat. Dinner starters included Gulash Suppe, with tender pieces of beef, carrots, and potatoes in a spicy paprika broth, followed by Gurkensalat, sliced cucumbers marinated with onions, garlic and parsley in a vinaigrette. Dinner continued with Käse Spätzle, roasted pasta with melted Swiss Emmenthaler cheese and Kartoffelpuffer or potato pancakes. Eating freshly made Kartoffelpuffer with applesauce was Sophia's favorite. The entrees included Wiener Schnitzel served with boiled potatoes and potato dumplings, and a plate of sausages including Bratwurst, Knackwurst, Bauernwurst, Weisswurst and Blutwurst. The birthday cake was another of Sophia's favorites - Schwarzwaelder Kirschtorte or Black Forest cherry cake with layers of chocolate and brandied cherries smothered in whipped cream. To take home and enjoy, they boxed an Apfel Strudel, flaky pastry dough filled with apples and walnuts seasoned with cinnamon and sugar. Sophia was amazed at the celebration and a serving of German culture was firmly implanted within the Gruneburg family.

John's level of knowledge went beyond his early age in that he experienced learning in a real world environment, not only exposing him to information, but also exposing him to experience. Thus, he retained what he had learned. He understood how language, math and science interacted to form a culture, which was reflected in his family's lifestyle.

John's first memory of being academically different from his peers occurred when he was in fourth grade and invited to his first sleepover at a classmate's house. The occasion was to celebrate his friend's birthday with other boys from their small Catholic grade school. The morning after the party found everyone gathered around the television with his friend's dad. John left the group and wandered into the kitchen where his friend's mom was grading exam papers. As a high school math teacher, she often came home with exams to grade. Without asking, John watched as she took a paper from the pile and proceeded to correct work that was incorrect. When it was time for the next paper, John explained that problems four, seven, and nine did not have correct answers. His friend's mother laughed as she lifted the paper from the pile. Glancing at the paper and then at John she asked how did he know the answers were not correct. John looked at the next paper and said, "This person also got numbers four and nine wrong. Should I correct the answers?" Handed a red pencil, John quickly corrected the math with the right answers. Just then his friend's dad entered the kitchen, saying it was time for breakfast. The mother looked at the dad and said, "This little guy just helped me correct Friday's algebra test". Holding up the papers, "This is tenth grade math!"

John's school years were filled with strong family ties, and the family's bond with Shuk Wa and Wenli grew stronger with each passing year. Traveling with his family was always special. John experienced cultures, new foods, languages. He was always learning. John's life was his classroom. When it was time to start talking about college John had a lot of options. His parents expected him to follow in their footsteps and prepare for a life in academia. Columbia would be an ideal place to start, but his parents openly discussed Harvard and Yale. Wenli seriously contemplated applying at Stanford, but the lure of the east coast prevailed and she set her sights on Harvard because of its Boston location. For John, deciding on the United States Naval Academy was not determined by some process of elimination or ranking based on specific criteria. It was his first choice, his only choice.

John told his parents about his interest in the Naval Academy during his sophomore year in high school and at his request the family planned a spring visit to Annapolis. John's sister was an active seven-year-old and Shuk Wa volunteered to stay with her for the weekend.

Springtime was perfect in Annapolis. The flowers and buds bloomed, the bay was dotted with sails and boaters, and tourists filled the shops and restaurants, which left a favorable impression on the entire Gruneburg family.

The tour of the Naval Academy was professionally done, all questions were answered, and as visitors they felt respect, if not admiration for the discipline and dedication they witnessed by the midshipmen. Still, John's parents raised many questions. Was it too regimented? Was John truly interested in a military career? Did weapons interest him? Why?

Weeks later, everyone agreed that participating in the Summer Seminar at the United States Naval Academy was the best next step for John and the family. Shuk Wa and Wenli observed this ongoing debate from the sidelines, carefully avoiding judgment. In private, Wenli and John had numerous discussions and Wenli was always a good listener and asked questions that challenged John to think deeply about his decision. Wenli enjoyed ending their discussions by saying, "May you have fair winds and following seas," to ease tensions between her and John on what had become a touchy subject for his family. While reading about the Naval Academy, Wenli discovered this nautical blessing whose meaning intrigued her. Fair winds referred to a safe journey, and following seas meant that the waves or current will be moving in the direction that you will be going. This nautical phrase seemed appropriate as John was to depart on this new voyage in life.

Finally, John's father reluctantly agreed to contact the office of their New York senator to discuss the nomination process and his son's interest in the Naval Academy. To his father's surprise, the senator answered his questions with enthusiasm and invited the family to visit his office in Washington.

The following month, John and his parents were sitting in the office of Senator Sam McDowell listening to a passionate testimony on the virtues of a Naval Academy education. Photos covering the walls revealed an international network of relationships with business and government officials, and the senator was proudly crediting his success to graduating from the United States Naval Academy.

Years of experience in the senate provided the senator with the ability to relate to the Gruneburg's work at Columbia University's School of International Affairs and the European Legal Studies Center. His knowledge and comments strengthened the credibility of Naval Academy graduates, reinforcing John's parents' growing respect for a Naval Academy education.

Soon his parents were off with staff members on a tour of the Capitol and John was standing in front of what the senator referred to as his Wall of Honor - past nominees of the senator who went on to graduate from the Naval Academy and continued their distinguished careers in government service. Senator McDowell encouraged John to pursue his dream and vowed to support his nomination to be appointed to the Naval Academy.

John submitted a strong Preliminary Application. He had superb Scholastic Assessment Test scores, passed the medical examination with flying colors, interviewed well at the Candidate Guidance Office, and had a solid official interview with New York's Blue and Gold Officer. Topping it all was the news that Senator McDowell designated John as his principal nominee for an appointment to the United States Naval Academy. John's enthusiasm sky rocketed as he awaited notification from the Admissions Board.

Finally, a letter arrived and John was designated as an official candidate for admission and received an invitation to attend the Summer Seminar at the end of his junior year. June arrived and Annapolis was hot and humid. John was greeted at the Naval Academy by a group of upper-class midshipmen who promised to challenge him physically and mentally throughout the week-long event.

John immediately understood the benefits of an education at the Naval Academy. The all too common juvenile behavior that frequented other educational settings was absent, replaced by a desire for achievement and camaraderie. Experiencing the challenges of the Naval Academy Summer Seminar was enough to convince John that the academy offered him growth academically and professionally. The seminar's six-day experience immersed John into a diverse gathering of high school students who were willing to be challenged physically and intellectually. The academy presented an environment to learn and apply oneself at an exceptional level that John appreciated and wanted.

Months went by, summer faded to fall, the application process was complete and still the discussion continued. Finally, in late October of John's senior year, a letter arrived. It was a Letter of Assurance, an Offer of Appointment to the United States Naval Academy. John's parents saw the joy, the pride of being selected early, the knowledge that he wanted to be part of this special breed of high achievers. It was a path different from the one they had chosen. It was his chosen path and they respected his decision and took pride in knowing that their son had met his first career goal with being accepted to the Naval Academy.

Now it was time to prepare for what the family was told would be a very challenging summer for John. Acknowledging that life at the Naval Academy would stretch John both physically and mentally. Testing his ability to function at his full potential with only six hours of sleep each night. John organized a routine that would prepare him for the schedule that he would experience during Plebe Summer. Everyone got involved. The excitement grew as June arrived and then it was time for John to leave his privileged life in New York City to travel 215 miles south to Annapolis, Maryland.

When someone tells you that you will not have a free moment or be allowed an independent thought for the duration of the Plebe Summer, you hear it, and you imagine what it will be like. Then you experience it. During the admissions process, John remembered that the Blue and Gold Officer emphasized that the Naval Academy would not choose anyone who was not up to the challenge. John recalled his words, "Recognize that attending the academy is a team effort, which means offering help when possible and seeking help when needed. Stay focused on what is required, and accept that you are doing it because you want to is of the utmost importance. You have to go out every day and prove that you want to be there."

For six weeks the only link to the outside world was John's daily stop at his mailbox and the thirty minutes of free time to write to friends and family. Days were a blur and post cards and letters were appreciated beyond imagination. His mailbox was never empty and his family's support and encouragement were a life line. Wenli always added humor to her daily notes that were written in French, German, or with Chinese characters, challenging John to respond using the same.

Finally, it was August and there was talk of Parents Weekend. Was this the end of this six-week experience? Had he made it? It was a warm, sunny Thursday and the noon formation was greeted by a larger than normal and very enthusiastic crowd. The temptation was to look into the crowd and search for familiar faces, but discipline prevailed and all eyes were focused forward. Each day the plebes marched from Tecumseh Court into Bancroft Hall, marching in precision formation toward King Hall where all midshipmen ate simultaneously three times per day. Today was different, as they entered Bancroft Hall, as the cheering faded into the distance, John's immediate thought was that in twenty-four hours his family would be waiting with open arms.

Friday morning arrived with a warm sun and clear blue sky and the clock slowly moved toward twelve and time for noon formation. At exactly 12:15 p.m. the plebes were dismissed by company and were directed to lettered signs in alphabetical order along Stribling Walk, the brick walkway leading to Tecumseh Court and Bancroft Hall. Rushing to the "G" sign and meeting his family was an exhilarating experience for John. He was a midshipman. Hugs were followed by photos, followed by more hugs. John's only thought was to head for the nearest gate as they moved toward Bancroft Hall. As he looked across a field of smiling faces, John stopped and asked, "Are you planning to eat lunch here?"

His mother held up tickets and said, "We all have tickets to dine with you in King Hall."

Wenli quickly added, "We understand that you can provide a tour of Bancroft Hall and show us your room." For his family, the highlight was visiting his room, seeing his cramped quarters, everyone carefully holding comments as they met with his company officers. As the group left Bancroft Hall and headed toward the gate, John reminded everyone that he must be back in his room by 10:00 p.m. that night.

Saturday morning found John's family in Tecumseh Court proudly observing the Morning Colors Ceremony, watching the flag being raised to the sounds of the Naval Academy Band. When it was time for morning formation, John's family knew exactly where to look for him. They watched with pride as the plebes marched in a formal parade to Worden Field. At the conclusion of the parade, the plebes were dismissed from Bancroft Hall and were on Liberty until midnight.

On Sunday, John's Liberty began at eight and the family participated in Mass at the Naval Academy Chapel. The family enjoyed Annapolis and John's mother cherished attending Mass at the chapel, making it a must with every future visit to the Naval Academy. John's Liberty ended at six with evening formation at Tecumseh Court, thus ending a Parent's Weekend filled with pride.

So began John Gruneburg's life at the United States Naval Academy. He liked the regimentation, the structure. Uniforms had always been a part of John's life, regardless if attending school or participating in athletics, there was proper dress that went with every occasion. Naval protocol for dress and uniforms was one area that made John feel comfortable. The Naval Academy's tightly structured program pushed John well beyond what he perceived to be his limits, and at the same time offered opportunities to hone individual interests to a level beyond his expectations. He was often reminded of an Einstein quote, "Once you accept your limits, you go beyond them."

Language skills, foreign travel, and lifelong family dinner conversations that centered on international politics influenced John's decision to select Political Science as his major. Demonstrating French and German fluency validated John's language skills and by testing out of advanced level courses qualified John to declare a Minor in Foreign Languages and to study Russian and Mandarin Chinese for all four years at the academy. Language skills and participating in the Political Science Honors Program also gave John an edge and influenced his selection to participate in the annual United States Naval Academy Foreign Affairs Conference.

Each year, the Naval Academy hosted the largest undergraduate foreign affairs conference in the United States. The mission of the conference was to provide a forum for students from civilian and military colleges to explore current international concerns. The conference theme was chosen by the Naval Academy and conference activities were supported by a select group of midshipmen.

Regardless of how many courses John tested out of, the sheer number of course offerings and the diverse selection kept even the best prepared midshipman in a stretch mode. When you stretched your abilities to achieve a goal, the reward was met with even loftier goals that always exceeded your expectations. There was an activity for every waking moment and it was the midshipman's main task to make every moment count. John enjoyed the pace, the structure, a schedule that presented an organized plan from 5:30 a.m. to 11:00 p.m. and the physical demands of the day left one's body so exhausted that the midnight taps were seldom heard.

The key benefit to being a Political Science major was the connection to Congress and other governmental offices. Members of Congress provided a unique opportunity to study public policies by coming into the classroom as guest lecturers and discussing political processes in a small group setting. Close relationships were established with specific members of Congress through internships and summer study programs. John was fortunate to have built an early relationship with Senator Sam McDowell and as the senator's principal nominee for an appointment to the United States Naval Academy, the senator was always proud to guide John through the halls of the Capitol building. The significance of being a Naval Academy graduate and the importance it played with the senator's career was always emphasized.

Then, a unique opportunity occurred that called John to demonstrate his level of French fluency. The chairman of the Armed Services Committee had arranged for transportation and military escorts through the Navy's Senate Liaison Office for committee members who were participating in a meeting in London with the Defense Committee of the House of Commons. At the last minute a second leg was added to the trip, which was a meeting with France's Chief of Naval Staff and the Executive Officer of the École Navale, the French Naval Academy in northwestern France. They needed a Navy officer with perfect French to make a presentation at the French Naval Academy and to act as a liaison while in France.

The last minute request left the armed forces liaison offices on Capitol Hill scrambling for someone who had that level of French fluency. Senator McDowell had seen John in action at the Naval Academy presenting in French to a group from the North Atlantic Treaty Organization. So, with little warning, John was on his way to the extreme western edge of Brittany France, to a sheltered bay in the city of Brest, the largest French military port on the Atlantic. The young midshipman charmed the French and the following summer John had the opportunity to intern in Senator McDowell's Senate office. Senator McDowell was proud to add John's photo to his Wall of Honor. John was honored to be added to that wall, and almost burst with pride when an additional photo was added of John and the senator at the École Navale.

As a legislative liaison and senate intern, John built a relationship with members of the Senate Select Committee on Intelligence. He also had the opportunity to work with the House Intelligence Committee and became friends with members of that committee. One young congressman, by the name of Joseph Spencer, enjoyed lecturing assignments at the Naval Academy and playing an occasional round of golf with the midshipmen. As a political science major and member of the golf team, John had the benefit of building a relationship with Congressman Spencer in both the classroom and on the Naval Academy Golf Course. It intrigued John to see the congressman use his influence to move nice weather meetings at the Pentagon to the Army Navy Country Club and the challenges of their Arlington golf course. It was impressive to see the congressman negotiate his way through a sensitive agenda item while playing a double dogleg par five hole, and coming out victorious on both ends.

Participation in sports was mandatory at the Naval Academy. While many midshipmen took on the honor and pressure of competing in team sports where the Navy fan base endlessly cheered for victory, John participated with the less celebrated varsity level cross country running, golf, swimming, and tennis teams. For many midshipmen, the late afternoon two-hour athletic session was a continuation of a demanding day. John found solace in this 4:00 to 6:00 time slot, providing a welcomed break, a period of trance-like meditation, regardless if he was running, swimming, or walking a golf course. John's upbringing taught him to enjoy sports in a respectful, dignified way that garnered all the satisfaction of competing without needing to be in the spotlight.

Congressman Spencer was also a jogger, golfer and tennis player and John became the congressman's enthusiastic partner whenever John was on Capitol Hill. John's Naval Academy experience went beyond the opportunity for a first rate education. It provided the means to build life-long friendships and professional achievement that opened many doors to a successful life. The hectic pace resulted in four years rapidly speeding by at the academy. Almost mechanically, John transitioned from plebe summer to a naval officer, accepting challenging assignments and increasing his desire to serve his country.

CHAPTER 3

Dr. Wenli Lau sat at her desk and looked out the window. Her mind kept slipping away to thoughts of John Gruneberg. John, her old and dearest friend was meeting her for lunch today. He would be here in a few hours and they planned to eat at the faculty dining room.

Wenli achieved remarkable success at Harvard and because of the school's advanced placement policy she tested out of many first and second level courses. She earned her bachelor's degree in three years and chose to stay at Harvard and complete an advanced degree.

Academia fulfilled Wenli's career aspirations. The academic world and university life were her niche and following in her mother's footsteps, Asian Studies seemed to come naturally. Wenli experienced no questions, no heart-wrenching decisions. Educational goals were achieved without fanfare.

For John, four years at the Naval Academy seemed to fly by quickly. Graduation set the stage for John's transition from midshipmen to ensign. As a Naval Academy graduate he was indebted to the Navy for a minimum of five years of military service. By accepting challenging assignments and demonstrating a knack for competent performance John quickly advanced to lieutenant. He adapted well to a straightforward Navy life and as a midshipman he became accustomed to the austere quarters of Bancroft Hall or the cramped space onboard ship during summer exercises. What mattered to John were the opportunities for growth and change.

After graduation John was assigned to the Navy's Office of Legislative Affairs. He was familiar with Capitol Hill and the Pentagon and was comfortable supporting and hosting congressional visits to Navy bases and naval air stations. At first, John's responsibilities included developing relationships between representatives of the Department of Navy and members of the United States Congress and their committee staffs. Months passed and John became more involved with preparing comments on legislation and responses to congressional correspondence. John approached his duties with confidence, secure in his ability to build rapport with members of Congress and senior officers.

Wenli and John stayed as close as the 430-mile separation would allow. They made their friendship a priority in their lives and carved out time to be together as often as they could. Travel to Boston by John or to Metro Washington by Wenli made for special occasions that fostered their friendship.

On this particular day, John was in Boston for a meeting at the Department of Naval Science at the Massachusetts Institute of Technology. A break in his schedule gave him the afternoon to catch up with Wenli. He was excited to see her in her element, which was why he suggested meeting her at her office and dining in the faculty dining room. Every time he thought of Wenli and her remarkable success at Harvard, he was filled with pride. She accomplished so much in such a short time.

John reached the Harvard campus and made his way to Wenli's office building. He told the receptionist that he had an appointment with Ms. Lau. After a brief phone conversation, the receptionist asked John to follow her. "Dr. Lau will see you now," she said.

John followed the receptionist down a long hall. Wenli's office door was open and as they approached her office, John caught a glimpse of her deep in thought before she lifted her head, smiled at them, and greeted John with a warm hello and quick hug. Instinctively, he smiled and hugged her back. He looked around. Wenli's office was full of museum quality furnishings; the far wall had a large window that overlooked a well maintained garden. Once again, John was filled with pride over Wenli's accomplishments.

Life at Harvard was different than on Capitol Hill, where Naval Liaison Officers were crammed into a small office in the basement of the Capitol building. Wenli's office impressed John, but he knew at this point in his career that he wanted more than an office. He wanted challenges, to do things that were important to his country, assignments that impacted national security. In John's mind, the intelligence community offered the challenges that he yearned for.

For years, John and Wenli had a running conversation. It didn't matter how long it had been since their previous meeting: they always picked up right where they had left off. Before it started, Wenli knew where this conversation was going— John's career aspirations. They had discussed them so many times over the past few years that Wenli braced herself once again as John expressed his yearning for a more challenging assignment.

John equated a challenging assignment with an assignment with the intelligence community. His fascination with the intelligence community frustrated Wenli. She did not understand it and saw the potential dangers such an assignment would involve. John, however, continued to justify his need for the challenges that the intelligence community offered him, neglecting to consider any of her concerns about intelligence work.

Over lunch, they talked and talked. Ever so patiently, Wenli tried to reason with John about his career path. She recalled his days at the academy when they had endless conversations about his future. Wenli, like his parents, envisioned John working in a world filled with global diplomatic challenges and opportunities. John, though, had gained a different perspective of a world filled with global threats. His parents and Wenli, for that matter, were comfortable knowing that he was assigned to the safety of a Washington office. But for John, this felt like entrapment and failure on some level. He wanted a more active role in dealing with global threats. He agreed that diplomacy was important, but tried to rationalize that conflicts were not always resolved through diplomatic channels.

Wenli continued to try and direct John's perspective on the importance of diplomacy in conflict resolution. In her mind, a life of diplomacy was a great calling and necessary in this fractured world, where the rush to action and judgement was too often impulsive and destructive.

Wenli advised John that his parents lived in a secure world filled with opportunities. They were prosperous and successful, but not wealthy. Their positions opened many doors and their circle of friends had similar beliefs. They were all academic achievers. Knowledge, research, writing in academic journals, publishing one's findings—these were their drivers. It was a rewarding, privileged life filled with travel and learning. Wenli told John that his parents always thought that he would follow in their footsteps.

John listened, but once again he tried to justify his need for a different kind of life. He acknowledged that his concept of service to his country was different than his parents. He reiterated to Wenli that his four years at the Naval Academy gave him another point of view. He was surrounded by competent midshipmen, colleagues who were dedicated to making a difference for their country. Ordinary was never acceptable. Everyone was in stretch mode, everyone was a high achiever, no one was out for individual gain, and the atmosphere was always one of a team effort striving to achieve a higher goal. To John, this defined a life of purpose. He wanted a career that continued to present these types of meaningful challenges. Wenli realized that John was seriously leaning towards a new path in his career. It was a path she had a hard time understanding, for she, like his parents and her mother, had chosen a path of scholarship and research.

Wenli tactfully told John that he had resolved his need for change before. This was not new. She stressed her position from previous discussions, that challenging assignments did not have to be dangerous.

Wenli tried to change the subject and brought up John's graduation. They talked about how graduation at the Naval Academy was more than a ceremony, it was an event. Phenomenal speakers, an abundance of pride, moments that produced tears and then cheers - it was an electrifying celebration. Wenli reminded John, that by graduation his parents had learned to accept his career choice and they shared his joy and felt his pride. She recalled that tears poured from his parent's eyes as they continuously smiled and Shuk Wa proclaimed that they were experiencing tears of joy. They all recognized John's personal and professional growth. Wenli remembered that she laughed and asked, "How could a young naval officer in a white uniform not be admired?" They were all in agreement that John's four years at the Naval Academy created bonds that would last throughout his lifetime. For his family there was no title that could have generated more pride; John was now an officer in the United States Navy.

She talked about their visits to the academy, how John's family always attended the 9:00 a.m. mass in the Naval Academy Chapel whenever they were in Annapolis on a Sunday. How they often roamed through the chapel after Mass, admiring the architecture and stained glass windows, studying the sculpture, enjoying the serenity under the dome that so dominates the Naval Academy skyline. Wenli reminded John of the time they made their way down to the John Paul Jones crypt below the chapel. John identified John Paul Jones as the Father of the United States Navy and credited him with the establishment of the Navy with his decisive naval victories. Leading the maritime forces of our young nation in the War of Independence.

Wenli recalled how they enjoyed debating the merits of his quotes. John argued that John Paul Jones set the standard for the United States Navy's principles of duty and honor.

Through his service, he demonstrated what it meant to defend the Constitution of the United States and the tradition of heroism was rooted in his quotes. Wenli questioned his desire for diplomacy and marveled at his willingness to sacrifice his life for his country with the quote: "An honorable Peace is and always was my first wish! I can take no delight in the effusion of human Blood; but, if this War should continue, I wish to have the most active part in it." She would ask what motivated such an individual. His quotes: "I wish to have no connection with any ship that does not sail fast, for I intend to go in harm's way" and "I have not yet begun to fight!" implied to Wenli an aggressiveness where John interpreted a willingness to defend our nation. John emphasized his spirit of readiness, to be on guard against aggression with his quotes: "If fear is cultivated it will become stronger, if faith is cultivated it will achieve mastery," and "Whoever can surprise well must conquer."

Wenli reminded John that his parents embraced the rule of law, the belief that laws should govern a nation. The principle of the rule of law is that all people, every member of society, is accountable under the law; therefore, citizens, individuals, lawmakers, government officials and military leaders, must all be constrained by the same law and live by the same code. John's parents wanted him to believe what they believed; namely, that the rule of law should drive conflict resolution. Wenli tried to reason with John, continuing to emphasize that there are challenges in resolving conflict through diplomacy. John continued to listen and expressed his appreciation for Wenli's willingness to always respect his point of view, even when it clashed with her opinion.

John explained to Wenli that when he was with her and Shuk Wa he was surrounded by academic achievers. Like his parents, they lived in an academic world, sanitized, without conflict, where credentials, status, and positions were knowledge driven. He treasured holidays and vacations with them, where he could escape to their island of serenity, a civilized world focused on social and humanitarian challenges, where conflicts always seemed to be resolved best through international law. John emphasized that his career choice presented a different set of drivers.

Wenli recalled John's early days at the Naval Academy. Reflecting back to his Plebe Summer and John's first introduction to the academy, and how his family was apprehensive about how he would adjust to a military life. It turned out that John's successes seemed to be a contradiction to what they expected.

She reasoned that growing up in a family that practiced and taught patience and self-discipline, John was a stranger to violent or aggressive behavior. Blessed with a natural muscular physique and a six-foot two-inch height, he was never bullied or intimidated by other students during his elementary or high school years. He treated everyone with respect and was often identified as having innate leadership skills and was comfortable taking the lead in school activities.

Wenli expressed to John that he was a person whom everyone could like, and they did. He was fortunate to be at ease when making friends and establishing relationships. He could work with anyone. He benefitted from an upbringing that placed a value on people. She proudly told him that she admired how he greeted the sanitation worker picking up trash in Central Park with the same energy as the president that presided over the governance of the park. She was filled with pride knowing that he had learned that it was important to respect everyone he encountered.

Wenli reasoned with John that his family members were not hunters and they did not own guns or weapons. She joked that knife skills were limited to learning how to julienne vegetables. Growing up, John never had toy guns or toy soldiers, never built model ships or had interest in firearms or weaponry. It was perplexing to his family that John was not only drawn to the regiment of the Naval Academy, but he excelled at weapons training and hand-to-hand combat skills. His parents saw him as a diplomat, not a warrior. And yet during Plebe Summer he surpassed most plebes on the firing range and qualified for a marksmanship ribbon when being certified in rifle proficiency using the M-16A3 assault rifle. As remarkable as that was, his family was amazed when he completed training for the Navy's standard issue sidearm and he also qualified for a marksmanship ribbon when certified in pistol proficiency using the Beretta M9 nine millimeter pistol.

She talked about high school. How John had excelled in gymnastics, running, swimming and individual sports like tennis and golf. He was competitive, but never encountered the physical punishment of sports like football or wrestling. He was unfamiliar with the pushing and shoving of contact sports like soccer and basketball. And yet, he surpassed most of his fellow plebes who were more aggressive when completing the Marine Corps martial arts training. John's coordination and ability to rapidly learn self-defense moves, where his dexterity and agility provided a natural skillfulness, allowed him to excel at self-defense. Wenli tried her best to explain that his military career choice was not what she, or his family expected, but they were learning, trying to understand what motivated him.

Wenli told John that she would always be there to listen, to provide a haven for John to discuss his future. John agreed that Wenli was the one person to whom he could talk without fear of critical remarks or negative feedback. They agreed that when future dreams and aspirations were the subject of conversation, they were both comfortable sharing their deepest feelings with each other.

Wenli reminded John about the time when he was approaching his last year at the Naval Academy and he had to indicate a preference as to where he would like to serve as a commissioned officer in the Navy. He had told her that he needed to request a first and second choice assignment.

Wenli was already working on her Doctorate degree, but as usual, freely offered her opinion. John had openly voiced his envy of friends who were destined to be Naval Aviators. Wenli scoffed at such desires and reinforced his first choice to pursue a national security research project in the Political Science Honors Program. She explained to John that she was so proud that they were in agreement that he should concentrate his studies on Asia and Eastern Europe, taking advantage of his foreign language expertise. Wenli asked, "Do you remember how you enjoyed telling me that my mother had already provided you with great insight into Asian culture? How you teased me, saying that you already had a keen understanding of the Asian mind? Knowing that I preferred using a purse holder to attach my purse to a table, saying that I thought if I placed my purse on the floor all my wealth would seep to oblivion." Wenli laughed and continued, "I chided you for joking about my culture, but I was filled with happiness because I knew you were serious about concentrating in part on Asian studies."

Wenli told John that when he finally got serious and stopped joking, he expressed a desire to study the subtle behaviors that influence a nation's national security decisions and how nations respond to perceived threats. You told me that your goal was to get inside the head of an adversary, knowing how they would react based on past decisions, understanding trends; knowing what they would do before they did it. Wenli reminded John, you smiled and said, "That's when you are right on, and you know you have figured them out."

John said he remembered when the day finally arrived and the Naval Academy's Superintendent handed each first-class midshipman a letter containing the information that defined their future assignment in the Navy. He agreed with Wenli that he was elated when he was granted his first choice and that the follow up meetings with the Department of Career Information and Officer Accessions in the Division of Professional Development assured him that he had made the right choice. Wenli reminded John that he was excited to learn that arrangements were confirmed that he would interface with intelligence organizations and work on national security issues with congressional committees as a legislative liaison.

John explained that his interest in the Central Intelligence Agency intensified when he had the opportunity to meet the CIA's Deputy Director. Recruited right out of college, it impressed John that the Deputy Director had dedicated his entire career to the agency.

John continued to espouse the virtues of the CIA and Wenli questioned the merits of his appraisal. Explanations did little to discourage her questioning. She raised numerous red flags when John explained that the CIA's mission was mainly to collect and analyze information, and only in rare occasions conduct covert operations. Words like clandestine and covert nurtured a fear of illegal activity with Wenli. John explained that the CIA only produced the plan and all covert action needed the approval of the President. The National Security staff provided the leadership and Senior White House Officials conducted a policy review and a legal review of every proposed mission. John explained that it was impressive to see how deeply CIA officials cared about protecting our nation, facing national security and intelligence issues on a daily basis, always pursuing the goal of keeping our country safe. Each judgment call was critical, knowing that their decisions saved American lives. John found the CIA to be a sophisticated, analytical organization, with incredibly dedicated people. Willing to make the supreme sacrifice when placed in harm's way, confident about gathering and analyzing information, understanding the importance of staying true to the facts. John told Wenli that these were the qualities that he admired and that he began to see himself being part of that organization one day.

Wenli made one final effort to voice her concerns. She reminded John that while he was at the academy, their discussions often ended with John justifying his preference for a Naval Academy education and Wenli questioning the need for him to take courses in the Weapons and Systems Engineering Department. To Wenli, the study of naval weapon systems, with a department's faculty comprised mainly of military professors selected from naval officers with doctorate degrees was a cookie cutter approach to creating more warriors and no diplomats. John's insistence that you needed to understand a country's military capabilities to negotiate peace from a position of strength did not convince Wenli otherwise. She would argue that training to develop and refine combat tactics and techniques, thus replicating an adversary's military capacity to wage war, was doing more than simulating a threat. Large scale military exercises could provoke an adversary to also engage in potential combat scenarios. What happens when perceived threats lead to aggressive action by an adversary? Where does it end?

Wenli challenged John with her questions, asking, "Do you entrust the safety and welfare of a nation to young men and women who believe that there is a correlation to being a warrior and being a patriot? Does building character rely on a willingness to take on difficult and dangerous assignments, or can a patriot step forward in a time of crisis to use diplomacy to resolve conflict?"

John countered Wenli's line of reasoning by reminding her that naval officers are bound to the highest personal and professional standards of duty, service, and honor. He explained how they hold fast to values that are instilled at the Naval Academy, unyielding dedication to their country and a desire and willingness to serve.

Wenli and John knew that they could always reach consensus when discussing the promotion of leadership at the Naval Academy. They both felt that our nation needed to be thankful for naval officers who will stand in defense of our country. Wenli admired John's passion for what the academy had taught him. Taking on the responsibility to lead while sharing with others the responsibility to make things happen, crediting others for their successes. With this realization, they looked at each other with understanding and relief.

They agreed that the afternoon's discussion had set a new record. John looked at his watch and then at Wenli. Immediately the thought came to mind that their time together was so enjoyable, they connected so well, and too soon this day would end and he would be back to Washington. They laughed as they agreed that they had both come a long way from their romps in Central Park. John expressed to Wenli that he especially appreciated her insight into his yearnings for a more challenging career. She knew he must go. She hugged him and bravely smiled at him as she once again said, "May you have fair winds and following seas." As John walked away he felt a feeling of strong gratitude that Wenli had remained his closest of friends.

Wenli watched John as he walked out the door. She stood still, deep in thought. John's fascination with the CIA alarmed her. Her intuition left her unsettled. She knew John well enough to know that he was going to pursue an assignment that was not in her comfort zone. She felt he was moving away from her and all he knew.

Looking heavenward, she softly whispered, "May you have fair winds and following seas, my dearest John." Then she slowly turned around and walked back to her office and the work that sustained her.

CHAPTER 4

As a legislative liaison John worked with members of the House Intelligence Committee and the Senate Select Committee on Intelligence. Meetings at the Pentagon and CIA enabled John to expand his network with members of the intelligence community and his assignments grew more secretive. Missions with Defense Intelligence Agency case officers relied on John for more than linguistic support. John's aptitude for analyzing foreign political and economic intelligence was his strength and his involvement with sensitive missions became more frequent. The emphasis was always on national security intelligence, often referred to as human source intelligence, utilizing assets funded under the umbrella of the United States Intelligence Community.

Time spent on Capitol Hill also familiarized John with the desire of Congress for improved information sharing within the intelligence community. The September 11th attacks resulted in Congress demanding to increase the capabilities of intelligence gathering organizations. The consensus was to expand the intelligence community's ability to conduct clandestine as well as covert operations around the world.

Clandestine operations required the operative to work in secret, collecting information, concealing sources, performing intelligence gathering in a stealthy, classified manner. The lack of qualified linguists at the Defense Intelligence Agency created the opportunity for John to become more involved with these sensitive missions, especially where the operation required advanced foreign language skills and the expertise to translate classified documents. Planting and servicing intelligence-gathering equipment became one of John's specialties. These missions required placing high-tech devices in embassies, infiltrating adversarial governments, and clandestine operations in locations controlled by our perceived enemies.

While participating in a planning meeting at the CIA, John was introduced to the head of a Special Operations Group that was responsible for covert operations in countries that supported factions who were hostile to the United States government. Members of this organization had secret identities and did not wear uniforms. The word spy was never used; they were operatives, selected from the special operations forces within the United States military, and they needed John's language skills.

John's fluency with French and German proved to be an asset and his political science major had allowed him to study Russian for all four years at the academy. John was very comfortable traveling through Eastern Europe and the former Eastern Bloc countries that bordered Russia, where the Russian language and culture were well rooted and still evident when dealing with government officials.

Covert operations presented an entirely different lifestyle for John. Clandestine operations dealt with concealment of the operation, while covert operations emphasized concealing the identity of the sponsoring organization. Covert action focused on influencing political or economic conditions in countries whose governments maintained an adversarial relationship with the United States government. These operations were conducted by the CIA and only authorized personnel knew of their existence. CIA personnel financially managed these operations through secret funds, leaving no trail or connection to the intelligence community or the United States government.

Covert operations seemed to be the opportunity that John was yearning for, challenging assignments that supported national security. Each mission was a unique experience. His identification did not show a rank or title, and he did not carry documentation that would associate him with the Navy or the United States government. He was on his own. Talents that were honed for years were put to the test; analytical skills combined with his ability to schmooze and build relationships in multi-national business communities proved to be very valuable. He gathered classified information and reported directly to the Joint Intelligence Center at the Pentagon. There were no written records and no reports.

John understood that he had to maintain a position of secrecy as he became more involved in classified business operations, and he proved to be effective at gathering needed intelligence. His work was rewarded by his assignment to the Office of Naval Intelligence, collaborating with an elite group in the Defense Intelligence Agency. Advancing within the agency, John was selected to join a team who were noted for their intellect, cultural knowledge, and multilingual capabilities. He was transitioning from intelligence gathering and analysis to a position where intelligence activities needed to be integrated to provide consistent support for national security operations.

When asked, John identified himself as a government liaison and his work at the Office of Naval Intelligence was never discussed with his family, friends or Navy colleagues. Get-togethers with Wenli were complex, she was not aware of his new role in the intelligence community, and yet her command of current events and world news gave John the impression that she knew exactly what he was doing. The simple mention of a city or country would stimulate an exchange that always led to questions and inquiries by Wenli. Never being one to easily give up, Wenli's questioning forced John to refrain from mentioning anything that could be remotely tied to one of his missions. He refused to lie to Wenli and he yearned for the days when their discussions were candid and unguarded.

Because of the sensitivity surrounding Defense Intelligence Agency operations, it was essential for all DIA personnel to maintain a Top Secret Clearance. At times classified information was derived from vulnerable intelligence sources whose identities were protected for fear of exposing their connection to an operation. These men and women lived a dangerous existence and the exchange of secret information always put their lives at risk. Because of the danger of revealing their identity, information connected with these sources could only be accessed through a formal control system called Special Access Programs. This Sensitive Compartmented Information was highly protected and accessed following strict Defense Intelligence Agency protocol. DIA personnel requiring access to Sensitive Compartmented Information had to undergo a Single Scope Background Investigation which included psychological testing, drug screening, security interviews, and passing the Defense Intelligence Agency's polygraph examination.

Whereas the DIA generally required a Counterintelligence Scope polygraph examination, John's situation was unique in that his assignments included operations with the Central Intelligence Agency, Defense Intelligence Agency, as well as the Office of Naval Intelligence. This situation required John to complete routine security vetting. Failing to pass any polygraph exam essentially guaranteed that an operative would be judged unsuitable for employment in the intelligence community.

For many, these screenings seemed intrusive, especially when one's personal life was brought into question, but not for John, whose record was without question. He always expressed a willingness to go beyond the norm to protect national security. Whether collaborating with a team or functioning as an individual operative, John's strength was his ability to adapt to the needs of the intelligence community.

It was the beginning of a new year and John received orders for his new assignment. He was to report to Camp Peary on the outskirts of Williamsburg, Virginia for advanced training. Assignments to the Armed Forces Experimental Training Activity, or "The Farm" as his contacts in the Department of Defense would say, was generally reserved for the one year basic operations course for new CIA recruits. This assignment was going to be different. Flights into Camp Peary were always through a private carrier and passengers were never identified. It was analogous to falling into a black hole. Upon arrival, he learned that members of his team included officers from the CIA's and DIA's Defense Clandestine Services. Their goal was crystal clear—develop interagency partnerships to ensure the protection of our national security.

Their training bordered on the extreme; real life scenarios blended the world of diplomacy, international business, and global university networks into an intelligence gathering whirlpool. It was difficult to tell when a training exercise began and when it ended. Downtime was nonexistent. Every operative was taught evasive driving tactics, handling vehicles under severe conditions, rapidly changing the direction of a car at high speed, crashing through blockade barriers, executing precision stopping maneuvers, even hotwiring a car, whatever was necessary to keep vehicles under control and to be prepared for the most brutal of real world environments.

CIA counter-intelligence measures were also emphasized. Designed to protect against intelligence activities by foreign adversaries, they included biographical directories that cataloged foreign citizens, disclosing background information on business or university contacts that cooperated with CIA operatives. Specialized training designed to prepare CIA personnel on the nuances of recruiting foreign agents who had access to, and were willing to provide, relevant intelligence information was an area of expertise also developed at Camp Perry.

Training sessions were intense. Sensitive issues were discussed in non-threatening team environments where the most guarded operatives often listened more than contributed to the conversations. Never knowing if it was a training exercise or planning a future mission, every encounter reinforced the CIA maxim to trust no one and nothing is what it seems. Personal welfare was never discussed. You approached each mission with the belief that duty, honor, courage, and commitment would guide one's actions.

Movies and television embellished the work of the CIA and the use of covert operations in hostile regions of the world. In real life the CIA operative did utilize any appropriate means to collect the needed intelligence, but missions were often in austere conditions, facing perilous situations in hostile foreign environments. It was a hazardous life, always living under a veil of secrecy. Hollywood made it look like a glamorous life, but in reality it was a disciplined, regimented, and an often dangerous existence.

Covert operations require a blending of the most elite special operations personnel with clandestine intelligence operatives, working together to conduct the most secretive of missions performed by the United States government. Missions that deploy operatives to high threat hostile countries. These operations call for the involvement of the CIA's Special Activities Division. Reporting to the CIA's National Clandestine Service, the Special Activities Division conducts operations claimed by no organization and deemed essential to our national security. Operatives are secretly deployed with limited support, and if they are exposed during the mission, the United States will deny knowledge of their operation. Their missions, eliminating subversive threats and eradicating terrorists are always supported and praised by Congress, but the actions to achieve the required results are often sensitive if not controversial. The most secretive of covert operations involve the infiltration of foreign governments, often buying confidential information contained in secret documents, or contracting sources to conduct military espionage. Extreme cases include sabotage and leading foreign forces whose goal is to overthrow a government that is antagonistic toward the United States. These operations are conducted knowing that disclosure of an operative or foreign agent would lead to brutal reprisals by the infiltrated foreign government. Operatives that serve with the Special Activities Division leverage their military, language, and technical skills to carry out extremely complex missions to defend against the most dangerous of threats to our national security.

John was proving to be a valuable asset. His security clearance was never questioned. He always passed the required psychometric, psychoanalytical, and polygraph examinations without incident. He was known as a stickler for following all covert operation protocols. His reputation was built on a history of mastering intelligence gathering techniques, and combined with his exceptional linguistic skills, made him an ideal candidate to be chosen for covert operations. With little fanfare, Johm became involved with the most secretive of national security missions.

Weeks flowed into months and in a flash it was late spring, and the Gruneburgs were having a party to celebrate the beautiful weather that New York City was experiencing. John and Wenli agreed to plan for a long weekend back home and arranged to play tennis at the clay courts in Central Park. Wenli was playing in a recreation league in Boston and John found that her level of play gave him an unexpected challenge. After the first set they sat overlooking the courts and their conversation turned from tennis to summer family vacation plans. Suddenly, Wenli told John that she understood that he could not talk about his work, his present assignments, and he need not be uncomfortable. She was aware that there were confidential assignments that he could not discuss. She just wanted him to know that she was not going to interrogate him about his work, but she did want to discuss how they could enjoy their time together when he was not on assignment.

She laughed, "I am interested in what you are doing, but I will stop asking my usual one hundred questions, so I want you to feel relaxed when we're together." John sat in silence, and then Wenli laughed again and asked if he was ready to play another set of tennis.

While playing through the second set, John thought about what Wenli had said. She had been gracious with her comments. His thoughts went back and forth with every volley. He knew he had to reply to her comments. She did not ask for a response, but he knew in his heart that he needed to grasp this opportunity and respond to her remarks. As the set ended, John walked toward Wenli and said, "You played really well. I enjoyed the competition. I may not be as lucky next time."

Wenli smiled, gave John a soft punch on his arm, and said nothing as she followed him back to their perch on the hill overlooking the tennis courts. For a few moments they sat in silence as John struggled, thinking how to best start the conversation. He looked directly into Wenli's face and as he made eye contact, she showed a slight smile, slightly lowered her head, then smiling broadly, she finally said, "I know there is something that you want to say. You were quiet throughout the entire last set."

John laughed and said, "You are always one step ahead of me. How did…"

Wenli interrupted, giving John another punch on his arm, saying, "I may not be one step ahead of you on the tennis court, but I know you, John."

John smiled and said, "I miss our candid discussions. Sharing our successes as well as our challenges. You are a brilliant woman, Wenli. Your understanding of world events…," John hesitated, and then continued, "you're so good at connecting the dots."

Wenli interrupted again, saying, "I told you that I will stop asking my usual one hundred questions. I understand." With that, John grew quiet, and Wenli immediately sensed that he was uncertain on how to proceed, and she said, "Don't stop now John, I'm enjoying this moment tremendously."

John grew serious, and said, "Our time together is very important to me and I definitely want to be included in your vacation plans. Do you understand, Wenli?"

Wenli smiled, and said, "I understand John, and I appreciate what you said today."

Before parting, Wenli hugged John tightly and looked into his eyes as she said, "May you have fair winds and following seas." John smiled at her broadly. He fully met her gaze and was filled with peace.

As they were leaving New York, John and Wenli agreed that they had solidified more than their summer vacation plans over this long weekend.

Months went by, and then John was told there was a need to support the findings of the Base Realignment and Closure Commission to consolidate military intelligence and clandestine operations within the mission of the Central Intelligence Agency. John was assigned to the Naval Postgraduate School in Monterey, California to work in the Operations Research Department to analyze world wide security challenges. John was to report to an old friend from the Naval Academy, Admiral Michael J. Lee. At the Academy, John spent most Wednesday evenings with the Chinese Culture Club whose purpose was to study the language, traditions, customs, culture and most of all, Chinese dietary pleasures. At the time, Admiral Lee was in charge of the Chinese Culture Club and John enjoyed his weekly dialogue with the group, practicing his Mandarin language skills.

Admiral Lee headed John's unit at the Joint Intelligence Center at the Pentagon and hand-picked John to lead a team assigned to utilize top-secret technology and mathematical modeling to simulate a number of Asian defense and intelligence scenarios. These simulations built on John's research at the Naval Academy where he studied the behaviors that influence a nation's national security decisions. This involved utilizing computer driven simulations to predict how a nation responds to perceived threats, calculating how they will react based on past decisions, understanding trends, predicting what they will do before they do it. This was an assignment that John had dreamed of for years.

Admiral Lee had established a close relationship with John and they enjoyed practicing both Mandarin and Cantonese dialects, often spending hours conversing in Chinese and studying Chinese military documents. One of John's favorite ploys was to call Wenli after he had spent days conversing in Chinese. He would initiate their conversation in Mandarin and refuse to switch to English. Enjoying the moment, he flaunted his ability to converse in Mandarin with the person who taught him his first words in Chinese. Wenli also enjoyed assisting John when he was uncertain of a translation, proud to share her expertise in understanding the subtle nuances that are found with regional dialects.

John had found his niche. The intelligence community offered the challenges that he was searching for when he left the academy. He knew that his work was important to his country and he accepted with pride all assignments that impacted national security.

CHAPTER 5

Time passed quickly at the Naval Postgraduate School and the pleasant climate and beauty of Monterey added a feeling of privilege to those who were assigned to the Operations Research Department. The work was challenging, but that made every success that much more rewarding. Admiral Lee respected John's contributions to his team and was proud to have him under his command. The admiral's closeness was especially beneficial when he received heartbreaking news about John's family and it was his responsibility to convey the sad news to John. As John's commanding officer, Admiral Lee was informed of the tragic death of John's mother, father, and sister in a car accident in New Hampshire. For John, this was incomprehensible news. It was inconceivable, beyond belief, that his family could have died so tragically. He was the one, they believed, who lived a dangerous life.

The next few days were a blur. Feelings of disbelief and sadness engulfed John. Grief overwhelmed him and the emptiness of the Gruneburg residence drained him emotionally. Comfort and consolation were found with Shuk Wa and Wenli, all others added to the numbness. John's sorrow was understood and the family's attorney, who was a close friend of John's mother and father, stepped in and dealt with the will, insurance, and the transfer of bank accounts, stocks, and property. John's family and Shuk Wa had engaged the same law firm and financial planner, so the question of trust was never an issue. John received endless offers of support from family friends. Colleagues and staff from Columbia University and hundreds of people offering their condolences said they were there for John, but he could not understand how they could ease his pain. The Funeral Mass at Saint Ignatius of Loyola Church left John exhausted and the following days found him sitting in the church in silence. Going to his parent's home was too difficult, being in the house alone intensified his emptiness. Shuk Wa's kindness was endless and she invited him to stay in her guest bedroom.

Reminiscing about time spent together comforted John. Including Shuk Wa and Wenli as part of the Gruneburg's extended family was the root of so many happy occasions; his parents valued their friendship as their greatest gift. There were so many memories. Sharing meals together, walking in Central Park and through their neighborhood, vacationing where they hiked and enjoyed the beauty of nature, understanding and being engulfed in cultures. Life was so good, so full of experiences that were treasured when they were all together. Wenli recalled John's last visit to New York, just a few months back, listening to John's father planning a trekking holiday to France and Spain, a family pilgrimage to Santiago de Compostela in northwestern Spain. Wenli remembered the happiness of the moment. Planning to hike the Way of Saint James was one of his father's dreams and he wanted to do it with his extended family, the next time John was on leave.

Shuk Wa and Wenli sat with John for hours, sometimes in silence, other times in sorrow, remembering the joy and happiness that John's mother, father, and sister brought to their lives. Shuk Wa and Wenli vowed that they would be there for John to create new memories. John listened and told them how much he appreciated their kindness, but openly explained his feelings of sadness and told them he was emotionally exhausted. Wenli listened as John only expressed a need for change and to serve his country. There were moments when John seemed to understand that Wenli wanted more, but then he would once again be overwhelmed with grief, and he would say that discussing their future plans would have to wait for another day.

John resumed his normal routine. Weeks turned to months and it was time for John to consider a new assignment. A decision was made not to sell the Gruneburg residence. The law firm would arrange a rental agreement and Shuk Wa would move personal items into storage.

John discussed his options with Admiral Lee and expressed a need for change, a new assignment that had challenges and strong implications of doing what was important for his country.

Admiral Lee spent hours listening to John and reluctantly told him about a recent request to identify staff for a new operation. This was a project that had to fall under the authority of a special branch of the CIA, a project that the Department of Defense did not have the authority to conduct. It would involve a total cloak of secrecy, maintaining a position where the United States would deny involvement in the operation. It would involve operations that were political in nature. There would not be any connection to the United States government; John would be on his own when carrying out these missions, knowing that the United States government would disavow any knowledge of the operation.

If interested, Naval Intelligence would create an alias and his assumed name would have no connection to the Navy, the United States government, or his personal life. He would no longer be John Gruneburg for the length of this assignment. Admiral Lee stressed the complexity of such an operation. Was John ready? He could possibly be facing a very dangerous existence, putting his life at risk, living with potential danger every moment of his life. Was he ready? His identity would be protected, sealed as Sensitive Compartmented Information, accessed only following strict Defense Intelligence Agency protocol through Special Access Programs.

John questioned the possibility of his identity being compromised. He already had a history supporting CIA operations. Wouldn't he be recognized? Admiral Lee reminded John that he was always assigned to the Office of Naval Intelligence and his personnel file would not have been available to other intelligence organizations. "Remember, when you work at Naval Intelligence, not many people know of your existence. Working on classified projects, always maintaining that realm of secrecy, you were successful and no one knew who you were or what you were doing." Admiral Lee assured him, "Don't worry John. Your records will be safely protected at the headquarters of the Office of Naval Intelligence at the National Maritime Intelligence Center in Suitland, Maryland."

A meeting was arranged and John traveled to Berlin to meet with the CIA officer who would offer him this position. John heard all the right words: loyalty, dedication, service. The message was what John wanted to hear; he would be making a difference and he would be saving American lives. John searched for details about the operation and received only vague responses. He would live in a so called safe house wherever a mission was needed. Financial resources and false identity would be provided. The structure of the overall operation would always be ambiguous. John was told that he would be the pointed end of the stick and have the authority to eliminate foreign terrorists. John thought deeply about what was being said. This was more than infiltrating an enemy's government, way beyond espionage to collect secret information. This was talk of assassinations and targeted killings to eliminate potential enemy combatants.

Assets, operatives, a focus on threats, it was a language that left no ties to humanity, leaving no clues to the identity of those who would be targeted. How would he communicate? He would receive information by accessing a specific safe deposit box and the contents would clarify the nature of each mission. Entry to the safe deposit box would always be controlled through the use of a retinal scan and iris recognition data. The location of each safe deposit box would be encoded in a business document; they would use an encrypted message with an eight-digit safe deposit box number that only he could access. The eight-digit number would also indicate the bank's location. The system was full proof.

John was emotionally vulnerable and Admiral Lee knew it and questioned if he was searching for an opportunity to help his country or escaping a painful time in his life. John said that he needed the change and the admiral respected his decision. John would secretly remain under Admiral Lee's command through his ties with the Defense Intelligence Agency. The branch of the CIA that John would be assigned to would not have any knowledge of who John really was.

John accepted the assignment and his training was more like imprisonment than instruction. He was subjected to days without sleep, long sessions under hypnosis, traumatized about what he was told was his past. Whenever doubt emerged, he was told that he volunteered for this mission, he came to them, and he wanted to save American lives. Was he a liar? He endured months of behavioral modification, experiencing water boarding, isolation, and endless days of being badgered about his dedication to the operation. In time, he became who they wanted him to be, following their orders, respecting what he perceived to be the chain of command, and in the end he lost all conscious memory of John Gruneburg. He was manipulated into silence, believing that it was his duty to do so.

He was often moved, always in a closed van, on private flights where he wore a hood during his entrance and exit to the plane. Even hearing protection was used to block out audio information that could reveal his location. Training was often in sterile environments with plain gray walls, no windows, no signage to indicate where he was. He was isolated.

Then, he was told that his training had come to an end. Was he ready to complete a mission, to follow the chain of command?

His early missions required him to stay off the grid, using his creativeness to improvise and make tactical decisions. His instincts carried him through each mission. He was highly trained in CIA protocols and his code of behavior was trumped by a shroud of top-secret orders. He was trained to be a malleable asset, but below the surface a conflict of good versus evil haunted him. He followed orders, carried out missions, and then suffered from nightmares, reliving in his dreams the horror of taking another person's life. Each mission triggered psychological pain and emotional stress. Flashbacks created anxiety and his nights became increasingly restless. He recalled violent experiences in his dreams that he could not erase. Then, he realized the reality of the situation. If he were captured or killed, no one would know whom he was. When he was alone he felt anxious and realized for the first time in his life that he was emotionally drained.

Working with members of the intelligence community lifted John's self-esteem, and gave him validation. He was making a difference. This assignment, however, was different. As his CIA assignments became more secretive, John had to distance himself from Wenli. Though their friendship remained close, the intimate sharing of their deepest concerns and aspirations was gone. He missed those days of talking openly with her. Now, he talked with no one. He was now socially isolated. Out of touch with Wenli, Shuk Wa, even his connections with the Navy were gone. There were days when every moment, every day-to-day task seemed to be scrutinized. He carried out each covert operation without leaving a clue that could be traced back to him, and yet he felt that he was under constant surveillance, as though someone was always watching to ensure that he completed each mission under a veil of secrecy. He could trust no one and that was the way it was meant to be. He maintained his silence knowing that the slightest crack in cover could lead to disaster and he was uncertain of the consequences if that should occur. Before the emphasis was always on national security intelligence. Now he was told that he was making a difference, he was saving American lives. When John tried to connect the dots to justify his actions, his dedication to duty was challenged. He was starting to doubt his decision to become involved in covert operations, but when he voiced his concerns, he was reminded that he volunteered for this mission; he came to them. He wanted to save American lives. It cut him to the core when they asked if he was a liar, always telling him: remember, you volunteered, you wanted to make a difference. So he squelched his doubts, soldiered on, and remained dedicated to the CIA.

When John reported to the CIA's Special Operations Group in Berlin, Naval Intelligence had already created his alias and the name in his file identified him as John Wolf. It was to stay that way for the length of this assignment. The name John Wolf and his falsified records had no connection to the Navy, the United States government, or his personal life. His identity had changed; he was no longer John Gruneburg.

Adding to John's confusion, the officer in charge of the CIA training operation informed him that he would now use the alias John Volkov, which was Russian for wolf. Throughout his training, he was repeatedly told that he was John Volkov, he was no longer John Wolf, and for the majority of missions John used French and British passports with the name John Volkov. He also used other passports with a simple translation of his first name - Hans Volkov for his German passport, Jan Volkov for Polish documents, Jonas Volkov for Lithuania, and Ivan Volkov for his Russian and Ukrainian travel documents. John was told that the Special Operations Group would use the code name Operation Azov for his missions. It was becoming emotionally trying to remember who he really was. Mentally, he no longer identified with the name John Gruneburg. He had lost all memories of Shuk Wa and Wenli.

For the length of Operation Azov, John Gruneburg's real identity was protected under the Navy's Special Access Programs, ensuring that his identity and all information connected with his name could only be accessed through this formal control system. Access to this Sensitive Compartmented

Information could only be granted by receiving permission directly from Admiral Michael J. Lee. All of John's personal information including his name, social security number, date and place of birth, mother's maiden name, medical, educational, financial, and employment records, driver's license, passports, and civilian and military photo ID's would be secured under the Special Access Programs. Paychecks would still be issued by the Department of the Navy to John Gruneburg, deposited into an account using direct deposit information that was provided by John before reporting to Berlin.

John Gruneburg's biometric records were transferred to his new alias John Wolf. This elaborate swap of forensic records included fingerprints, dental records, DNA profile, retinal scan, and iris recognition data. All of John Gruneburg's forensic information would now be tied to John Wolf and no one would be able to obtain these biometric records and trace them to John Gruneburg without direct permission from Admiral Michael J. Lee.

Operation Azov was targeting wealthy Russian businessmen who were funding opposition to the Kremlin's continued campaign to retain control of the oil and natural gas industries. These billionaire investors were organizing Russian entrepreneurs with business interests and sizeable investments in the energy sector to work toward the privatization of the industry. John was aware that Kremlin friendly oil magnates were in favor of government control of the industry. It did not make sense to target the entrepreneurs. What was the threat to America?

The CIA had been gathering intelligence on the Russian oil industry for decades. Details regarding investments by American and European financiers were of particular interest, especially when the investors were dealing with what were perceived to be state-owned monopolies. Dependence on Russia's large reserves of oil and natural gas as a key driver of the European economy also troubled those who were not supportive of the government's leadership. Exports of oil and natural gas were reaching record levels on global markets resulting in a robust expansion of the Russian economy. The need for international investment opened doors for CIA operatives to infiltrate major industry sectors and Russia's aging infrastructure allowed for projects that built strong relationships with major American companies. Because the Russian government was actively promoting its energy sector, looking for large investments in what was in many ways an underdeveloped industry, wealthy investors interested in expanding the country's production and refining capabilities were greeted with open arms by Russian entrepreneurs. State owned companies welcomed venture capitalists as shareholders. Corruption was rumored to be especially strong in government controlled oil and gas industries that were finding expanding markets in the West.

It was winter and the howling winds along the Black Sea made for a cold evening. John's next mission sent him to the city of Sevastopol where the major base of the Ukrainian Navy is located. Improvements of coastal infrastructure along the Black Sea between Ukraine and Russia were becoming contentious because any threat, real or imagined, to the Russian Navy's strategic bases riled the Moscow government. This area was home to the Black Sea Fleet and recent Russian naval activity was driven by newly developed harbors used to ship oil and natural gas through the Black Sea to European ports along the Mediterranean.

This evening's plan was to scout the premises of the hotel where John's target was attending a series of business meetings hosted by the Russian government to attract energy sector investments. Arriving at the hotel, John intended to survey the area and get acquainted with the hotel's general vicinity. Then, the unimaginable happened. John's plan was compromised when pro-Russian separatists confronted a group of locals who were protesting increased Russian influence in the area. The protesters were unexpectedly met by gunfire from an armed militia and John was caught in the middle of the crossfire. This attack ensued when the protesters tried to force their way into the hotel. John was hit by two rounds in the back just below his right shoulder. Protected by a heavy wool overcoat and a sweater under his suit jacket, the bullets penetrated through his clothing and lodged in his back. The combination of John moving away from the incident and the force of the bullets knocked him down and his head slammed onto the stone pavement, knocking him unconscious.

Left for dead by the militia, his body was later dragged away by the protesters. When they discovered he was alive, they took him to a local doctor who was sympathetic to their cause. Fortunately, John had a well-developed muscular back and the bullets entered on an angle lodging in the muscle and avoiding deeper penetration toward his vital organs. The protesters soon realized that no one recognized him. He looked and was dressed like a businessman. Searching through his clothing they discovered that he was not carrying identification papers. Confused and suspicious, they questioned if he really was a businessman. Wouldn't he have a wallet with credit cards, local currency and some kind of identification? The doctor removed the bullets, treated the wounds, and voiced his concern that he had remained unconscious. Possibly they should inform the local authorities.

Days later in the local hospital, John became conscious and when questioned by the doctor and the police he had no recollection of what had happened. His memory was gone. They repeatedly asked for his identification papers. They wanted to know where he was staying. What was he doing in Sevastopol? Stunned by their questioning, John had no answers; he was feeling drowsy and soon fell fast asleep.

Slowly awakening, John lay motionless, eyes closed, listening to the voices in the room. They were speaking Russian. Someone was saying that his condition was normal, he had been knocked unconscious, he had been shot, this was normal behavior, called acute stress reaction. He was lucky to be alive. The retrieved bullets were probably fired from a small caliber handgun. The lack of consciousness and responsiveness to questioning was normal.

This explanation was being questioned by what seemed to be an angry voice. He said that John's insistence that he did not know who he was only antagonized the skeptics who continued to question the complete lack of identification. He said the rumors were starting to fly. He must be hiding something. Possible involvement in a variety of illegal activities was raised, but then no one could link John to any criminal behavior. They decided to contact all local hotels, looking for a lead to his identity.

When the room emptied, John continued to lay motionless. What did they mean by acute stress reaction? They said a psychological shock caused this traumatic event, that he had been shot. How could he have been shot? His mind was blank.

Once again someone entered the room. There were introductions and the angry voice was told that the hospital's neurological specialist had examined the patient. The specialist explained that it was common for victims of acute stress disorder to experience symptoms of psychogenic amnesia as a result of a traumatic event. If symptoms of acute stress reaction lasted for more than a month the memory loss may be diagnosed as post traumatic stress disorder, and the inability to recall personal information may last for years. Even though he had a severe head injury and was knocked unconscious, the MRI showed no structural brain damage and the clinical data indicated that the brain activity was in line with psychogenic amnesia. John listened. He remembered yesterday's questioning and understood what they were saying today, but he had no recollection of falling or being shot. He could feel the pull of the bandage on his back and moving his right arm caused pain across his shoulder. Why couldn't he remember his name?

The following morning brought more questioning and John learned firsthand that the angry voice belonged to a Ukrainian government agent who was sent to investigate the situation. John sensed his frustration and began to understand the seriousness of the situation. They wanted answers and he was incapable of providing what they wanted. John spent his days challenging himself to remember, which created feelings of anxiety, which spilled into his nights which were becoming more and more restless. He was having dreams and flashbacks of very violent experiences.

That afternoon the government agent received word that the desk clerk at a local hotel, the Villa Nikita, did report that a hotel guest had not returned to the hotel and his room for three days. The hotel's policy was to hold the passports for all guests and the hotel manger had turned over a German passport for a Hans Volkov. An officer was on his way to the hospital with the passport. When the officer arrived, John immediately heard the government agent say, "This is him. Do you agree? This man that you are caring for is Hans Volkov, look at the photo on this German passport." His voice grew louder with each statement. "Go back to the hotel and with the hotel manager I want you to search the room. Bring everything belonging to Hans Volkov back here immediately."

Seconds later the government agent came charging into John's room announcing, "You are Hans Volkov." John had overheard the entire conversation, but was still startled at the intensity of his voice. "Do you remember now? Do you remember that you are Hans Volkov?"

John sat in the bed trembling, only able to answer, "No."

When the officer returned from the hotel he was carrying a leather attaché case. Handing it to the government agent it was immediately opened and the contents were laid at the foot of John's bed. There was a document that seemed to be written in German and the government agent handed it to John. "Do you know what is written here?" John looked at the document and began reading it out loud in German. He read it naturally, without effort. The government agent immediately asked, "Is it German? Can you read German? What does this document say?"

John explained that it looked like marketing information from a company with the name Energy Sector Futures. They were representing clients that were interested in making investments in the Russian oil and natural gas industries.

Handing John another document the government agent said, "Tell us what this document contains."

John began to read the document again out loud in German; he hesitated and then continued, "It mentions a Credit Suisse Bank at Uraniastrasse 4 in Zürich, Switzerland. They will be the transfer agent for all financial transactions." John stared at the document, he was seeing a pattern and it contained an encrypted message with an eight-digit safe deposit box number to be accessed by Hans Volkov. Was he imagining that the document contained an encoded message?

The government agent asked, "What else? What else are you reading?"

John responded, "It says that Hans Volkov is authorized to contact the bank as a representative of Energy Sector Futures."

The government agent snapped at John, "Are these your documents? You can read and speak German. Do you work for this company Energy Sector Futures?"

John looked at the documents and then at the government agent, "None of this has meaning to me. I am not familiar with the name Hans Volkov or a company named Energy Sector Futures."

The government agent then handed John a leather billfold and asked John to look inside. John unzipped the case and pulled out a significant stack of banknotes - Ukrainian hryvnia in one hundred and two hundred denominations, Russian rubles in one thousand and five thousand denominations, Swiss franc banknotes in one hundred and two hundred franc denominations, and one hundred, two hundred and five hundred Euro banknotes. The government agent looked at John and said, "This Hans Volkov is carrying a large amount of money. Is this your money? Are you Hans Volkov?"

Once again, John looked at the government agent and said, "I don't know."

The government agent said he would be back tomorrow with more information and left the room. John sat staring into space. None of this made sense. He could not remember anything about the documents that were shown to him and he did not know the name Hans Volkov. And then there was the document that seemed to be encrypted and where did he learn to read and speak German?

Early the next morning, the government agent had an interpreter call Energy Sector Futures in Munich, Germany. A person who claimed to be the receptionist answered the phone and when an inquiry was made about Hans Volkov, she said the call was being transferred to the Director of Marketing, Miss Monica Schmidtski. Listening to the conversation on a conference phone, the government agent told the interpreter to ask if Hans Volkov was employed by Energy Sector Futures.

Miss Schmidtski immediately asked, "Who is calling?"

When the interpreter explained who the government agent was and there had been an incident resulting in Hans Volkov being shot, the Director of Marketing asked for them to please hold until she was able to get the Vice President of Marketing on the phone. It seemed like many minutes had passed and the government agent was growing impatient. "Where are they? What are they doing?"

Just then the phone clicked and a voice said, "Good morning, I am Heinrich Kochmandt, Vice President of Marketing. Hans Volkov reports to my marketing team. Please, may I have details of what has happened to Hans?"

Through the interpreter, the government agent explained the events of the last four days. There was a pause and then the government agent told the interpreter to ask, "What do you want us to do with Hans Volkov?"

There was another long pause and finally Heinrich Kochmandt raised the question, "To be certain that I understand correctly, are you saying that Hans does not recognize the name Hans Volkov or Energy Sector Futures? And you have identified him by his photo on his German passport? There is no mistake, he matches this photo?"

The government agent became irritated by the questions, "Yes! Yes! We have confirmed his identity from the photo. I have already told you that. What do you want us to do with Hans Volkov?"

Sensing the government agent's irritation, Heinrich Kochmandt replied, "I will have Miss Monica Schmidtski leave for Sevastopol this morning to arrange the transfer of Hans back to Munich. Is the number that you are calling from the number where we can reach you? We will call within the hour with Miss Schmidtski's travel details."

The government agent, pleased with the response, said, "Yes, this is the number that you should call. Thank you! We will be awaiting your call." With that the phone went dead on the German end of the line.

CHAPTER 6

As soon as he ended the call, Heinrich Kochmandt turned to Monica Schmidtski and said, "We have a crisis."

What was said to be a company called Energy Sector Futures located in Munich was really the front for the CIA's Special Operations Group in Berlin. John had been recruited by Heinrich Kochmandt who at the time was the CIA Station Chief in Madrid and he had become John's Supervisory Training Officer. Kochmandt reported to the Head of Operations in Berlin, who in turn, reported to the CIA Deputy Director for Special Operations whose office was located in New York City. They were all involved in Operation Azov and John was their key asset. Keeping Operation Azov a secret was vital to their professional survival.

Monica Schmidtski was assigned to the Berlin office to monitor the performance of operation assets throughout Europe. In simple terms, she tracked the psychological well being of each CIA operative, studying their patterns of self control, keeping an eye on their social relationships, and charting their mental state in relation to the purpose of each mission. A trained psychologist, Schmidtski first met John when he was assigned to the Special Operations Group in Berlin and had monitored his involvement with Operation Azov from day one.

It was not an easy assignment to track a highly trained CIA operative who was an expert at staying off the grid. These individuals were always involved with top-secret missions and trusted no one. Schmidtski held John Volkov in high regard. She respected his dedication to the chain of command, following orders, completing each mission. She was aware that John would only take another person's life when he knew it was vital to national security. The action of taking a life always had to be justified for a greater good, saving American lives. John's conduct had to be morally right. If the mission was morally right, then any method of achieving it was acceptable. Despite his dedication to the agency, she knew that John struggled with his role in the CIA's Special Operations Group.

Kochmandt looked shaken and he told Schmidtski that he needed to understand what was going on with Volkov before he talked with the Head of Operations. "Do you believe this? Is Volkov just playing them along until we can get him out of there? If he was shot and was concerned about blowing his cover, this might be a clever tactic. They're talking about post traumatic stress disorder and for all they know he's a businessman who apparently got shot in the back. And he survived it! What are they talking about? Do you understand this part about the head injury and being knocked unconscious and an MRI that showed no structural brain damage? How did they determine that the clinical data from the MRI substantiates their diagnosis of psychogenic amnesia? Are you buying this or is Volkov going to get the best actor of the year award?"

Schmidtski stood there silently and then she sensed that Kochmandt wanted answers. Hesitating, she finally said, "I won't have answers to your questions until I see him in person. Should I make my travel arrangements? I think we can all agree that we should get him out of Ukraine as soon as possible. Should I bring him back here or take him to the safe house in Munich or Zürich?"

Kochmandt stood there staring at her, frustrated that she wasn't agreeing that this had to be a scheme that Volkov was pulling off to protect his cover. Finally, he answered, "Yeah, make your travel arrangements. I'll go talk to the Head of Operations."

Kochmandt was standing in front of the office of the Head of Operations thinking about how to start the conversation. Suddenly the door opened and a big, burly man with wavy gray hair stood looking into Kochmandt's eyes. It was Stephen

Spearfoot, a twenty-eight year CIA veteran who spent the last six years in Germany assigned to the Berlin office. "What's up Kochmandt, you look lost?"

Kochmandt hesitated and then just blurted it out, "I think we may have a problem, Sir."

Turning, the Head of Operations went back into his office and Kochmandt followed without saying a word. Closing the door Kochmandt went to sit down and the Head of Operations growled, "Don't get comfortable! I don't like it when someone comes into my office saying we have a problem. What are you talking about, Kochmandt?"

Standing up straight, Kochmandt explained, "It's John Volkov. He was in Sevastopol targeting the billionaire businessman who the Russian Oil Minister said was going to expose Operation Azov. This is the wealthy guy who was funding the opposition to the Kremlin's efforts to retain control of the oil and natural gas industries. Volkov was shot when a group of pro-Russian separatists confronted protesters trying to force their way into the hotel where the wealthy oil magnate was gathering support against Russia's control of their energy sector. When he was shot he fell hard, slamming his head onto the pavement, and was knocked unconscious. We were contacted by the Ukrainian authorities. They have Volkov, and they're telling us that Volkov has totally lost his memory. He didn't even recognize his own name. They confirmed his identity with his passport photo. We think Volkov was concerned about blowing his cover and created this memory loss scheme to give us time. Schmidtski is leaving for Sevastopol this morning to get Volkov out of Ukraine."

Standing silently, the Head of Operations stared at Kochmandt. He finally broke his silence saying, "None of this can come back to this office. What are you going to do about this wealthy Russian? He cannot go to the press about Operation Azov. Do you understand? Are you going to take care of this?"

Kochmandt quickly responded, "Yes Sir. We'll take care of it. I'll give you an update tomorrow."

As soon as Kochmandt left the office, the Head of Operations was on the phone. He needed to contact the Deputy Director for Special Operations at his office in New York and inform him about Volkov's condition. They needed to get Volkov back into action. They needed to take care of the wealthy Russian businessman. Kochmandt also had to be certain that none of this information would get to the CIA Deputy Director for Global Operations in Washington.

Schmidtski scheduled an 11:30 a.m. flight on Ukraine International Air from the Berlin Tegel Airport to Odessa, Ukraine. She would arrive around 1:00 p.m. and would have an eight-hour drive to Sevastopol, Crimea. She reserved an Audi A6 rental car, booked a room at the Villa Nikita Hotel and all charges were made using her Credit Suisse Bank Card issued to Energy Sector Futures. She kept a travel bag in the office and left for the airport immediately. She told the receptionist to call the government agent and tell him that she will be going directly to the hospital. She should arrive around 9:00 p.m. their time and she could meet with him at that time or at his convenience the next day. She left a travel itinerary for Kochmandt with a message that she would call him from Sevastopol.

The drive from Odessa to Sevastopol was challenging with heavy truck traffic on poorly maintained roads. Even in a comfortable Audi A6 it was a tedious journey. Schmidtski was tired when she arrived at the hospital. It was late, almost nine o'clock, and the receptionist wasn't pleased to hear that she wanted to see a patient at that time of day. Schmidtski explained who she was, that she just travelled from Odessa, she needed to see Hans Volkov for a brief period of time, she would make arrangements for his release the following morning. Reluctantly, the nurse in charge said she could stay for fifteen minutes, but not a minute longer.

Monica Schmidtski was an attractive "thirty something" who spent every free minute in a pool swimming laps or in a gym on a treadmill. She was fussy about what she ate and her morning routine started with a stop at the bathroom scale. Her job was her life. Its challenges were endless. She was constantly travelling and learning - languages, cultures, ethnic foods, and yes, the personalities. Everyone was so driven. She enjoyed interacting with Volkov. He was quick to assist with translations or understanding a culture. She could always count on his cooperation.

Walking into Volkov's room she made eye contact, smiled and with a somewhat humorous tone in her voice, speaking in German she said, "How are you this evening Mr. Volkov?"

Starring into her face, Hans Volkov thought for a moment. He wasn't sure about a correct response, but he responded in German, "You're new, you haven't been here before."

Recognizing the look of confusion on Volkov's face Schmidtski calmly said, "That's correct Hans. I just arrived from Germany." She hesitated for a moment, then she continued, "I'm your coworker, Monica Schmidtski. Do you remember me?"

Still starring at her with a look of confusion, Hans answered, "No." Schmidtski was about to respond and then Hans said, "It has been difficult. I haven't been able to remember," he paused and then with hesitation, "It has been frustrating, I cannot remember who I am."

Sensing his frustration, Schmidtski assured him by quickly responding, "Don't worry Hans. It will all come back in time. I am going to return tomorrow and we will discuss a plan to go back to Germany and put you on a quick path to a full recovery. You need to rest well tonight. Will you be alright until tomorrow morning?"

Coming closer, Schmidtski reached out and put her hand on his, "We will take care of you Hans. Your memory will come back. Have faith." Looking at Hans she repeated the question, "Will you be alright until tomorrow morning?"

Hans looked at her with a slightly more relaxed look on his face, and he said, "Yes."

Before leaving the hospital, Monica Schmidtski spent time with the nurse in charge, asking questions, reviewing the doctor's diagnosis, listening to the nurse substantiate what they had been told on the phone. The consensus was that Hans Volkov's symptoms were consistent with what would be expected of someone who had been knocked unconscious, was shot, and lost a lot of blood. The hospital's neurological specialist diagnosed him with acute stress reaction. His behavior only reinforced the diagnosis. Thanking the nurse, Monica asked her to leave a note stating that she would return in the morning.

Exiting the hospital, Schmidtski reached into her bag for her cell phone and immediately hit the speed dial for Heinrich Kochmandt. Answering the phone, Kochmandt blurted out question after question. Finally, Schmidtski interrupted, "Heinrich, listen to me! I was just with Hans and this is real! He is not capable of going back on this mission. Heinrich, do you understand? He did not know who I was. He is not acting."

With a deep sigh, Schmidtski continued, "Heinrich, it has been a long day and I'm exhausted. I will go back to the hospital tomorrow morning and I will call you then. I need to get to the hotel. I am very tired."

Heinrich Kochmandt sat staring at his cell phone. Should he call the Head of Operations? It was late, what would he tell him? Finally, he hit the speed dial and almost immediately the Head of Operations was asking, "Do you have good news for me Kochmandt? Have you taken care of the wealthy Russian?"

Hesitating for a second, Kochmandt responded, "No Sir. Sir, this is complicated. Volkov is out of commission. I just spoke with Schmidtski. She was with Volkov. He did not know who she was. She said that Volkov is not acting. He definitely has lost his memory. He must have gone off the deep end Sir and totally lost it."

After a long silence the Head of Operations said, "You told me that you would take care of this. I want an update tomorrow. Do you understand, Kochmandt?"

Now it was the Head of Operations who was contemplating his next move. He looked at his watch. He sat thinking. He did not have many options. Finally, he dialed the cell phone for the Russian Oil Minister. The phone seemed to be ringing forever and then in Russian he heard, "Hello!"

The Head of Operations quickly responded, "This is Stephen Spearfoot. I have a problem. I need your help."

Interrupting, the Russian Oil Minister said, "I told you not to call this number."

The Russian Oil Minister heard the stress in the voice of the Head of Operations who began to plead, "Please, listen. We failed to take out the target in Sevastopol. We need your help. We cannot risk the exposure of Operation Azov. We need you to take him out."

The Russian Oil Minister listened intently and then he asked, "What happened to your agent? You think you are so clever. I have had reports on the fiasco in Sevastopol. Now you want me to clean up your mess? What about this agent? What are you going to do about him? You cannot have all these loose ends floating around Europe. What about Kochmandt? Your people are getting nervous. Your end of this deal is starting to unravel. We need to start shutting this down. Eliminate every potential source of a leak. Do you understand, Spearfoot? It is not only your head that will roll. I cannot afford that this gets out to the press. Send Kochmandt to your safe house in Munich tomorrow and then have your agent meet him there. I will take care of the rest. Do you understand? Are you listening?"

"Yes, I hear you. I'll do it. Kochmandt will be in Munich tomorrow and Volkov will arrive two or three days later."

Spearfoot sighed, not necessarily a sigh of relief, but a feeling of gratitude that the Russian Oil Minister would cooperate.

Then the Russian Oil Minister said, "Spearfoot! One more thing, understand this, never call me at this number again, never!" And then the line went dead.

Looking at his watch and then at his phone, the Head of Operations called Kochmandt. As soon as he answered, the Head of Operations said, "I want you to go to the safe house in Munich first thing tomorrow. I am working on a solution. Tell Schmidtski to bring Volkov to Munich as soon as possible. I'll give you more details when you get to Munich. I have more calls to make. Good night."

Kochmandt heard the click. Cradling his cell phone in his hand he began to gently toss it from hand to hand, thinking, feeling relieved, and wondering, "How was the Head of Operations going to solve this problem?"

CHAPTER 7

Getting out of bed before dawn, Schmidtski was searching the Internet, updating her understanding of acute stress reaction and the symptoms of psychogenic amnesia. Her findings were obvious - she would be dealing with a person with severe memory loss. Hans did not appear to be violent, he actually seemed calm when she left him. Would he be compliant with her requests to travel? Would he accept her suggestions? Would he cooperate and follow her lead?

After settling her account and Hans Volkov's account at the Villa Nikita Hotel, Schmidtski was off to the hospital. It was 8:35 a.m. and she had already called the hospital and arranged to meet with the doctor at nine. She was told that the Ukrainian government agent would also be waiting for her.

After meeting with the doctor, he assured Schmidtski that Volkov was physically on a path to a full recovery. He was eating well, his appetite was good and the wounds on his back were healing. He should avoid physical activity for a few weeks and most importantly, he needed mental rest. He should not be put into stressful situations and would need medical attention in Germany. She was rather surprised at the straightforwardness of the hospital discharge process. By 9:45 Schmidtski was told that Volkov could be released as soon as she settled all obligations with the hospital's financial department. Watching over the morning's events with keen interest, the Ukrainian government agent listened attentively to every conversation. As soon as the medical staff completed their release procedures, the government agent asked if he could meet with Schmidtski and Volkov. Taking an envelope out of her purse and handing it to the government agent, Schmidtski told him that they were grateful for his courteous and prompt action in contacting Energy Sector Futures in

Munich. Schmidtski asked if he would accept a monetary gift to possibly benefit the police department's orphan fund. Smiling, the government agent insisted that such a gift was not necessary, as he slipped the envelope into a suit pocket. Schmidtski assured the government agent that she would contact him when they returned to Germany and provide an update on Hans Volkov's condition. Volkov watched Schmidtski's every move and listened closely as she talked and was impressed with her tact and skill as she interacted with the medical staff and the government agent.

As soon as they were alone, Schmidtski opened a travel suitcase and explained that it contained Volkov's suit and other clothing that was left in his hotel room. She asked him to change while she settled the hospital account and then they would leave. When Schmidtski returned to the room Volkov was dressed and standing by the suitcase. Schmidtski reached for the bag smiling at Volkov, "Are you ready to leave Hans?"

Feeling comfortable with the morning's events and Schmidtski's apparent concern for his welfare Volkov answered, "Yes, I'm ready."

Schmidtski picked up the suitcase and headed toward the hospital's main exit. Volkov broke the silence saying, "It's strange, but I'm not even sure if I truly understand where we are going."

Sensing his apprehension, Schmidtski quickly responded, "Don't worry, Hans. It will all come back. It will just take time. We will start our journey today, returning to Germany by train. Traveling by train will be more restful and it will give you time to relax." As they reached the car Schmidtski once again looked at her watch. "It's 10:35 and it will take at least eight hours to drive from Sevastopol to Odessa. We'll stop for lunch in a few hours. Try to relax. Would you like to listen to music?"

Hans hesitated, and then he said, "I understand that your name is Monica Schmidtski and I am your coworker."

Hesitating again for a moment, he said, "I haven't been able to remember anything about you. I have no memory of Energy Sector Futures, or Munich or even Germany. Do you understand what I am saying?"

Monica responded, "Yes, Hans, I understand. Your memory will come back eventually. Think positively Hans. You remembered my name so that is progress. Give it time."

Monica continued to converse in German, half afraid to switch to English. "We will take an overnight train from Odessa through Moldova to Suceava, Romania. Then we'll make a connection to Vienna, Austria. Will you be alright traveling by train?"

Sensing his uncertainty about what to say she continued, "We'll listen to classical music. I have one of your favorites, Vivaldi's Four Seasons Violin Concerto. It will be relaxing for both of us." The music did relax him and it brought a smile to his face. Monica took a deep breath as she saw that Hans was beginning to settle.

As soon as they arrived in Odessa, Monica went to the ladies room and called Heinrich Kochmandt's cell phone. She quickly gave him an update and emphasized that Volkov was definitely experiencing severe memory loss. Heinrich explained that he was in Munich and would meet them at the safe house in a few days. Monica explained that they were at the train station and were booked on an overnight train from Odessa to Suceava. She would contact him in a few days from Vienna.

Comfort was a rarity on the long journey from Odessa to Suceava and the seating was not the best as they continued on the rocky connection to Budapest. Finally, on the last leg of the journey they were able to get first class seating for the three-hour trip from Budapest, Hungary to Vienna, Austria. As they neared the end of the journey, Monica stood and stretched as they approached Vienna. "We will arrive at the Wien Westbahnhof, Vienna West Station, and I need to call

Heinrich Kochmandt before we depart for Munich. Do you remember that Heinrich Kochmandt and I created a tradition whenever we travel through Vienna? I generally avoid cakes and pastries. Heinrich insists an exception must be made when you are in Vienna. He raves about their quality and is very particular about his selections. We have enough time between trains to walk to the K&K Hofzuckerbäckerei. It is easy to find, located between Saint Stephen's Cathedral and the Vienna State Opera. Heinrich's favorite is apple strudel or as he would say "apfelstrudel." He tells me that it is the national dessert of Austria and it would be diplomatically irresponsible not to pay homage to this delicate pastry that the Viennese have perfected. Heinrich is also partial to Gerstner's Sachertorte, a fantastic chocolate cake that is associated with Vienna by anyone who has traveled to Austria. Do you remember any of this, Hans?"

Shaking his head back and forth Hans smiled and responded, "No, Monica, I don't remember anything about Vienna."

Monica continued, "When you see a Sachertorte you'll probably remember. It is definitely one of Vienna's most famous specialties. The freshly baked chocolate cake has an aroma, and with the dark chocolate icing, it is just irresistible. When I call Heinrich, I'll ask if we should bring him an apple strudel or a Sachertorte. He always responds that it is too difficult to choose so I best bring one of each."

Monica continued to talk while she pulled out her phone, "I'll give him a quick call and then we'll be off." To her surprise there was no answer and after a long series of rings she heard a click and was transferred to voice mail. Leaving a message, she asked Heinrich to call her. She looked at Hans and thinking out loud said, "That's unusual." Looking at her phone she began to key in a text message asking about his choice of dessert. A few minutes passed and finally there was a ping on her phone. "It's a message from Heinrich." Opening the message, she read it in disbelief. "Do not bring desserts. Come directly to Munich." She looked at Hans and said, "Something is terribly wrong."

Monica saw the confusion on Hans' face. She immediately made the decision not to say anything more about Heinrich. She remembered what Heinrich told her many times, "You must be prepared for emergency situations and if you're questioning the way an agent is responding to you, ask a security question." Heinrich was always very exact about this procedure and being a graduate of the University of Wisconsin, he made her practice the security question, an unbearable amount of times. Looking at her phone, she hesitated for a moment, before sending the following text message to Heinrich. "Do you believe that Bucky Badger is extinct?" If the answer was yes, or no it was a sign to go into crisis mode. The answer should be, "He lives on in the hearts of his fans." Waiting and looking at her phone Monica became increasingly restless. Finally, she heard a ping and received the message, "Come directly to Munich."

Once again she stared in disbelief at her phone. She immediately hit the speed dial for Heinrich's cell phone, listened, and then the call went directly to voice mail. She knew almost instinctively that something was wrong and felt a knot developing in her stomach. Again she hit the speed dial for Heinrich's phone and waited and again was transferred to voice mail. Heinrich had reviewed this procedure so many times and she never took it seriously. She needed to make a decision. Feeling anxious, she finally dialed the Berlin office and the receptionist answered. Monica immediately asked the question, "Have you heard from Heinrich today?"

With a nervous voice the receptionist said, "Monica, haven't you heard? He was found in the Munich safe house this morning. He was shot in the head execution style. I wasn't supposed to say anything to anyone. They are still investigating. No one else is in the office right now. Are you alright? Where are you?"

Monica quickly responded, "I'm on my way to Berlin. I'll be in the office tomorrow."

Monica looked at Hans and saw the confusion on his face. They made eye contact and he said, "Did you just say that you were on your way to Berlin? I thought we were going to Munich."

Monica knew that she had to act fast without stressing Hans. What would Heinrich do in this situation? Her mind was spinning madly. Finally, with a big smile she looked at Hans and said, "Slight change in plans. First we're going to Zürich then to Berlin."

Hans immediately asked, "To Zürich, Switzerland? Why?"

Monica got really excited. "That is very good Hans! You remembered that Zürich is in Switzerland. That is really good! Do you understand? I didn't say Switzerland."

With her mind racing she knew that she had to get Hans to his safe deposit box in Zürich and somehow explain to him that they may be in danger. Why did she receive a message from Heinrich's phone telling her to come to the safe house in Munich? Who would have sent that message?

Hans watched as Monica rapidly flipped through a variety of screens on her phone with an intense look on her face and then she yelled, "Yes! We need to hurry to catch the 1:30 p.m. Vienna to Zürich train. We can do this." With that she was up and moving toward the train platforms. Turning, she was relieved to see that Hans was following her. "Come on, Hans, we can do this."

Reaching the train platform, they boarded the first class car and in a matter of minutes the train was pulling out of the station. Still excited, Monica turned to Hans and without thinking said in English, "Hans, we need to talk."

Surprised, Hans looked at Monica and responded in English, "You're speaking English. Why did you change languages?"

Monica smiled broadly. "Hans, you remembered. You remembered that you can speak English. Your memory is coming back, Hans." Calming down, Monica took a deep breath and then continued "We need to rest. This will be an eight-hour trip. When we get to the Zürich Hauptbahnhof (Main Station), we will discuss our next steps. For now, we better rest."

Monica closed her eyes, questions were spinning in her mind. Who would have killed Heinrich Kochmandt? Who answered her text message using Heinrich's phone? Why were they asked to come to the Munich safe house? Was she in danger? Why would she be in danger? She calmed herself and concentrated on a plan for when they arrived in Zürich. She must not shock Hans by disclosing her concerns.

Half asleep, she continued thinking. Was it wise to go to the safe house in Zürich? It might be best to stay in a hotel without making a reservation and use cash instead of a credit card. Would their movements be traced to Zürich because of the online purchase of the train tickets? They had to be careful. She needed to prepare Hans for what he would find when he opened his safe deposit box. Where should she start?

Monica had not slept well on the train from Odessa to Suceava and it was too uncomfortable to sleep from Suceava to Budapest. It had been over two days without sleeping well and now it hit her. The rocking train, a comfortable seat, and a warm pleasant temperature in their private compartment relaxed her. She closed her eyes and was sound asleep in minutes.

"Monica, Monica, we will be arriving in Zürich. You need to wake up."

Still in a dream-like state she heard the voice again, "Monica, Monica," and then she realized it was Hans. He was gently prodding her, trying to wake her up. She sat straight up in her seat, opened her eyes, and she immediately asked, "How long was I sleeping?"

Hans smiled. "For most of the trip, you must have been tired. Are you alright? You seem tense. Are we going to speak

English for the rest of the journey? I made a list of questions. I thought it would be good to start a diary."

Monica sat in stunned silence. Were they in real danger? Hans had no idea of his true identity. How should she explain that they work for the Central Intelligence Agency?

Hans made direct eye contact and repeated, "Are you alright?"

Monica snapped out of her daze and immediately started to explain their plan. "There is a good hotel only 100 meters or so from the Hauptbahnhof. We will stay there tonight. Once inside the station we will follow the signs for Bahnhofstrasse and Hotel Saint Gotthard is just a short walk at Schützengasse 15. I will check us in and we will use French." Speaking in French she asked, "Do you understand?"

Without hesitation Hans responded in French. "I understand what you said. I just don't understand where I learned to speak French."

They checked into the hotel as planned and as soon as they got to their room Monica said, "There is a reason that we need to stay together in one room and I need to establish some ground rules. You must not leave the room without me. Do you understand?" Without waiting for a response, she continued, "I am really hungry so I'll order room service for us. The menu is probably in that folder on the desk. And I really need a shower. I'll first order the food." Pointing to a bed she said, "You sleep there. I want to be close to the bathroom."

As they were eating Hans reached for his small note pad, "May I ask some of my questions?" Without waiting for an answer, he said, "What exactly do I do at Energy Sector Futures?"

Monica thought for a moment then she said, "Remember, you were asking about the different languages that we were speaking? We work for a government agency and it is important that we can communicate using the local language in many European countries. It is also important for us to spend time in a country without people knowing who we are. We sometimes do confidential work that other governments don't know about."

Hans placed both hands in front of his chest and asked, "Which government do we work for?" Hans and Monica talked for hours. Patiently answering question after question, Monica skirted around the true nature of their operation and never reached the point of telling Hans what his real role was in the agency and why he was on assignment in Sevastopol. When they finally turned off the lights to go to sleep Monica promised that she would provide greater detail after they visited the bank in the morning.

Following her normal routine, Monica was once again out of bed before dawn. She explained that their first stop would be to the bank where Hans had a safe deposit box. "This bank has a very sophisticated security system and the majority of their clients maintain secret access to documents or objects that are, let's just say, of a secretive nature. Security is their prime concern and they will utilize a retina or iris scan for you to gain access to your safe deposit box. They don't provide details about their system, but you are the only person who can access the items in your box."

They left the hotel at 9:00 a.m., walking the short distance to Uraniastrasse 4, the location of the Credit Suisse Bank in Zürich. Asking for the security manager, Hans handed his German passport to the manager and received a warm greeting "Welcome back, Mr. Volkov." Following the manager to the back section of the bank, the manager keyed a code into a steel vault door and they proceeded into a vault lined with safe deposit boxes. Hans was asked to sit in a specific chair and the manager maneuvered what looked like a medical device for eye examinations in front of his face. "Please use the chin rest to be comfortable and look straight ahead." There was a quick buzz and then the manger's response, "Thank you, Mr. Volkov." Within a few minutes a safe deposit box was placed on the table in the center of the room and the manager said, "Mr. Volkov, I will leave you now and please press this buzzer when you are ready for my return." Monica quickly sat at one of the chairs at the table and motioned to Hans to sit in the other chair. Opening the box Hans reached in and pulled out a stack of passports. Monica explained, "These are the passports that I talked about last night. While traveling in Ukraine and Sevastopol you used your German passport with the name Hans Volkov and because of the geographical location of your assignment you spoke Russian and German." Opening the French passport Monica continued, "Now that we are in Zürich, it would be best for you to use the alias John Volkov, this French passport and to speak French and German. We use our language skills and various passports to fit in with the local community and avoid the appearance of being a foreigner or tourist. Put all the passports in your attaché case and we will discuss them later."

Reaching back into the safe deposit box Hans took out three plastic zip-lock bags. The first contained a one-inch stack of Swiss banknotes in one hundred and two hundred franc denominations, the second bag contained an even larger stack of Euro banknotes in one hundred, two hundred and five hundred denominations, and the last bag had two stacks of United States one hundred dollar bills with a $10,000 wrapper around each stack. John looked at Monica and said, "This is a lot of money."

Without any sign of emotion, Monica pointed to the attaché case, "Put them in, we will talk later."

The last item in the safe deposit box was a leather folder. Laying it on the table, Hans opened it to find a series of papers, all with the title *Operation Azov* as the heading, and each page had large sections of blackened out text. Hans looked at Monica who recognized his look of confusion. "These are redacted documents." she said. "They contain top secret, classified information, and all sensitive information was removed.

The intent is to protect the secret information and one of the methods is to blacken or delete text. It is called redacted text. You were provided the essential information to complete each assignment and all the highly sensitive information that you didn't necessarily need to know was blackened out. These sanitized documents had the classified text blackened out and were then photocopied to provide you with a document with all the sensitive information removed." Monica got the impression that her rushed explanation was probably causing more confusion and she said, "Put them in and we will go over each one in detail later."

Looking at her watch she said, "Please close your attaché case and I will press the buzzer." Once again Monica looked around the room and said, "There are no cameras in here. Stay calm. Are you ready to leave?"

When they were once again in the lobby, Monica scanned the walls and noticed the cameras pointing in every direction. Reaching the sidewalk outside the bank she said, "We'll return to the hotel and secure the contents of your attaché case in our room safe. We have one more stop and possibly, just possibly, we may need to hurry because of the security cameras in the bank." Monica quickly added in a firm voice, "I know that you don't completely understand, but you must trust me right now. Please, Hans, may I count on your cooperation?"

Shaking his head Hans said, "I don't understand any of this, but I do remember that you said since we are in Zürich I should be called John Volkov, use my French passport, and speak French and German. Is that correct? Should we stop using English for now?"

Monica laughed for the first time in days. She smiled at John, saying in French, "I am not sure that your memory is coming back John, but you are absolutely right. We will switch to French and I will now call you John."

John smiled back at Monica and said, "Remember, Monica, you are the only person that I know so who else can I trust?"

John's comment surprised Monica, and then she thought, "He's correct. Right now, I'm his only connection to the outside world. I am the only person that he can trust."

As soon as Monica and John left the bank, the manager was on the phone to Berlin. When the receptionist answered, the manager asked, "May I please speak to Stephen Spearfoot?" When Spearfoot answered the phone, the manager simply said, "Following your instructions Sir. I'm calling to report that we had two clients at the bank this morning who accessed one of your company's safe deposit boxes. Their names are Monica Schmidtski and Hans Volkov."

Spearfoot responded immediately, "Do you know what they took from the safe deposit box?"

The manager responded, "No, Sir. There are no security cameras in any of our vaults."

Spearfoot responded, "Thank you for this information."

Hanging up the phone Spearfoot looked at his watch and thought out loud, "It's too early to call the Deputy Director for Special Operations at his office in New York City."

Leaving the hotel, Monica looked at her watch and it was already 10:35. She said to John, "We are going to a safe house that Heinrich Kochmandt leased last year. You have a room there with clothing and other personal items."

Walking only a few blocks, they approached a well maintained apartment building. Upon entering the outer lobby, they were greeted by a doorman. In perfect French, while showing him her passport, Monica said, "Good morning, we are going to our flat."

The doorman immediately responded, "Yes, of course. I remember you, Miss Schmidtski. Thank you for remembering the staff with your gift at the end of the year. Your generosity was appreciated." The doorman opened the door to the main lobby and thanked her again.

In the elevator Monica smiled and said to John, "Always remember to take care of the people who provide you with a quality service." She pressed the number six on the elevator panel and the elevator door closed. Once inside the apartment, Monica showed John his room and opened his closet saying, "These are your suits and shirts and luggage. We'll come back to these shortly, but first I want to show you something."

While walking into the next room, Monica continued, "This is Heinrich Kochmandt's room and there is a safe behind the back panel in this closet." Monica slid a wood panel to the side exposing a safe that had a display for an eight-digit code and a numeric keypad below. "Remember you said that there was an encrypted message with an eight-digit code in the letter you were carrying?"

John said, "Yes, but I thought it referred to a safe deposit box number."

Monica responded, "What was the number?"

John paused and then responded, "The message referred to a code that has six prime numbers."

Monica then said, "And this safe requires a code that is eight numbers in length."

John replied, "That's correct! Then the code could be the first six prime numbers in sequence: 2, 3, 5, 7, 11, and 13. Try 23571113."

Monica keyed in the numbers. "It doesn't work."

John said excitedly, "Wait! The message said the code was six prime numbers in reverse order. Try 13117532." The lock clicked and the safe opened.

Opening the safe, they saw a shelf holding a stack of documents. Picking up the top document, she hesitated, and stopped to look at the cover. In large black letters it was labeled *Operation Azov* and below in red capital letters, *TOP SECRET*. Monica opened the document and to her surprise none of it was redacted. She took the stack of documents and placed them into John's attaché case and continued to search through the safe. She found a number of CIA identification badges and one was for New York City and there was a cell phone that apparently belonged to Heinrich. She placed everything into the case. Next, she found what looked like a diary with financial information and records of Swiss bank account transactions.

Sliding open a drawer inside the safe Monica said, "Don't touch it." Lying in the drawer was a Beretta M9 nine millimeter pistol. Monica quickly closed the drawer. Then she looked through the passports and envelopes filled with a variety of currencies. Monica looked at John and said, "We don't need any additional money. I need to wipe our prints off of everything and we need to close the safe. While I'm doing that you should go to your room and pack clothing for at least two weeks. Can you do that? Choose the suitcase with the wheels and remember your back, you cannot lift the suitcase when it is packed."

Leaving the apartment Monica's mind was racing again. She was thinking of Heinrich Kochmandt. He would talk about emergency procedures and she always thought it was some kind of joke. She remembered him saying that it was always good to have a GET OUT OF JAIL FREE card when you were playing Monopoly or working for the CIA. His words were ringing in her head, "Monica, you need to be prepared for emergency situations." Was that what they found in his safe, his emergency reserves?

Now she was thinking about the security cameras in the bank. Were they safe in Zürich? They needed to get back to the hotel and evaluate what they had found. Maybe she should call the Berlin office. Could she be overreacting?

Back at the hotel Monica organized everything on her bed and thought about dividing the work. What should she give to John? The diary was best. She did not want him to start with the Operation Azov file. John was already looking over her shoulder and she knew she needed to get started. "John, do you feel comfortable reviewing Heinrich's diary? Try to create a summary. Are you comfortable with that?"

John just picked up the diary and said, "Yes!"

Monica picked up the cell phone and scrolled through the address book. She found nothing unusual until she came to Bethanne Longfield - CIA Deputy Director for Global Operations in Washington and her cell phone number. "John, I found a number that will be useful. Heinrich has the cell phone number for the CIA Deputy Director for Global Operations."

John didn't even hear what she was saying when he interrupted, "Monica, this financial summary shows that twenty million dollars was transferred from Central Intelligence Agency accounts to a number of Swiss bank accounts. There are also financial records of bank transfers from what looks like Russian names to the same bank accounts. There are statements about corruption in the Berlin office and illegal use of CIA resources by the Head of Operations in Berlin and the Deputy Director for Special Operations. Do you know these people?"

Monica stopped what she was doing and listened to what John was saying. Were this diary and Heinrich's death connected? Should they leave Zürich? Looking at her watch, it was just after 1:00 p.m. They did not have enough time to make the 1:34 train to Paris. Was she panicking? Then, looking at John, she hesitated and said, "I think we should be careful and go to Paris. I know a number of small hotels. It will give us time to evaluate all this information. We do not need to hurry. We can take the 3:34 p.m. train from Zürich and arrive in Paris before eight. We will have lunch at the Hauptbahnhof and dinner in Paris."

John sat there in silence. Was something wrong? Was Monica telling him everything? Why did she seem so anxious since she made those phone calls in Vienna?

Monica was uncomfortable with John's silence. She waited a short time and then asked, "Are you alright, John?"

John was still silent and finally said, "I'll cooperate, but we need to talk on the train. I need to know what is happening."

Monica hesitated and said, "We will use our French passports and speak only French. Do you understand? We will travel in the first class car, but we will still be surrounded by people. We shouldn't discuss this on the train. We will have time when we reach Paris and I will explain why I have been concerned about our safety."

At the Hauptbahnhof Monica purchased first class tickets using cash. She explained that they were booked on the Lyria 9226 and would be served a late lunch in the first class section. "We should arrive at the Paris Gare de Lyon at 7:37 – it's only a four-hour trip." Before leaving the station, she stopped at a kiosk that sold cell phones and purchased two phones with an international calling plan. Deep down she knew it was time to call Langley.

It was 3:00 p.m. in Berlin and Stephen Spearfoot looked at his watch and dialed the Deputy Director for Special Operations at his office in New York City. Listening to the phone ring Spearfoot was thinking, it will be 9:00 a.m. in New York and the Deputy Director should be in his office. Finally, there was an answer and Spearfoot began, "We located Schmidtski and Volkov. They're in Zürich. They were at the Credit Suisse Bank this morning and accessed Volkov's safe deposit box. We're not certain about where they are staying, but we're searching Zürich's security camera system. We'll locate them."

There was a long silence and finally the Deputy Director for Special Operations said "You told me that you were going to take care of this. I told you that this cannot come back to this office. Do you understand? Take care of it!"

The phone went silent and Spearfoot stood there staring into space. Should he call the Russian Oil Minister? He tried to weigh his options and finally dialed the number and waited. The ringing went on and on and finally he was connected to voice mail. "This is Spearfoot. I need your help. We found Schmidtski and Volkov. They're in Zürich. I need your help with this." And then the voice mail cut off. Spearfoot stood there staring at his phone. Did he provide enough information? Would there be a response to his request? Did the Russian Oil Minister understand how desperate he was? Spearfoot dialed the number again and there was a partial ring, then a click, and then a dial tone. He tried again and got the same result.

The Gare de Lyon is located in the east end of Paris on the north bank of the river Seine. As the train arrived in the station, Monica explained that she arranged for accommodations in a small hotel in the west end of Paris on the south bank of the river Seine. The neighborhood is formally called the 7th arrondissement, or district. It is home to the Eiffel Tower and the rue Cler, a pedestrian friendly market street where they could easily blend with local Parisians and throngs of tourists. With a smile she announced that they would stay at 29 rue Cler at the Grand Hôtel Lévêque. "Don't let the name fool you John. The only thing grand about this hotel is its location."

Because of the distance to the hotel and John's recuperating back injury, Monica arranged for a limo service to take them to rue Cler. The subway would be difficult because of the luggage and John's injury, and the taxi stand would be packed at this time of day.

Settling into their simple room with twin beds, a small bath and a view out of their street facing windows, Monica locked their valuables in the closet safe. She turned to John and said, "It is almost 9:00 p.m. Would you like a light dinner and then we can go for a walk and talk? While walking, we can talk comfortably, and be sure that no one can overhear our conversation."

They walked south on rue Cler for two blocks to the Avenue de la Motte Picquet, turned right, walked another three blocks, and then it came into view, the Eiffel Tower, at the far end of the Jardin du Champ de Mars. Monica paused and said, "I always find it so beautiful, the lights magically twinkling in the night." Looking at John, she knew he wanted answers.

"Let me start by saying that Heinrich Kochmandt always respectfully referred to you as a soldier, only your battlefield was not the norm. He believed that you were fighting a war to protect American values, to ensure the national security of the United States. He was dedicated to this cause and he honored your commitment to each mission. You carried out missions that were known only to a few people. Operation Azov was a top secret program. You were the first agent to complete what they referred to as behavior modification. They wanted to provide foolproof results for the most demanding missions. Mistakes were unacceptable, preparation was exhausting, every detail was checked and rechecked, making certain that each mission ended with success. You were able to meet this high standard. You never failed."

"When you look through the Operation Azov file, you will see individuals who were targeted, who were eliminated, to remove whatever threat they presented to the United States. You were on assignment in Sevastopol, on such a mission, and then you were accidentally shot. Falling to the ground, you hit your head, and were knocked unconscious."

John cleared his throat and then said, "When I saw the Operation Azov file I remembered the faces. I have been having nightmares and those faces are always there. I have not been able to escape the memories of those missions."

Monica listened to John as they walked for over an hour, oblivious of their surroundings. After a period of silence, Monica looked at John and said, "Tomorrow we will search through the documents, look for answers, and then we will decide what is next."

The morning came and they went about their task to read each document, sometimes whispering, pointing to excerpts, making notes. The afternoon faded into early evening. Stretching and holding back a yawn, Monica looked at John and said, "We need to make some decisions. Let's go for a walk."

Reaching the Jardin du Champ de Mars they found an area where they were alone. Monica looked at John and said, "It is mid-morning at Langley. I am contemplating our next move. I decided to call the CIA Deputy Director for Global Operations. I will call the cell phone number that we copied from Heinrich's phone." Calling the number Monica anxiously waited for an answer and then she heard "Hello." As soon as she heard the voice Monica said, "This is Monica Schmidtski. You don't know me. Is this Bethanne Longfield?"

There was a pause and then a question "May I ask how you got this number?"

Monica took that as a "Yes" and continued. "I have information about a rouge operation and corruption in the Berlin office."

Bethanne Longfield did not respond to Monica's comment, but asked, "Where are you? You need to return to the Berlin office. They have been searching for you for days. They are concerned for your safety. Do you know where Hans Volkov is?"

Monica was surprised by the lack of response to her comment and she hesitated and then asked, "Why are you asking about Hans?"

Longfield, curious about Monica's reaction to her question, hesitated for a moment, then said, "The Deputy Director for Special Operations believes Volkov killed Heinrich Kochmandt. They have a taped phone conversation where Kochmandt says Volkov might have gone off the deep end and totally lost it."

Monica felt a flash of anger. Taking a deep breath, she said, "That is ridiculous!"

The Deputy Director for Global Operations sensed the anger in Monica's voice and said, "You need to come in. You need to come in with Volkov. We need to sort this out."

Monica was feeling anger, then fear, then frustration and she said, "Did you hear what I said? I have information about a rouge operation and corruption in the Berlin office. It may not be safe for me to come in."

Longfield asked the question again, "Where are you? Do you want me to meet with you?"

Confused and frustrated, Monica said, "I'll get back to you" and ended the call.

Monica looked at John as he stared. She felt a rush of confusion and disbelief. What should they do? She explained the phone conversation, tactfully downplaying the accusation that he killed Heinrich, emphasizing that they must see how implausible it is to accuse him.

They continued to walk, constantly checking their surroundings, being careful not to be overheard while discussing their options. Then Monica's cell phone rang. They were startled and looking at the display Monica gasped and said, "It is Bethanne Longfield calling back."

Monica answered the call and was shocked by the question she was asked, "Are you and Volkov in Paris? I had your last call traced to a cell phone tower in Paris. This is important. Are you in Paris?" Longfield continued, "I just finished a call to New York with the Deputy Director for Special Operations. He told me that the Head of Berlin Operations did not come into the office this morning. They found him dead in his apartment. At first it looked like an apparent suicide, but their investigation showed that he was murdered. This is the troubling part. The method used to kill Stephen Spearfoot is exactly what Volkov was trained to do. The Deputy Director for Special Operations believes Volkov killed Spearfoot and you assisted him. That is why you must verify that you are in Paris. Have you been to Germany in the last three days?"

Visibly shakened, Monica responded, "No! We started in Ukraine, traveled through Moldova to Romania and then to Hungary, then Austria, Switzerland, and finally Paris. We have been traveling for four days and have not been to Germany."

Longfield responded with a tone of urgency in her voice, "I need to see the documents that you have. I could have someone meet you."

Monica quickly responded, "I don't know who I can trust. When can you come to Europe?"

Longfield hesitated and asked, "Are you willing to meet with me? Are you willing to come in peacefully?"

Monica nervously asked, "Why do you say peacefully? I just don't know who I can trust."

Longfield quickly responded, "You can trust me, Monica. I will get answers. I must go to New York City tomorrow. I will be staying at the Hilton Times Square Hotel. You can call me there or on my cell phone. You need to keep changing your location and get rid of your cell phone. If I tracked you, you may be vulnerable. Will you call me?"

Monica said, "Yes" and ended the call.

John immediately asked, "Can we trust her?"

Monica looked at him, questioning what she should say, and then said, "Yes. I think we can trust her. She recommended that we change our location. She said she is going to New York City tomorrow."

Monica stood there, silently looking at John. Thinking, what to do next, but before she could finish the thought, John said in an excited voice, "You said this all began for me at the CIA facility in New York City. That's where I need to go to find out who I really am. It should be safe to meet with Bethanne Longfield in New York."

Monica was not sure how to respond. She was deliberating that it would be best for them to split up and then she questioned if John could manage on his own. Was he ready to deal with an airport? She looked at John and said, "Will you be able to do that John? I mean are you capable of traveling on your own?"

Hesitating, John considered her question and understood her concerns. He responded, "If you help me with the planning I know I can do it. It seems to come automatically, I mean my understanding of traveling, once I start the journey. Does that make sense?"

Monica exclaimed in an excited voice, "We need to get back to the hotel and pack. You can only manage an overnight bag; your suitcase is too heavy." As they walked toward the hotel, Monica continued to plan and explain things to John. She would take the diary and financial records and go to Langley and he would take the Operation Azov file and Heinrich Kochmandt's identification card key for the CIA facility at 750 East 71st Street in New York City. They would take the subway to the airport and she would make certain that he was on his flight before she left him. Monica grabbed John's arm and said, "Are you sure that you can do this?"

On the way to the airport Monica checked the available flights and then in an excited voice, "You can fly from Paris to Montreal, Canada and then take the train to New York City. That will give you time to review your plan for New York City. Remember, use your French passport and speak nothing but French until you're on that train to New York."

At the airport, Monica purchased a first class ticket for the following morning on the Air France non-stop flight, AF 348. It would be leaving the Charles de Gaulle airport at 6:10 a.m. Paris time and arrive at Montreal's Pierre Elliott Trudeau International airport at 7:30 a.m. Montreal time. It was going to be a seven hour twenty-minute flight.

Arriving in Montreal, John would clear customs speaking French and at the terminal exit ask the taxi cab driver to take him to 895 rue de la Gauchetiere oust, the Gare Centrale in Montreal. He would then travel from Montreal to New York City on the Amtrak Adirondack line leaving Montreal's Gare Centrale at 10:20 a.m. heading south through the Hudson River Valley and arrive at 9:10 p.m. at New York's Penn Station. Crossing the Canada / United States border John would use his French passport for the Custom Department inspection. It would be a ten hour fifty-minute train trip giving John time to rest and plan his next steps.

When he reached New York City, the Penn Station would still be crowded at that time of the day with people hustling in every direction. John should find the 7th Avenue exit, take the escalator to ground level, and then make his way across the street and check into New York's Hotel Pennsylvania at 401 7th Avenue at 33rd Street.

Monica passed the itinerary to John and asked, "Are you comfortable with each step? Remember, you can ask for assistance in the Montreal airport and the train stations."

John smiled at Monica and said, "I'm amazed how easy it was for you to plan this."

Monica laughed and said, "You made this trip numerous times. It will probably all seem familiar once you get started. Remember to call Bethanne Longfield when you get to New York. It would be best to call her at 7:00 a.m. that first morning from your hotel and arrange to meet with her before she goes to the office. It is important that you get the Operation Azov file to her before you go to the CIA facility at 71st Street. Are you ready?"

John took a deep breath and said, "Thank you! I'll do my best to meet with Longfield the first morning that I am in New York City. Are your plans set?"

"As soon as you board your flight I'm taking the metro to the Paris Gare Du Nord and then the Eurostar high speed train from Paris to London's Saint Pancras Station. I'll cross the street to the Kings Cross Station and take the local train to Cambridge. From there I'll take a taxi to the United States Air Force base at Lakenheath. I have a close friend there and he'll arrange to get me on a military flight to Joint Base Andrews in Washington. I'll be safe once I get to the air force base and I have a lot of friends who I can trust in the District of Columbia. We need to put an end to this John. I'll contact Bethanne Longfield as soon as I get to Washington."

It was early morning John was lying in his bed at New York's Hotel Pennsylvania thinking about how well Monica's plan worked. He arrived in New York without a glitch, remembering Monica's parting words telling him that he had made that trip numerous times and it would probably all seem familiar. There was a certain déjà vu when John entered Penn Station; he seemed to know exactly where to find the 7th Avenue exit. On his way to New York City he studied a city map and John had a strong sensation that he had seen this map many times and was quite familiar with the layout of the city. Maybe these were good signs that his memory was coming back.

John looked at his watch. It was 6:00 a.m. and the plan was to call Bethanne Longfield at seven o'clock and ask to meet her at 8:00 a.m. at an agreed location. John showered and dressed in the only suit that he carried in his overnight bag. He was ready. At 7:00 a.m. he dialed the number for the Hilton Times Square Hotel and asked for the room of Miss Longfield.

There was a pause and then she answered, "Yes."

John's excitement was growing because everything was going as planned. He took a deep breath and said, "This is John Volkov or you may know me as Hans Volkov."

Longfield immediately interrupted and asked, "How did you know where I was staying?"

A little surprised by the question, he remembered, "You told Monica Schmidtski that you were traveling to New York City and she could call you at the Hilton Times Square Hotel."

Again there was an interruption and Longfield asked, "Is Monica with you? Where are you now?"

John wanted to discuss meeting with her before she went into her midtown Manhattan office, but she kept asking questions. Keeping his composure John said, "I last saw Monica at the Charles de Gaulle airport in Paris and I am in New York, not far from where you are staying. I would very much like to meet you and give you a document that you said you needed to see."

Longfield's voice was excited when she said, "You can come to my office. Is this afternoon a good time for you?"

John immediately responded, "No, not at your office. I would like to meet you under the large clock in the middle of the main hall in the Grand Central Terminal. Can you meet me there at 8:00 a.m. this morning?"

Interrupting, Longfield said, I cannot meet at eight. I have appointments most of the day, downtown at the Javits Federal Office Building, meetings with the Department of Homeland Security and Immigration and Customs Enforcement. Believe me, John, I want to meet with you, but I cannot reschedule these meetings. I need to return to my hotel before going into the office later this afternoon. Are you willing to meet at 4:00 p.m.?

John immediately asked, "Under the large clock in the Grand Central Terminal?"

Longfield responded, "Yes, I can meet you there at 4:00 p.m. today."

There was a pause and then Longfield asked, "How will I know you?"

John quickly responded, "I will be holding an 8½ X 11 beige envelope in my right hand with it placed over my left shoulder. I will see you at four." John paused for a second and then ended his call. Immediately he questioned himself. Was he too abrupt? He gathered himself wondering was it safe to meet Longfield at four? Would she be alone? Was the Grand Central Terminal a safe meeting location? John grappled with this change in his plan and finally decided to call room service, order breakfast and then study his notes for the rest of the morning. The morning went by slowly with John constantly checking his watch. Finally, it was after three and John thought, he better get ready to leave for the Grand Central Terminal. He gathered his papers, picked up his attaché case, looked at his watch. It was 3:20 as he left the hotel room.

Exiting the front entrance of the Hotel Pennsylvania, John turned right and went north on 7th Avenue. At the end of the block he turned right onto 33rd Street. Heading east he crossed 6th Avenue, passed the Empire State Building, continued across 5th Avenue, then Madison Avenue. When he reached the next corner he turned left and went north on Park Avenue. Nine blocks later he was standing in front of the Grand Central Terminal at 42nd Street and Park Avenue. It was 3:40 p.m. John had that feeling again - these streets seemed so familiar.

John had read on the train that the classic meeting place for New Yorkers was under the large Seth Thomas clock in the middle of the main hall in the Grand Central Terminal. When he arrived in front of the circular information booth, the large clock was above him. He immediately appreciated that Bethanne Longfield had asked how she would recognize him as hundreds of people rushed by almost in waves as various trains arrived at the station. It was certainly a busy location.

As soon as her meetings ended, Bethanne Longfield left the Javits Federal Office Building. Afternoon traffic was light and the taxi ride from 26 Federal Plaza in lower Manhattan to midtown took less than thirty minutes. Longfield was back at the Hilton Times Square Hotel by 3:15 p.m. Opening the safe in her room she collected documents to take to her office and then left for the short trip to the Grand Central Terminal. Exiting the hotel at 234 West 42nd Street, Longfield turned right and went east on 42nd Street, crossed 7th Avenue and at Broadway crossed the street to the Times Square / Grand Central Shuttle subway station. The 42nd Street Shuttle operates as part of the former Interborough Rapid Transit Company line and serves only two stations, connecting Times Square to Grand Central under 42nd Street. It is the shortest subway line in the system, taking only two minutes from station to station.

When Longfield entered the main hall in the Grand Central Terminal she moved toward the information booth. There was a person standing under the large clock holding an envelope just as Volkov had said. He was younger then she thought he would be. She approached him and holding out her right hand said, "Good afternoon Mr. Volkov, I'm Bethanne Longfield. Thank you for being flexible with your schedule."

John immediately responded, "Good afternoon, Miss Longfield. Thank you for being so prompt. He handed the beige envelope to her and said, "It's all in here. You'll see."

Longfield immediately responded, "Come into the office with me John. We can resolve this together."

John started to turn and he said, "I still have one more stop to make." He then told Longfield, "If you care about the agency, then do something. Make sure that document gets to the right people."

As John started to walk away, Longfield said, "Thank you, John!" John quickly moved away from the clock going west toward the 45th Street Passage and then blended in with the crowd as they moved into the passage. Longfield stood watching as he disappeared into the crowd asking herself, "Where is he going now?"

Bethanne Longfield held the beige envelope tightly as she walked the few short blocks to the CIA's midtown location. Entering her office, she closed the door and opened the envelope. As soon as she saw the cover, she sat down in her chair staring at the document. It was labeled *Operation Azov* and below in red capital letters, *TOP SECRET*. She quickly paged through the document and while still turning pages picked up the phone and told her assistant to call Langley and arrange for a Top Secret fax to be transmitted from the New York office.

As soon as John reached 45th Street he looked at his watch. It would take approximately twenty minutes to walk the thirty blocks up Park Avenue, and then he would turn right and cross

Lexington, then 3rd Avenue, 2nd Avenue, 1st Avenue, and finally York Avenue. He should be there before 4:30 p.m.

Going north on Park Avenue, the sun was to his left and already low in the sky. It was early spring and every time that John crossed a street he went from the shadows of the buildings on Park Avenue to the brightness of the late afternoon sun that was beginning to set in the west. Finally, John reached 71st Street and as planned, he turned right and headed east until he arrived at 750 East 71st Street. He entered the building, looked for the employee entrance and swiped Heinrich Kochmandt's card key to pass through the turn style. There was a security line to the left for employees with laptop computers, purses and attaché cases and John filed into a line to the right for wallets and cell phones. John walked through the metal detector screening area, crossed through the lobby and accessed an elevator using Kochmandt's card key. Sliding the card key across the sensor on the elevator panel, he pressed the tenth floor button and the elevator door closed.

Employees and guests entering the building were monitored by security cameras and the officer on duty recognized John from this week's security posting and as instructed on the posting he immediately called the Deputy Director for Special Operations. The Deputy Director immediately called the Training Director on the tenth floor and said, "Volkov is in the building and we think he is headed your way."

"Don't worry", the voice on the other end of the line said, "I'll meet him at the elevator." As the Training Director opened his office door and stepped out into the hall, the elevator pinged at the other end of the hall.

When John reached the tenth floor the door opened and he saw a person in a white lab coat standing alone at the end of the hall. It was the doctor, the Training Director for Operation Azov. John immediately recognized him. He was overweight, looked old and tired with beads of sweat on his brow, nervously running his right hand through his gray hair and then he made eye contact with John. "Hello, John! You have come home. This is where it all began for you. Do you remember?" The doctor turned, unlocked a door with his card key, and John followed him into the room, the door closing behind them.

John recognized the voice. It was the doctor who had badgered him, telling him that he had volunteered; he wanted to make a difference. Reaching into his lab coat pocket the doctor said, "I have something for you, your dog tags. You came to us, do you remember? You were John Wolf and we turned you into John Volkov. Your mission was to save American lives. Do you remember?"

John looked at the dog tags. Looking straight into the doctor's face he noticed the beads of sweat growing larger on his brow. John took a deep breath and said, "I remember! You used me for your personal gain. You sacrificed innocent lives. I remember! I understand what you did."

Once again, John looked at the dog tags. Something was not right, he was starting to remember, his memory was coming back. Then it hit him, the realization that John Wolf was also an alias, and then he thought, "They really don't know who I am."

Looking back at John, the doctor asked, "So are you going to kill me?"

John quickly responded, "No! They would give you a star at Langley and you don't deserve that. I'm leaving you to be tried, to be haunted by the disgrace that you brought to this agency, to your country. You were the liar! You were driven by personal greed. You were not saving American lives! You will be held accountable for what you did."

Just then the Deputy Director for Special Operations pounded on the glass panel on the door. He tried to force the door open. Then, he fired his gun at the steel mesh reinforced glass and the glass began to shatter. He was still coming after John.

John ran to a door at the opposite end of the room, opened the door and ran down the hall toward a door marked exit. He opened the door and ran up the steps to another steel door. When he opened the door he realized he was on the roof. He looked at his options. There was no other exit. The slight glow in the west indicated that the sun had just set and the remaining dim light left him in near darkness. Looking over the edge of the building, the East River was in front of him, ten stories below.

Then the door opened behind him and a person appeared in the shadows and opened fire in John's direction. John knew that the relentless pursuit by the Deputy Director for Special Operations would not stop. He continued to fire. John was not armed, he had no weapon. He heard a bullet wiz by his ear. He looked around one more time. He had no choice. He took a running start and jumped over the edge of the building toward the East River, falling into the darkness of the night as the gunfire continued to ring out behind him.

CHAPTER 8

It was challenging for John to keep his emotions from skyrocketing out of control. The realization that he remembered who he was, the adrenalin rush of being shot at and jumping from the roof to save his life, and finally, finding his way to 81st Street put him on an emotional roller coaster. There were moments when he was experiencing a feeling of elation, and the next moment, he was agonizing over the fear that he was being followed. That he could be endangering Shuk Wa. What had he done? Rambling at times, and then falling into periods of deep thought, John tried to explain to Shuk Wa what had occurred during the last two hours, the last two weeks, the last two years. Shuk Wa listened as John excitedly told his story. Beginning with his dramatic exodus from the CIA Training Facility on 71st Street. John tried his best to explain it all to Shuk Wa.

"Jumping from that roof was not brave. It was an act of desperation. Survival was my only thought, regardless of the risk of a ten story fall into the East River. At that moment, it seemed to be my only option. My mind was racing, memories of who I was and what I had become bounced in and out of my mind, and I was driven by the belief that the agency would not stop their chase until I was dead. It seems oversimplified to say it, but it was as if I were waking up from a bad dream, and getting off that building was my only way out."

"Hitting the water was like being thrown into a concrete wall. My entire body felt the pain. When my plunge into the depths of that cold water finally ended, I lay there motionless. Knocked senseless by the impact, it took time for me to realize that I was alive and needed to get to the surface to take a breath of air. My descent from the roof to the water was just a matter of seconds and I am sure that I drifted under water in a dreamlike state for what seemed to be a long period of time. When I surfaced it was like I was being raised from the water after baptism. I had escaped a bad dream and I felt elated, joyful to be alive, to have escaped death one more time."

"I immediately felt the pull of the current and the salty taste of the water in my mouth. I was totally disoriented for a period of time, floating into the darkness. I could hear traffic to my right, above the blackness of a wall, and to my left it seemed quiet and less threatening. Half swimming, half floating, I bobbed along feeling the pull of the tidal current and the realization of the coldness of the water hit me. I needed to get out of the river. Straight ahead were the twinkling lights of the Queensboro Bridge and to my right was the East River Esplanade. Across the river to my left was a complex of brightly lit buildings and the shoreline slowly faded into shades of gray and I could see an outline of trees through the darkness. I was floating toward South Point Park on the Southern end of Roosevelt Island. It looked safer to head in that direction, across the river. The darkness looked inviting."

"I was evaluating my options and as fortune would have it I saw what appeared to be a small landing straight ahead, just ahead to my right. Was it safe? Was I too close to 71st Street to exit the river? The chill of the river drove me to the landing and as I pulled myself out of the water the darkness and cold night air engulfed me. I was adjacent to the 63rd Street Pedestrian Bridge. The Esplanade was dark and deserted and I moved quickly through the shadows onto the ramp and crossed over FDR Drive to York Avenue. The pedestrian bridge exited at the South end of Rockefeller University. The street was lined with trees, and I felt safe in the shadows. Right in front of me was a large container where students could leave clothing for the homeless. The container must have been at capacity because there were plastic bags piled to the side and I saw my chance for dry clothing. I rummaged through the bags; I found sweatpants, sweaters, an old jacket, and even a woolen skull cap. I changed in the shadows with lightning speed and in a matter of minutes was heading North on York Avenue carrying a bag with my wet clothing."

"I stayed on the sidewalk under the trees bordering the campus and when I reached 64th Street, the fear of moving in the direction of 71st Street entered my mind. I turned left and headed West on 64th Street and felt comfortable because the one-way traffic was coming in my direction. It was a quiet street, little traffic, with only a few people out walking their dogs. At 64th and 2nd Avenue a large group of young people were coming out of a building. I noticed a sign for the College of Mount Saint Vincent and I blended into the back of a group as they crossed 2nd Avenue. When I reached Lexington Avenue I turned right. The one-way traffic moved fast on Lexington Avenue and it was comforting that it was coming toward me. The sidewalk grew crowded at 68th Street at Hunter College and I avoided looking up, knowing there would be street cameras because of the subway station."

"As I walked up Lexington Avenue it all started to come back to me. Good memories of the times that I visited this neighborhood with my family. At 77th Street I thought of the many times that I entered and exited the 77th Street and Lexington Avenue subway station. When I reached 81st Street I instinctively turned left. I crossed Park Avenue and at Madison I could see the Metropolitan Museum of Art straight ahead. When I reached your block, I remembered your name, your closeness to my family, and the many times that I visited you in New York. The dragon above your door was such a welcoming sign. I knew I had found a friend and safety. It was the first time that I knew who I really was in two years. What I failed to think of was the danger that I might be bringing to your door."

As the Chair Emeritus of the Department of East Asian Languages and Cultures at Columbia University, Shuk Wa Lau maintained more than a position. Her ongoing research, concentrating on the political and legal structure of a geographical area that historically used a common writing system, kept intact her reputation as a scholar and expert in her field. Her passion was mentoring graduate students who specialized in an interdisciplinary approach to Southeast Asian law and business. She was renowned for guiding graduate fellows through teaching and research projects that included her second love, the Metropolitan Museum of Art.

Born in the year of the Dragon, Shuk Wa exemplified the characteristics associated with her Chinese sign; she was an extroverted bundle of energy, confident, and she loved every challenge and the inevitable success that naturally followed. She was generous with her time, attracted many friends, but cherished solitary moments, and self-sufficiency trumped the need for close bonds with friends or colleagues. Her year of birth presented her with the unique characteristics of the Metal Dragon, individuals who succeed through determination, burn the candle at both ends, take risks, demonstrate a knack for organizing, enjoy the opportunity to lead, and find delight that others want to follow her lead. She earned respect!

The entrance way to every residence of her block on 81st Street was the gateway to accumulated wealth. Every door, every window, was protected fashionably with ornamental ironwork. Good taste surpassed the need for protection; designs that kept out intruders were works of art in addition to their utilitarian purpose. Not one entrance gave the appearance of a prison. Shuk Wa's front door was over the top in the uniqueness category. A sculptured metal dragon positioned over the entranceway symbolically guarded the door below, with its steel bars shaped into a classical diamond pattern that presented a look of elegance rather than the bars of a jailhouse door. The dragon both welcomed guests and warned adversaries that a Metal Dragon resided beyond the door.

In Asian philosophy, people born in the year of the Dragon are to be honored and respected, and Shuk Wa seemed to work diligently to prove to be deserving of the accolades bestowed on Dragons.

John's family had complemented a Dragon perfectly. His Mother, born in the year of the Monkey, proved to be the best friend to a Dragon. His Father, also born in the year of the Dragon had been the mirror image of Shuk Wa's finest attributes. John was also born in the year of the Monkey, and his sister was also a Dragon. They all had enjoyed traveling together, never accepting the convenience of a tour or the comforts that tourist destinations offered. Off the beaten path, mingling with people they would meet along the way, they were the most comfortable in remote places.

And now, listening intently and somewhat confused, Shuk Wa had one pressing question to ask. Reaching out and holding John's hand, she said, "Why did we not hear from you for the past two years?"

Making eye contact, John heard the concern in Shuk Wa's voice. Taking a deep breath, he hesitated for a moment, and finally said, "This is all going to sound far-fetched, and it has been difficult for me to accept and to comprehend what I have been doing for the last two years. When I last stayed here, I was being reassigned from the Joint Intelligence Center at the Pentagon to what I was told was a clandestine unit that conducted missions that were vital to national security. I was in a state of mind that I needed to hold onto something good, something that was worthwhile, that would make a difference, and the words vital to national security were just what I wanted to hear. The training was intense and I am not even certain if my memories are real or imagined. I remember sessions involving hypnosis and being exhausted, remaining in a hypnotic state for days. This is the part that really gets far-fetched. I was given all these aliases and had passports for many European countries. I do not understand how they did it, but they enabled me to think more quickly, to be decisive, acting almost mechanical, achieving success with each mission. They seemed to control me as if I were programmed to be this person who achieved success with each mission regardless of the personal cost. I lived with the name of an alias, John Volkov and I honestly began to believe that I was that person. For the last two years they convinced me, somehow manipulating me into believing John Volkov was my real name. Their constant badgering exhausted me mentally. It is hard for me to believe, to accept, that I forgot that I was John Gruneburg. Somehow they altered my memory, maybe it was the hypnosis, the many sessions that I was in a hypnotic state. I only know that it left me without memories. Then I recently learned that I had a CIA file and I was told what was supposed to be my real name, John Wolf, but that was an alias that the Navy created. When I got to New York, it all started to come back to me. I started to remember my past. Then, at the CIA Training Facility I finally remembered who I really was. Are you getting this? Stop me if you get confused.

Shuk Wa moved her hands toward John and turned her palms up while shrugging her shoulders.

John continued. "They convinced me that their training made me incredibly bright. I would open a passport, fall right into the role of the alias, speaking any needed language, regardless if it was English, French, Dutch, German, Russian, Czech, Polish. I had no understanding of how I could speak fluently, without hesitation, without knowing, no memory, of how I learned these languages. Enough about how this training confused me mentally, what is more important for you to understand is that I became a highly-trained covert assassin carrying out missions that I was told would make our country more secure. The last two years have been very difficult. I realized that I was an assassin, programmed to be a very effective lethal weapon that was trained to instinctively inflict deadly action. My reflexes are so sharp, so fined tuned, I respond to a fight as if I am just reaching out and catching a ball. It is frightening to know what I am capable of and how

I have been used. So now I am hunted. For some reason they want to eliminate me. To be dead, gone, and out of their case files. I am afraid that it may be very dangerous for me to be here. I need to move on, and I am sorry to say this, but I need your help. Is Wenli still living in Shanghai?"

Shuk Wa sat in silence, and finally realized that John was waiting for a response. He had talked for so long and so fast, she had sat almost motionless, listening intently, absorbed in what he was saying. Not in disbelief as John had suggested, but bewildered by the extent of it all. John was always a credible source and his life at the academy and the missions that followed were always extraordinary, way beyond everyday life. This was different. This was like one of those action films that she never really liked. It was more than a nightmare. This story bordered on the edge of the horrific, a place where Shuk Wa had no interest in going.

John stared at Shuk Wa, waiting for a reply. "Is Wenli alright?" "Is she …"

Shuk Wa interrupted. "John it has been two years. Every holiday, every birthday, every visit to this house, haunted her by not knowing where you were or what had become of you. John, she is living in Halifax, in Nova Scotia, in eastern Canada. I think in her heart she has buried you many times, but yet she has kept you alive, with hope as perennial as the grass."

John sat silently for a moment. "I need to move. I need to adjust my plan. I know this will sound strange, but I feel if I stay here both of our lives will be in danger. May I explain my plan?"

Shuk Wa smiled for the first time. "With what you have just told me it would be good to hear a plan. It cannot be any crazier than what I have heard for this past hour."

John was surprised at her response. "I am serious, he said. We may be in danger if I do not move."

Shuk Wa looked at John and said "John, please explain."

Without hesitating, John said, "My belief is that there is a very small circle in the CIA who really knows my true identity. I am being hunted under a number of aliases and what is listed in my CIA file as my real name is another alias. The people who recruited me, trained me, and put me on a path to be an assassin, are all dead. My main contact in Berlin is dead. He was the CIA Officer in charge of our operation and reported to the Head of Berlin Operations who is also dead. I was originally recruited by that CIA Officer when he was the Station Chief in Madrid; he was my Supervisory Training Officer. They provided all the aliases and I believe they created the CIA file that claimed yet another alias as my real name. The CIA and even the Deputy Director for Special Operations in New York consistently refer to me by my alias, John Volkov. The only person who told me what he thought was my real name, was the Training Director for Operation Azov. It was not until I faced that doctor, the Training Director who ran the program's behavior modification program in the training section of the CIA building on 71st Street that I finally remembered who I really was. I then realized that he did not know my real name, only my alias John Wolf, the false name in my CIA file. He had no idea that I was John Gruneburg. I remembered him telling me that I will no longer be called by the name in my CIA file. He actually handed me what he said were my dog tags and called me by the name in the CIA file. He said I came to them as John Wolf. I had volunteered for the assignment and they made me John Volkov to protect me and my country. The other interesting point is that those dog tags had my blood type as O negative."

"I remembered everything. He had told me that my missions would save American lives. I volunteered for that program because I believed him. When the CIA recruited me and that fake name was placed in my file, it must have been set up to protect the Deputy Director in case my mission failed. He was working with a corrupt Russian Oil Minister and embezzled millions from the agency. One of my first assignments was to assassinate a Russian Minister in Berlin and I had no idea that I was killing the one person who could expose the Deputy Director's fraudulent scheme. If I were caught, the alias on my passport would lead to a name in my file, a person who did not exist. The O negative blood type on the dog tag was the trigger for me. My blood type is A positive. They never checked it when I gave them the information to create the fake CIA identity. For two years I could not remember who I was because they had suppressed my real identity and brainwashed me into believing I was serving my country. I lived with the aliases, struggling to remember who I really was."

John hesitated, took another deep breath, and continued. "So here I am, hunted, in someone's discarded clothing, possibly putting both of us in danger by sitting here and talking."

John hesitated again, and then with his tone of voice growing more intense, he said, "Do you understand what I am saying? I think I can travel using my own passport. The name John Gruneburg will not set off alarms. That name is safe to use. The problem will be that surveillance cameras will be using facial recognition and my face and my identity will be tied to the aliases in the CIA forged passports. I need to stay off the grid. I need to stay away from transportation hubs and facilities with security cameras."

John stopped talking and the two sat in silence for what seemed to be a long time, and then Shuk Wa asked, "Have you slept recently? You look exhausted. You need to rest and then we can plan the next step."

John reluctantly agreed to lie down for a short period of time. He was asleep in seconds.

As soon as John went to sleep, Shuk Wa turned on the television to watch the nightly news. Half staring, half in a trance, she saw John Gruneburg's face flash onto the screen and the CIA story was being explained. Shuk Wa was stunned, almost in shock. Never doubting John, she hadn't grasped the urgency of the situation, the seriousness of the danger in which he may be involved. The horrific had become reality. John truly needed her help.

CHAPTER 9

It had been a long day with early morning meetings cascading into the afternoon and evening. Congressman Joseph Spencer was tired as he flopped into his most comfortable chair, padded and well cushioned, it looked out of place in a congressional office. Reaching for the remote, Congressman Spencer tuned to his favorite news channel and picked up a mug of green tea, getting ready for a half hour of relaxation. With a folder filled with the evenings' must-read documents in his lap, he leaned back, sipped his tea, and focused on the news.

He started paging through the stack of documents, half listening, half watching the news, when he saw BREAKING NEWS flash across the screen and a voice over, "Live from New York, two senior CIA Officials were arrested this evening, including the Deputy Director for Special Operations for the Central Intelligence Agency in New York. Stay tuned for further details as they become available." The congressman stared in disbelief. What looked like plain clothes law enforcement officers led a well dressed man to an unmarked car, directed him into the back seat, closed the door, and the car sped away. This was not a good way to end the day.

As a member of the House Permanent Select Committee on Intelligence, Congressman Spencer knew he would need answers before he got a call from the Speaker of the House of Representatives. He immediately reached for his phone and dialed his friend from the Senate Select Committee on Intelligence, Senator Sam McDowell. As soon as the phone rang, the senator looked at the name with the incoming call and knew what he would hear as soon as he said hello.

"Have you seen the evening news? Do you know anything about this CIA problem?" Congressman Spencer blurted out the questions without even saying hello to the senator.

The senator paused for a second, and then responded, "I just got off the phone with CIA headquarters, they are being smug as usual and I was about to call you. We need more information and we need it fast and I'm afraid we're not going to get the details we need from the CIA. We need to set up a meeting with your friend George Harthmann and find out what the National Security Agency knows about this operation. Will you be at tomorrow morning's meeting of the Board of Visitors at the Naval Academy? Arrange for us to see Harthmann before that meeting. We cannot skip the meeting. As the appointee from the Senate Armed Services Committee, it is my responsibility to organize the team to write the annual report to the president and that's the first item on tomorrow's agenda. Many of the new board members, especially those appointed by the president and vice president want to have an active role, assisting in writing sections of the report and organizing the board's findings and recommendations. As the designee from the House Armed Services Committee I am counting on you to coordinate your four colleagues who were appointed by the Speaker of the House of Representatives. Make sure they have no hidden agendas. This is not political. They need to understand this is a public relations campaign and we need to paint the best possible picture with this report. We need to set up teams to work on the various sections of the report. Think about inquiries into the morale and discipline at the academy. Another group can work on curriculum, instruction, academic challenges. Make sure they emphasize the continuous need for the latest technology. The last group can work on facilities, equipment, fiscal and financial reports. We need recommendations that are on the top of every admiral's list."

The senator stopped for a moment and then asked, "Are you getting all of this Joe?" Without waiting for an answer, the senator continued, "We are scheduled to start at nine and have lunch at the Officer's Club. This will give the admirals the opportunity to express their needs to board members who are assigned to report on their specific areas. Invite George Harthmann to meet us at the Officer's Club at eight. That should not set off any alarms. I have to make a number of calls. I will see you in the morning."

The senator was gone and Joe sat there with the phone still to his ear. Without much thought he found George Harthmann's name on his phone list and dialed his cell and started tapping his other hand nervously, "Come on, George, pick up," thinking out loud as the phone rang. Finally, there was an answer.

"Good evening, Congressman Spencer. How can I help you, Joe?" George Hartmann knew that an evening call from a congressman was not going to be a social call and having heard about the CIA debacle in New York, he had a good idea where this conversation was headed.

Congressman Spencer got right to the point. "I just got off the phone with Senator McDowell. He would like you to meet with us at eight tomorrow morning at the Naval Academy to provide details about the CIA operation that was reported on this evening's news."

There was a period of silence and then George asked, "Who will I be meeting with and why at the Naval Academy?" The congressman quickly responded, "Just the senator and me. We have a meeting at nine with the Board of Visitors at the Naval Academy and the senator is the Chair. He cannot miss the meeting. We will meet you at eight at the Officer's Club and the senator will even buy you breakfast. Are you available? Please do not say no."

With a laugh George responded, "Anything for you, Joe. I will see you at eight."

The next morning it was rainy and chilly; Annapolis was blanketed in an early morning fog. This kind of weather also paralyzed Metro Washington traffic and the senator and congressman knew that the only way to deal with the wet roads was to get an early start. When the congressman pulled into the parking lot behind the Officer's Club he noticed two men standing under umbrellas. As he got closer he realized it was Senator McDowell talking with George Harthmann. The rain had slowed to a drizzle and the congressman contemplated if he really needed an umbrella. It was just a few minutes after seven and the parking lot lights were still on giving a glisten to the falling drizzle. As the congressman approached the others he yelled, "I thought I would be the first one here this morning. How long have you been here?"

Senator McDowell started without answering the question. "George was just asking me if this meeting is off the record and he was concerned that you may have planned to record the conversation. What do you have to say to that congressman?"

Joe reached out and grabbed George's hand, "Thanks for making the early morning trip George. Why off the record? I'm afraid that we will need to answer a lot of questions before we put this baby to bed."

George looked at the senator and with a smile asked, "Do you mind if we go for a walk? I understand you know your way around these grounds."

The senator quickly shot back, "Why not inside? I could use a cup of coffee."

George shrugged his shoulders, "Please give me five minutes, but away from the possibility of someone overhearing our conversation."

As the senator started walking, he turned to George and said, "The clock is ticking, I suggest you get started."

Thinking out loud George responded, "Where does one start?"

The senator quickly retorted, "I would suggest the truth. What is this about?"

Without hesitation George started, "You need to focus on the CIA Deputy Director for Global Operations who is investigating a rouge Berlin operation and has apparently recovered documents that confirm the theft of twenty million dollars from the agency. There were two CIA Officers connected to the Berlin operation and both were recently murdered in Germany. The Deputy Director for Special Operations was implicating a CIA agent with the murders. While investigating the murders, the Deputy Director for Global Operations found evidence that the CIA agent was framed. Her continued efforts led to the discovery of a rogue operation, the black op that was reported in last night's news. It was reported that this unauthorized operation implicated senior CIA officials, including the Deputy Director for Special Operations who is stationed in New York. It was alleged that this was a government assassination program that may have, in some cases, targeted non-combatants. It is my understanding that the CIA Deputy Director for Global Operations will be contacting the Senate Select Committee on Intelligence to make a statement and disclose the truth about the operation. As you know, CIA headquarters in Langley, Virginia is doing their best to prevent any further news on this operation."

Sensing a break in the conversation Congressman Spencer quickly said, "You mentioned the Senate Select Committee on Intelligence. Was there mention of including the House Permanent Select Committee on Intelligence?"

George took a deep breath and looked at the congressman. "This is damage control, and as long as it is off the record, there are members of the House Permanent Select Committee on Intelligence that cannot be trusted. There have been leaks in the past. There are members on that committee that will leak information for political purposes."

Congressman Spencer, getting a little animated said, "I hope you are not telling me that the NSA is listening to private conversations of congressmen."

George quickly responded, "If a congressman goes into a meeting knowing that the content of the meeting will include documents that are marked Top Secret and then chooses to ignore the oath of secrecy and disclose information from the meeting, it is being kind to say they cannot be trusted. Treason may be the more appropriate label. Do you understand what will happen if this continues in the news? We do not need to feed the conspiracy theorists and give Hollywood the chance to rewrite history. We cannot have a confidential meeting, reviewing classified documents, with some of the present committee members who are intent on leaking information to the press."

George took a deep breath and continued, "This is an embarrassment to the CIA. There may be criminal activity, and they will not disclose embarrassing information to Congress. They will look for a scapegoat and will want to wrap up the inquiry. They will discuss clandestine operations that may include covert and top secret missions, and because of the secrecy of the operation, the information is not available, or cannot be disclosed. They will tell you that the facts have been exaggerated, dedicated civil servants were deceived by foreign operatives, Americans were the victims, and they were duped in what was designed to be a training mission."

George hesitated, took another deep breath and said, "Senator McDowell, Congressman Spencer, I apologize for getting so emotional. You do not need a lecture at this time of the morning. I will get you additional information. What is your schedule for the rest of the week?"

Senator McDowell patted George on the back, "If you weren't emotional about your job, you wouldn't be here today. Believe me, George, we value your frankness. What about breakfast? The Officer's Club is a great place to start the day."

George smiled broadly, "Thank you senator, but it is best that I say no. There are a few of your board members..." George hesitated, "I would prefer that they did not know that we were meeting this morning."

Congressman Spencer reached out and grabbed George's hand and said, "Thank you again for your time and your honesty. I will get back to you later this afternoon. I promise that I will get you back out here to play a round of golf with the Naval Academy golf team."

CHAPTER 10

Shuk Wa tossed and turned most of the night, unusual for someone who normally slept soundly for a minimum of eight hours. Throughout the night Shuk Wa thought about her options, waking momentarily, and then drifting back to sleep. Almost in a dreamlike state, she began to plan. The priority must be to get John out of New York City. She understood the danger in mentioning his name on the phone, with e-mail or texting. She needed to contact Wenli, but she could not disclose last night's events. Quietly leaving her bedroom, she silently went down the stairs and entered her office and closed the door behind her. Her plan was to call Wenli and arrange to meet her under the guise that it had been an extremely bad winter and she needed a springtime holiday.

Security cameras would be an issue with John. Travel by train, plane or bus would require going through a terminal, and in New York City, every terminal was under twenty-four-hour security camera surveillance. Her only option was to drive in her own car.

Halifax was in the Atlantic Time zone, one hour ahead of New York, so if she called at 6:00 a.m. Eastern Time, Wenli would be into her 7:00 a.m. routine, getting ready for work. The next question was where should they meet? If she said Boston, Wenli would fly in and she would expect her Mother to take the train. She needed a location to which they both needed to drive.

Shuk Wa wanted to suggest a location that would evoke past memories, good memories, holidays that were enjoyed and treasured. With a smile on her face she knew she had the place.

It was six o'clock and Shuk Wa dialed Wenli. When the phone rang Wenli was surprised. No one called her at this time of the morning and when she looked at the phone's display and saw Shuk Wa Lau she was even more surprised. Wenli quickly picked up the phone, "Good Morning, Mom! What's up? Are you alright?"

Shuk Wa quickly responded, "Good Morning, Wenli! I'm fine. It has been a brutal winter and I was thinking of spring and I thought how much I was missing you. I've been thinking about an early spring holiday to Maine, spending a few days shopping in Freeport and three or four days enjoying the serenity of Acadia National Park and Bar Harbor."

Wenli hesitated for a moment then asked, "Are you sure you're alright? How is work? Is everything alright at work?"

Shuk Wa responded in a flash, "Wenli, I'm fine! I just need a break from this winter, a break from the city, it would be good to see you and spend some time together."

Wenli was listening and thinking at the same time. This was not like her Mother who never, ever did impulsive holidays. Everything always had to be planned. Wenli asked, "Do you want me to come to New York this weekend? I could fly down Friday night."

Shuk Wa quickly interrupted, "I appreciate your offer, but I would like to get out of the city for a relaxing holiday. It would be nice to have a change of scenery."

Wenli thought for a moment and then said, "Why Maine? It's a little far to go for a long weekend."

Shuk Wa quickly responded, "It is only a six-hour drive and I could be in Freeport this evening. I could do some shopping tomorrow and travel on to Bar Harbor the next day. You could join me on Friday."

Wenli quickly responded, "Don't you think that is a little far for you to drive on your own? You could fly into Boston and make a connection to Bar Harbor. Are you alright Mom? This all seems a little rushed. Do you want me to come to New York?"

Shuk Wa could sense that Wenli was worried and she instinctively knew that she had to redirect the conversation. "I am really alright, Wenli." Shuk Wa calmly said and then added, "I know it has been a hard winter for you. We both work too hard and we really don't spend that much time together since you moved to Halifax. This year more than most, I am looking forward to spring and I would really enjoy sharing the earliest days of spring with you. I want to go to Bar Harbor because we have enjoyed so many holidays there over the years. The beauty of Acadia lifts the spirits, the fresh salt water air, and the warmth of a bowl of good lobster chowder at the end of the day. I need that kind of change right now. Will you be able to join me on Friday? I really am looking forward to seeing you."

Wenli took a deep breath, "Alright, Mother. Now you are making me feel guilty for questioning your reasoning. Who would have thought that my Mother would turn into a drama queen in her old age, or should I say her senior years?"

Shuk Wa quickly interrupted, "Please don't get into labeling or name calling. I raised you to be above that kind of language." Taking a deep breath Shuk Wa added, "I will take that as a yes and I will e-mail details about Bar Harbor later today. Thank you for being such a wonderful daughter!"

Wenli laughed, "It will be good to see you, Mom. I better finish getting ready for work and I have a lot to get done if I'm taking Friday off. I will look for your e-mail message. Travel safely, Mom, and keep your cell phone on."

Shuk Wa quickly responded, "I will, Wenli, and I will call you this evening from Freeport."

Wenli added, "I will be waiting for your call. Bye, Mom!"

Leaving her office, Shuk Wa quietly walked to the entrance of the living room where John was still sound asleep on the couch, wrapped in the blanket that she covered him with last night. Looking at her watch, then at John, her thought was to let him sleep. Her mind was racing. He will need a good breakfast when he finally wakes up, and she needed to make reservations for Freeport and Bar Harbor. She looked at her watch again. Time was not a problem. It was early and there was no need to worry about reservations at this time of the year. She was sure that there would be vacancies. With that, she quietly moved to the kitchen.

The smell of potatoes frying with onions, blended with the aroma of coffee, filled the kitchen and slowly drifted toward the living room. John stirred and immediately froze, intently listening, thinking about where he was, and wondering if it was safe to leave the warmth of the couch. The sounds from the kitchen seemed normal and his growling stomach was responding to the aroma permeating from that direction. John slid off the couch and without a sound moved toward the kitchen. As he got closer, he could see Shuk Wa working in the kitchen. He stood motionless watching her every move, listening for other voices in the house. They seemed to be alone. John thought for a moment that he should be leaving. It was dangerous for him to stay and maybe even to have come here. He hesitated, then he decided to say something to avoid startling her. "Good morning, Shuk Wa! I believe I slept longer than I thought I would. I have been thinking. I should leave."

Shuk Wa quickly interrupted, "I have a plan, John. I will drive you to Maine today. We will leave after you have breakfast and take a shower. Your clothes are still in the upstairs back bedroom. We haven't changed a thing since you were last here."

John put his open hands in front of his chest, palms facing Shuk Wa, unconsciously showing a sign of rejection to Shuk Wa's idea. "Wait! Wait! I don't want you to get involved."

Shuk Wa once again interrupted. "Be rational, John, you said it is not wise to use public transportation. It started raining during the night. Your photo has been broadcast on the local news report identifying you as the missing CIA agent."

John interrupted, "What did you just say about my picture being shown on the local news? When did you see this?"

Shuk Wa sighed, thinking that she should not have mentioned last night's news story. "It was on the late night news. It was just a fifteen second news story." While Shuk Wa was talking she placed a potato, onion, and egg frittata on the table in front of John. There was already a plate of breakfast sausages, a pot of coffee, and two place settings on the table. Shuk Wa motioned to a chair and said, "John, please have breakfast and I will explain my plan. I must tell you one very important point. Our accountant filed your federal, state and city taxes just over two weeks ago using this as your home address. This has been your legal mailing address for the last two years. Your bank statements come here, all of your personal mail, even your alumni magazine from the Naval Academy comes to my address. If someone were looking for John Gruneburg, they would have been here already. Do you agree?"

As Shuk Wa was talking, she calmly sat down in front of one of the place settings and motioned to a chair. "I think we should say a prayer of thankfulness for this food and for your continued safety." With that, Shuk Wa reached out her hand toward John. John had forgotten how special life had been. He had forgotten the warm and caring atmosphere that always awaited him in Shuk Wa's home. In silence, John sat down, reached out for Shuk Wa's hand and she began to pray. John was in a dreamlike state, options racing through his mind. It all seemed too good to be true. Was the peace that he was feeling going to last? Was someone going to crash through the door at any minute?

After the prayer, Shuk Wa continued talking, passing the frittata, then the sausages, feeling relieved that John was starting to eat. "Last summer Wenli and I decided that we would take a road trip out West this coming August. We are planning," stopping in the middle of the sentence and hesitating for a moment, she continued, "That really doesn't matter. I purchased a new car to be used on the trip. It is the fanciest car that I have ever owned. It is a Mercedes Benz and I keep it in the museum parking garage. Because of my position at the Metropolitan Museum of Art I have free parking privileges. It is just across the street. I enter the parking garage at Eightieth Street and Fifth Avenue. The museum opens at ten, but I can access the car in the garage at nine. It is a very nice car, a GLK 350 SUV. They call the color polar white. Wenli and I joke that the car has only seen sunshine. It has never been out of the garage in the rain or snow. I purchased the car on the west side, on Eleventh Avenue," again stopping in the middle of the sentence, she hesitated. "I'm sorry, John, once again that doesn't matter." Taking a deep breath Shuk Wa continued "I called Wenli and she will …"

John interrupted in the middle of her sentence. "What did you say to Wenli? Did you call her using your landline or cell phone?"

Shuk Wa immediately understood John's concern. "Don't worry, John. I understood what you said last night, that it would be dangerous to mention your name in a phone call, a text message or in an e-mail message. I did not tell Wenli that you were here. I never mentioned your name. I told her that I needed a holiday away from the city."

John interrupted once again. "Did she accept that? She is coming to Maine? I still think that I may be putting you and now Wenli into a situation that is too dangerous. I'm afraid it is beyond your imagination. I have seen what these people are capable of doing."

This time Shuk Wa interrupted John, speaking in a different tone of voice than before. "John, I must explain something to you that Wenli and I have discussed in detail, and I do not want this to sound emotional. John, you must understand that our entire social structure was centered around Columbia University and the Gruneburg family was the center of that social circle. Wenli and I have greatly missed your mother and father and of course your sister, Aimée Marie. We have missed you, John. Wenli and I have sat in that back bedroom crying, missing you so very much, not knowing where you were, sometimes thinking the worst, but always holding onto the hope that you were alive. It has been difficult for us and now I am thrilled to see you. Wenli will be overjoyed to see you; the greatest danger for us is the thought of losing you, of not seeing you again."

John was overwhelmed. He felt the intensity of their friendship, and yet in some ways it all felt foreign to him. He was remembering his closeness to Shuk Wa, and yet when he became comfortable with her kindness and concerns for his safety, he immediately reverted back to the fear of the unknown. What was going to happen to him?

Shuk Wa sensed that John was in deep thought and she seized the moment and said, "Get a shower and pack enough clothes for a few weeks. You have a number of suits in your closet. We will dress as if we are going to a business meeting while we are traveling. Your bag needs to look like you are taking a combination business trip and holiday. I will give you a garbage bag for those clothes. We will take them with us."

John interrupted her. "I think you have been watching too many spy thrillers. You sound like you really know what you are doing. Please don't enjoy this, Shuk Wa. This will be very dangerous. I will take a shower and pack. Should I be ready to leave by nine?"

Shuk Wa ignored his comments and continued. "John, do you remember that you have a safe in your bedroom closet? Your passports are in that safe. Do you remember the combination for the safe?"

Momentarily John was a little stunned and he excitedly asked Shuk Wa, "Are you saying that I have a safe in this upstairs back bedroom that you keep talking about and I have a passport in that safe?"

Shuk Wa quickly responded, "That's correct! Do you remember the combination? If not, you gave it to me before you left the last time you were here."

John hesitated and then asked, "And that was two years ago?"

Shuk Wa responded, "Yes, John, almost two years have passed since you were here."

While in the shower John was thinking of alternatives to Shuk Wa's plan and every time he came to the same conclusion. This was the best way for him to get out of the city. He could leave in her car alone, use cash for expenses, and get out of the city, but then what would he do? Sooner or later he would need to use a passport if he was going to leave the country. Did he want to try to disappear into rural America? Where would he go? What would he do? Shuk Wa's plan would give him time, but was it also going to put her life at risk?

What about the news? Should they be checking the local and twenty-four-hour news stations? Shuk Wa convinced John that sitting around watching news channels would just make her paranoid. It was best to get on the road and he could scan news stations in the car using her laptop computer. She thought it was best to leave the city. The rain had subsided to a light drizzle making it a good time to leave.

Then there was the safe and the passports. Before Shuk Wa mentioned the safe, John had no recollection of leaving his passports at Shuk Wa's house. But, as soon as he looked at the safe, he remembered the combination and the contents. It all came back in a flash. Those moments were unsettling and he questioned his grip on the true reality of the situation. He fluctuated from good memories to the fear of the present and was emotionally drained.

Shuk Wa cleaned up the kitchen, packed her bag, laptop, cell phone and all her travel essentials. Dressed in a blue business suit, she was ready to go. As soon as she saw John with his bag she said, "I will walk to the parking garage and get my car and pick you up in front of my house. It will take me about fifteen minutes. I have to go around the block because of the one way streets."

John quickly interrupted, "Should I come with you?"

Shuk Wa quickly responded, "No! There are security cameras all around the garage and you would need to show identification to get into the garage. Be ready to bring the suitcases to the car. Here is the key to lock the front door behind you. Make sure that you lock the dead bolt. It's just drizzling now. Are you ready to leave?"

John took a deep breath and said, "I'm concerned about driving in the direction of the CIA training facility."

Shuk Wa interrupted John saying, "I have the route planned. We will avoid immediately going east to stay away from the area around the CIA training facility. My plan is to go down 5th Avenue to 79th Street and then make a right into Central Park, go across the park and come out onto West 81st Street and go straight ahead to Broadway, turn right and go North on Broadway through the Columbia University Campus to West 125th Street, make a right hand turn and continue on 125th Street across Manhattan and then exit on the right for the Robert Kennedy Bridge. The GPS will take over from there and we will be in Freeport in about six hours and we will avoid the East side neighborhood that concerns you. My car has this navigation system that uses GPS technology to provide detailed driving directions and maps and even displays gas stations along the route. I'm sure that you are familiar with that kind of system."

John smiled thinking about how she was adapting to technology and yet in awe of its capabilities in a very smug way. John took a deep breath and his voice got very serious as he said, "I am overwhelmed with your kindness. This is going way beyond what anyone should be doing for me."

Shuk Wa interrupted and said, "We can talk later. It is best that we get an early start." Shuk Wa's voice turned serious. "Until we get out of the city and through the Connecticut traffic and onto Interstate 95, we need to concentrate on the highway and the traffic. No discussions until we get onto

I-95 away from the heavy traffic. I will purchase a number of morning newspapers. There is a news stand on 5th Avenue on the sidewalk in front of the museum, and you can use my laptop to access the web sites for the local news station. My laptop is totally mobile and you can connect to the Internet as soon as we are away from the busy Metro New York traffic."

With that Shuk Wa picked up her briefcase, handed John a key and she was out the door. John looked at his watch, 9:05 a.m., then at the key and the suitcases gathered around the front door, then back to his watch. She will be back by 9:20 he thought, and then he smiled thinking for a moment that "she's unbelievable" and then his thoughts grew grim. "Was it safe to leave? Would someone be waiting right outside the door? What if a surveillance team had been watching the house, waiting for him to leave?" John looked at the key, then at the locks on the door, shuffled the suitcases, and then opened the door to check the locks from the outside. He looked around. People were hurrying through the drizzle and the temperature was not that cold, but it felt damp. He looked around again, scanning up and down the street, checking out the windows across the street, looking toward the roof tops. A few taxis went by and most people were walking briskly toward 5th Avenue, probably going to work.

John closed the door and walked around the room turning off the lights. Moving back toward the door, he looked into a mirror to the right of the entrance way. He stared at his image. It was like a dream. Why did he leave this caring comfortable environment? How did he get into this situation? The more that he remembered about his past, his time with his family, Shuk Wa and Wenli, the more that he doubted that the last two years could be anything other than a bad dream. Would he have a future?

Just then John heard a "beep beep" outside the front door, and opening the door, saw Shuk Wa in her car. Picking up two suitcases, John moved to the back of the car, pulled open the hatch back, and placed the suitcases in the back of the SUV. John quickly returned to the house gathering the last few items, Shuk Wa's computer case and two umbrellas. Looking around the room to make sure that he had everything, John closed and locked the door, placed the remaining items in the car, closed the hatch and was quickly in the front passenger seat. As soon as his seat belt clicked, Shuk Wa put her foot on the gas pedal and the car was pulling away moving toward 5th Avenue. Then, she looked at John, visibly flushed and said, "I forgot how to turn the windshield wipers on. This is the first time that I had to use them. Look on the back seat. I got you three newspapers, the *New York Times*, the *New York Post*, and the *New York Daily News*. Are you alright?"

John quickly responded, "Thank you for the newspapers. I turned off the lights and checked to make sure the door was locked. Are you alright driving in this rainy weather?"

Shuk Wa responded, "Let's concentrate on getting safely out of the city and on our way to Maine." Shuk Wa was focused on the road, driving at the speed limit, giving her full attention to driving her car. The passenger compartment grew quiet, the sound of the wipers beating to the noise of the morning traffic, and the occasional sound of "recalculating" from the navigation system. They were soon on 125th Street and then the navigation system sounded, "Exit on the right for the Robert F. Kennedy Bridge in one-half mile." They were on their way.

It was almost eleven as Shuk Wa exited off Interstate 95 onto Interstate 91 North to Hartford when she asked, "Are you alright? It is one hour to Hartford and I know a great Chinese restaurant just off the Interstate. Can you make it to Hartford without a rest stop?"

John was pleased that there was a break in the silence, as he said, "I'm alright Shuk Wa. Do you need to take a break before Hartford?"

Shuk Wa quickly responded, "I'm alright. The restaurant is the Feng Asian Bistro and it is on Asylum Street in downtown Hartford. They make the most exquisite Kobe beef and rock shrimp dumplings. Please input the restaurant in the navigation system. It's easy, it has a touch screen."

Reaching forward, John was already changing screens on the display as he said, "I think I can do that."

As soon as they exited Interstate 95 Shuk Wa relaxed and started to talk. Suddenly she said, "John, I want to tell you something about your mother and father. It is a story that I never told you, a story that will help you to understand why helping you means so much to me."

John listened intently as Shuk Wa started her story.

"You know I grew up in Hong Kong and received my Doctorate from Hong Kong University? I came to New York and Columbia University not knowing a person in the city. My husband was a proud man, a man who believed that he should be the center of my world. Our marriage was in many ways arranged by my father and my husband's father. They worked together at the Peninsula Hotel in the Tsim Sha Tsui district in Kowloon. It was the finest hotel in Hong Kong and the owners were rather advanced thinkers for the time. The Peninsula owners recognized my academic talents when I was a young girl and rewarded my accomplishments by making it possible for me to attend Hong Kong University. As long as I excelled academically they made certain that my tuition and university expenses were always paid. They encouraged me, opened door after door, throughout my education. My parents did not really understand what I was achieving. To them, it was all important that I got married, and so I did. I married the son of my father's friend and when I received my doctorate degree and had offers to come to New York and establish the Department of East Asian Languages and Cultures at Columbia University, my family thought I was foolish to even think about the position. They thought my dreams were that of a school girl, not the kind of ambition that a Chinese wife should have. I was a young mother, very proud of my beautiful daughter, only to face disappointment from my husband and my family because my first child was not a boy. I wanted more than Hong Kong was offering, a better life for my child, better opportunities to grow as an individual. So I came to New York with Wenli and started my journey at Columbia University. My husband stayed in Hong Kong, threatening to divorce me if I were to leave. Your parents befriended me and helped me in so many ways. They recognized my potential and were by my side with every challenge that I faced. I remember sitting with your mother and father, with you and Wenli happily playing in front of us, and I said that I was going to take an Americanized name, possibly Mary Anne. An immediate protest was heard from your mother and father and they convinced me that my strength was my Chinese cultural heritage and the names Shuk Wa and Wenli were part of the inheritance that I brought to the classroom. They reinforced and supported my uniqueness as a Chinese woman in an American society. Because I was accepted by the Gruneburgs, I had value as a person, a professional, and a friend to other colleagues at Columbia. Their friendship made the difference. They helped me survive and then flourish in an academic setting. They helped me understand how to be a good mother. Wenli and I owe so much to your family and over the years we grew to feel that we were part of your family structure. Helping you now is what I cherish and I want you to understand that I am here as your family, maybe a surrogate family, but your family nonetheless."

For over an hour Shuk Wa had been silent and now she was talkative, reinforcing how much she cared, and John was finding this sudden burst of compassion overwhelming. His emotions went from joy to fear, from a feeling of security to grave concern for the unknown. He was beginning to think he had turned into a Doctor Jekyll and Mr. Hyde personality. There were moments when he felt very uncomfortable with

Shuk Wa's kindness and then a few moments later felt filled with gratitude and comfort, very much appreciating her help and assistance. He was riding an emotional roller coaster. John took a deep breath and said, "It has only been two days since I escaped from the …," John hesitated. He was not sure how to describe his situation. "Somehow my memory was blocked and it is almost like the past years were a bad dream. I remember you and relate to your kindness, your caring attitude, and then I flash back to the reality of the last two years, and I am haunted by my past. I mentally go from peace and serenity to horror, fear and anxiety. It is very unsettling and I feel like I am two people living in one body."

Shuk Wa calmly responded, "Be patient, John, and accept that the person whom they are looking for is gone. He disappeared in the East River."

John took a deep breath and responded, "That is a nice thought, but there are times that I fear for the worst."

Shuk Wa interrupted as she pulled into the restaurant parking lot. "We can talk about it more after lunch. For now, relax and enjoy the next hour."

In many ways it was a relief for John when they pulled into the parking lot. Entering the restaurant, he heard the owner speaking Mandarin Chinese. John surprised Shuk Wa when he joined the conversation and his use of the Mandarin dialect and pronunciation impressed the restaurant staff. The lunch was a welcome break from being in the car and the friendliness of the staff made John temporarily forget about his predicament. Then, standing up to go to the restroom, reality hit home as he instinctively looked for surveillance cameras, scanning the room to evaluate the patrons. There were no cameras, the restaurant was almost empty, and he felt somewhat relieved and comforted knowing that Shuk Wa was familiar with this oasis.

On their way out of the restaurant, Shuk Wa said, "We have about a three-hour drive remaining and we need to talk about room accommodations for this evening. This morning I made a reservation for the Hilton Garden Inn, right in the center of downtown Freeport. It is just a short walk from L.L. Bean and the hotel is very popular with tourists. My question is, are you comfortable sharing a room with two double beds and only one bathroom?"

John was somewhat surprised by the question. "I'm alright with that arrangement, if it is acceptable to you." After a few moments John added, "I did not pack pajamas or a robe."

"No problem! We will go shopping at L.L. Bean as soon as we get to Freeport. Do you prefer cotton or flannel?" Shuk Wa's responsed.

They readjusted the car's navigation system and found the ramp for Interstate 90 East and continued on their journey. In less than an hour, they exited onto Interstate 495 North and eventually rejoined Interstate 95 just south of the New Hampshire border. They continued on Interstate 95 into Maine, they then exited onto Interstate 295 for the last hour of their journey, finally reaching the Freeport, Maine exit.

Arriving in Freeport it was just past four in the afternoon and Shuk Wa drove straight to the L.L. Bean parking lot. Pulling in at the far end of the lot, away from the store's main entrance, Shuk Wa calmly said, "I think it is best that you stay in the car and look at the newspapers. I'll get the pajamas. Is extra large the right size?"

John said, "Yes," and with that Shuk Wa was out of the car, across the parking lot, and into the store. John saw a group of people exiting the store, talking and laughing, and he reached to the back seat and grabbed a newspaper and opened it in front of his face. John was paging through the pages of the *New York Times* looking for a headline related to the Central Intelligence Agency. He did not find anything that referenced the CIA or a missing agent. Glancing toward the store, he felt a tinge of guilt. Forgetting to pack pajamas, he was becoming a burden.

He thought of Shuk Wa and said out loud, "Unbelievable," and then went back to searching through the paper.

Suddenly the driver's side car door opened. John did not hear or see Shuk Wa approaching. Somewhat startled, John was getting ready to say something when Shuk Wa said, "Now we can go to the hotel and I will check in."

John quickly interrupted, "I have been thinking about the expenses for this trip."

Shuk Wa quickly interrupted him. "I will update you on your finances this evening. Money is not a problem." Pulling out of the parking lot Shuk Wa laughed. "I shouldn't be laughing John. I know we need to be vigilant, but I keep forgetting that there are many things that you don't remember. You gave Wenli and me access to your checking account two years ago, John. Money is the one thing that is not a problem for any of us."

Just a few blocks later Shuk Wa announced, "this is it," as she pulled into a parking lot across the street from the hotel. "May I suggest that, once again, you wait in the car, I will check us in, and then we can go directly to our room?"

Fianally settled in their room, Shuk Wa had another suggestion. "Since we are in Maine, may I suggest a lobster roll for dinner? Linda Bean's Maine Kitchen is just a block away and they have this colossal lobster roll, large chunks of lobster on a toasted roll with just a touch of herb dressing. You can stay in the room, search the Internet, and I'll get the food. I did not sleep well last night and after today's drive I believe I'll be ready for bed right after dinner. Do you mind spending the evening looking through the newspapers and browsing the Internet? You can even check out the twenty-four-hour news channels."

Listening to Shuk Wa's suggestions, John began to arrange the newspapers and once again he was hit with feelings of gratitude, then fear for Shuk Wa's safety and the uncertainty of their present situation. As he opened the laptop on the desk, he repeated his concerns and they agreed that it was best for him to search the news outlets for new information.

After the fabulous lobster rolls, Shuk Wa showered and was in bed just after eight, apologizing profusely for being so tired. Shuk Wa mentioned that she called Wenli while waiting for the lobster rolls to let her know that she arrived in Freeport safely. They would see Wenli tomorrow evening in Bar Harbor. Then, the room grew quiet and Shuk Wa was asleep in minutes.

John scanned the news channels listening intently, but there was no mention of the CIA. Paging through the newspapers, only the *New York Daily News* had a photo with the caption, "Deputy Director for Special Operations for the Central Intelligence Agency is arrested in New York", and the story just briefly mentioned a missing CIA agent. Searching the Internet, John found last night's BREAKING NEWS story and to his surprise his photo was not on the screen longer than a few seconds. There were no additional follow-up stories. Mentally exhausted, John crawled into bed and instantly fell asleep.

Hearing someone moving in the room, John turned slowly, ready to respond to an unknown threat. Making eye contact with Shuk Wa, she immediately responded, "Good morning, John! Are you alright? You look like you have seen a ghost." Without waiting for a response Shuk Wa continued, "I've been up for about an hour. I slept really well. I'm going out to the Starbucks. It's just a few blocks away. Do you have a favorite morning beverage?"

John cleared his throat, "Good morning, Shuk Wa, and thank you! May I please have black tea with milk. The way you make it."

Shuk Wa nodded and said, "Yes, John, I'll bring you a Chai tea. I'll be leaving now. That will give you some privacy and time to get ready." Shuk Wa smiled and then she was out the door.

As soon as the door closed, John was out of bed heading for the shower, thinking he had to be showered and dressed by the time Shuk Wa returned. When he was dressed John sat down at the laptop and returned to the web site for New York City local news, always being careful to do a general search for the city and never searching specifically for the Central Intelligence Agency. Once on the web site, he would open various news stories, never going directly to a CIA story. John was very aware that he could establish a cyber trail. Returning to the local news section he immediately noticed a headline from yesterday's late night news. Controlling his excitement, he systematically opened each story on the list and finally to "UPDATE: POTENTIAL CIA SCANDAL." Opening the link, he scanned through the story, then clicked on the video link to last night's news story. About twenty seconds into the story, his picture was there again, briefly for a few seconds, with the voice over saying, "After two days of searching the East River the missing CIA Agent has not been found." That was it. John was tempted to repeat the video, hesitated, and then decided to go to the next story. Clicking on the remaining stories on the list, he stared at the computer in a trance. Analyzing what he had heard, he quickly surmised that they were still searching for him, only mentioning the East River as the search area, and after two days the agent had not been found. What could he determine from this latest story?

After knocking on the door, Shuk Wa entered, announcing to John, "Breakfast is served, full leaf Chai tea, blueberry oatmeal with skim milk, and a Greek yogurt with berries parfait. You cannot get a healthier breakfast than this." Looking at John, then the laptop, and back to John, Shuk Wa asked, "Are you alright, John? You seem to be lost in deep thought this morning. Is everything alright? Did you find anything in the newspapers or on the Internet?"

John took a deep breath and said, "They are still searching for me. My photo is still being shown on the New York City late night news. They reported that they have been searching for two days. I'm not sure what it all means. They may not be giving details to the news outlets. They may have leads that we don't know about."

Shuk Wa sensed that she needed to change the subject. She hesitated and then said, "It is three hours to Bar Harbor from here. We can finish our breakfast and be on our way. I made a reservation at the Harborside Hotel; it is downtown on West Street, with beautiful views of Frenchman's Bay. You'll be able to see the sun rise over the Atlantic each morning. We have a two-bedroom suite, you'll have your own bedroom and bath, and there's a gas burning fireplace in the sitting area, so we can sit and talk this evening."

John continued to stare at the laptop. "I'm concerned, Shuk Wa. They may be closing in on us and we don't even know it. You may be in serious danger and you're planning a holiday."

Shuk Wa quickly interrupted. "I know you are in danger, John, it took me a while to grasp the seriousness of this situation, but I get it. I understand the danger and you must understand that I'm truly concerned about your safety. My thought, better yet, my prayer, is that your name will be cleared in time and this will all pass. We have avoided surveillance cameras, you have not been outside this room, we are in Freeport, Maine, hours away from New York City and the East River where they are searching for you, and no one is pounding on our door. We are doing our best to avoid any potential danger." Taking a deep breath Shuk Wa calmly said, "We need to leave for Bar Harbor right after breakfast." With that she moved to the small table in the corner of the room, put down the food, and said to John, "Please have a seat over here so I can say a prayer and eat this oatmeal before it gets cold."

John came to the table and sat down while saying, "I appreciate your help Shuk Wa. I get overwhelmed with the potential danger and my concern for you."

Shuk Wa said, "I know John," as she grabbed his hand and said a blessing before eating.

They were on the road for about an hour, heading toward Bar Harbor, when Shuk Wa's cell phone rang. Hearing the ring Shuk Wa immediately flipped on her turn signal, pulled onto the side of the road, stopped the car, and anxiously said, "It's Wenli's ring tone". Answering the phone with a smile and noticeably happy, Shuk Wa said, "Good morning, Wenli! Where are you?"

John, could hear Wenli laughing, "I'm at the Saint Stephen, Calais border crossing area, waiting in line to cross over into Maine. There are about four cars in front of me so I thought I would call. I should be in Bar Harbor by noon."

Shuk Wa laughed with joy, "That is great. It is just a few minutes past nine. What time did you leave Halifax?"

Wenli interrupted, "Sorry, Mom, I am moving up to the International Customs Station, gotta go. I'll call when I reach Bar Harbor. Bye!" And with that a dial tone could be heard.

Shuk Wa smiled broadly, "Wow! We will see her at noon. There is a not so pretty Chinese restaurant on Main Street called China Joy and they make this great dish called Lobster with Ginger and Scallion. Wenli really enjoys it. They have an Asian menu not given to tourists. I must call to let them know that we are coming so that they will be prepared to serve us." Shuk Wa quickly paged through her phone and in seconds was speaking in Mandarin making the noon reservation for three. She smiled at John, "Good. That is settled and we will have a relaxing lunch."

Pulling back onto the highway Shuk Wa said to John, "We need a plan. Wenli does not like surprises and you are going to be more like a shock than a surprise. It is eight hours from Halifax to Bar Harbor. She probably left at four a.m., almost the middle of the night. She will be tired, John. We definitely need a plan."

John had been quiet since they left Freeport and Shuk Wa appreciated seeing John smile when he heard Wenli's voice. "She is going to be thrilled to see you." Shuk Wa said and then added, "I will meet her in the hotel parking lot. I already called the hotel and we will be able to check in early. You can stay in the room and check the Internet and I will meet Wenli. We will pick up the lobster, and have lunch back in our room. That will give me time to explain. Do you agree?"

John sighed deeply and said, "I appreciate not going to the Chinese restaurant, but I still feel very guilty that you are so caught up in this calamity, and now Wenli will be involved. Are you sure about this?"

Shuk Wa interrupted him, "You are part of our family, John. We are moving forward. We're in Maine and still no incidents. Tonight we can talk and plan and help you determine your next step."

John sighed deeply again and asked, "When did Wenli move to Halifax? What is she doing now?"

Shuk Wa was relieved to hear the question and smiling broadly said, "Wenli is the Executive Director of the Confucius Institute in the Sobey School of Business at Saint Mary's University in Halifax. She has been the Head of the Foreign Exchange Department and International Activities Office for over a year. The last time you saw her she was traveling to Shanghai to expand the Chinese language program for international student's at Fudan University. She has been successful building partnerships with a number of Chinese universities by offering graduate level programs to interested English speaking students, including courses in Chinese history, the Chinese economy, and Chinese law. I am proud to say that she has also built a relationship with the College of Business at the University of Hong Kong. In addition, Wenli is also working with the European Quality Improvement System to attain globally recognized standards for their exchange program in Toulouse, France." Shuk Wa laughed. "She will enjoy hearing you speak Chinese. Keep in mind, John, that she has always admired you and she has told me many times that you inspired her to excel academically."

Crossing the bridge over the Mount Desert Narrows, the salt air permeated the car's interior. Bar Harbor was just ten minutes away. After arriving in Bar Harbor, Shuk Wa registered them at the Harborside Hotel and John carried the suitcases to their suite which was spacious with views of Frenchman's Bay and Bar Island in the distance. The accommodations were certainly comfortable and Shuk Wa praised the benefits of having a gas burning fireplace in the sitting area to take the chill out of the evening air and encourage conversation.

The silence was broken with Wenli's ring tone and Shuk Wa held the phone up and said to John, "We should be back in about half an hour", and then as she walked out the door John heard her say, "Hello Wenli, where are you now?"

Wenli responded, "I just crossed the Narrows onto Mount Desert Island. Where are you?"

Shuk Wa responded, "I'm at the Harborside Hotel and I'll meet you in their parking lot."

As soon as Shuk Wa saw Wenli's car, she waved her arms enthusiastically like a teenage schoolgirl and greeted Wenli with a big smile. Getting into the car Shuk Wa immediately said, "Thank you for coming so far my dear girl. We are going to the China Joy Chinese Restaurant."

Wenli immediately interrupted her. "Mother! Are you alright? You do not seem to be," Wenli hesitated, "You seem under pressure. I've been worried."

Shuk Wa quickly interrupted, "I'm alright. I have no health problems. I understand that you have been worried. Please, let's go to the restaurant. I will explain."

Wenli interrupted, still not moving, "What is there to explain? Mother, what is going on?"

Shuk Wa calmly said, "Please, Wenli, I'm rather hungry and I ordered Lobster with Ginger and Scallion and they are expecting us at noon." Shuk Wa was relieved as Wenli pulled out of the parking lot and turned right for the short journey to the restaurant. As they pulled into a parking place in front of the restaurant Shuk Wa said, "I am going to explain something, you must not interrupt. Please just listen for a minute, it is important."

Wenli immediately interrupted her, "Mother!"

Shuk Wa gave her daughter "the look" and slightly raised her hands, palms up.

Wenli responded, "Alright, Mother, I will listen."

Shuk Wa calmly and quietly said, "Two nights ago, sometime after eight, John Gruneburg came to our house." Wenli looked shocked, but said nothing. Shuk Wa continued. "It is a very complicated situation and he desperately needs our help. He will need your patience. This is not easy to explain. John is back at the hotel."

Wenli interrupted, "What? What did you say?"

Shuk Wa continued, "Stay calm, Wenli. You need to stay calm. John may be in real danger and his life may be at risk. You must understand the seriousness of the situation."

Wenli asked, "Why is he in danger?"

Shuk Wa continued, "John was on a special operation with the Central Intelligence Agency and somehow became the target of the Agency and he is now paranoid that the CIA is trying to kill him."

Wenli said, "Mother, can any of this be true? Do you think John is alright?"

Shuk Wa continued, "I also had my doubts when John told me his story. But, when I saw his photo on the late night news, the headline said he was a missing CIA Agent; it was then that I understood his danger was real. Wenli, he jumped from the roof of a ten story CIA training facility into the East River to escape. I don't know how he survived." Shuk Wa stopped and they both sat there in silence and then Shuk Wa continued. "I know it is hard to believe and I understand that you will have questions, but we need to help John. We need to be patient and listen to him."

Wenli said, "What does he want us to do?"

Shuk Wa took a deep breath. "That is part of the problem. John thinks he may be putting our lives in danger."

Wenli interrupted, "Is that true? Are you talking about someone breaking down our door and possibly using gun fire? Does John have a gun?"

Shuk Wa spoke firmly, "They are searching for him in the East River. He had numerous aliases as a CIA Agent. They may not know that his real name is John Gruneburg."

Wenli shook her head, "This does not make sense. It does not seem plausible."

Shuk Wa said, "Let's get the food and go back to the hotel and John can start answering your questions."

Wenli responded, "Mother, my stomach is flipping. I'm not sure that I can eat. I'm not sure that I want to go back to the hotel. I'm very unsettled with this entire story. What are you asking me to do?"

Shuk Wa responded, "John needs our help!"

Wenli interrupted, "To do what, Mother? What does he want us to do? What are you asking me to do?"

Shuk Wa sensed that she reached an impasse and opened the car door, got out of the car and said, "I'll get the food and then we can continue talking. Please just stay calm." With that Shuk Wa was out of the car and entered the restaurant.

Wenli sat there thinking, "How can someone stay calm with this situation? This is crazy! What is my Mother thinking?"

Not much was said as they returned to the hotel. While Shuk Wa embraced the challenge of helping John, Wenli's immediate response was to push back, questioning everything, not seeing how they could assist John, even saying that this was his mess to sort out. Shuk Wa never lost her patience, her hope, her belief that Wenli would understand the merits of helping John resolve what must be wrongful information on the part of CIA officials.

Shuk Wa anticipated a reunion filled with hugs and warm embraces. Instead Wenli greeted John in a friendly, yet somewhat aloof manner. John recapped the same story that he had told to Shuk Wa two days earlier, trying his best to convey the confusion that he experienced when he entered the training facility on 71st Street. Wenli questioned how his absence could have lasted for almost two years, how could his past, his caring friends, and his time at the Naval Academy could not have mattered? How could his memory loss be so severe that he did not know who he was? How could seeing 81st Street and the MET miraculously restore his memory?

John had no answers, only emphasizing that he had led a troubled, tortuous life, always knowing it was abnormal not to have past memories. Wenli grilled John about the last two years, reminding him that when they last met in New York he said he would be back in six months; he would see her and Shuk Wa when he had his next leave. He agreed that they would plan a hiking vacation.

John offered no excuses. Wenli seemed only to grow more irritated when John could not justify his actions. She wanted to know, to understand, why he agreed to be part of such an operation. He continually emphasized that he wanted to be assigned to a clandestine unit that was tied to gathering information. It was never his desire to be involved with missions to assassinate anyone. Pressing him, Wenli said that she doubted that he could kill anyone. It was not the John Gruneburg that she knew.

John sat in deep thought for a moment, and then he said, "You may not like what you are about to hear, but you must listen and try to understand. Somehow, I truly do not know how, they turned me into a highly-trained covert assassin carrying out missions that I was told would make our country more secure. To the CIA, I was an asset that eliminated threats. They never talked about people or how my actions impacted other people's lives. I dreaded falling asleep because I had nightmares, reliving every mission, seeing the faces of my victims. I was programmed to be a very effective lethal weapon that was trained to inflict deadly action."

Wenli immediately shot back with the question, "How do you know that these memories are true and not part of a bad dream?"

John stood, turned his back to Shuk Wa and Wenli, and slowly opened and then took off his shirt. "The two scars on the right side of my back are from bullet holes when I got caught in the middle of a skirmish in Ukraine. The dreams were real. The memories are real." John turned and saw Shuk Wa staring at him, a look of disbelief on her face, then he caught sight of Wenli. Tears were flowing down her face that showed anguish and despair. A lump welled in John's throat as he fought to stop the tears that were pooling up in his eyes.

Wenli looked at John and calmly said, "I am very tired. I got up at 3:00 a.m. this morning and drove eight hours to get here. I am exhausted. I must go to bed. I cannot talk about this anymore today."

Shuk Wa was slightly startled when the sound of the bedroom door closing seemed louder than expected, but she remained motionless and quiet. John put his shirt on, slowly and deliberately buttoning each button, not saying a word. There was silence for a long time and then John finally spoke. "It was a mistake for me to come here, it is not fair to you and Wenli. I did not intend to cause her such sorrow. She is right; this is my agony, my pain to bear, I should not be inflicting my suffering and misery on you and Wenli. It angers me that I have brought her sadness and caused nothing but unhappiness."

Shuk Wa and John sat in silence for a long, long time and soon the bay changed to a darker shade of blue and small waves caught fleeting flashes of gold from the sun in the western sky. Shuk Wa took a deep breath and said, "I understand why she is angry and you need to see this situation from her point of view. I needed to listen more closely to what she was saying and I failed to understand her line of questioning. You must pay attention to what I am about to tell you and you must understand why I am telling you this." Shuk Wa hesitated and then said, "You suffered from amnesia for almost two years and Wenli was asking how you could not remember your past, your friends. Do you understand, John? She was wondering how could you not remember her, your best friend? When she came to New York, we would sit in that back bedroom holding onto our memories of you, crying because we feared the unknown, and yes, crying because we missed you. Do you understand, John, that she spent two years in agony, missing you, not knowing where you were, and you were telling her that during that time you did not even remember that she existed? Do you understand, John?"

John sat in silence looking at Shuk Wa, slowly nodding his head up and down, acknowledging that he understood. Shuk Wa sat there looking at John. Had she said enough? Taking a long deep breath, she said, "There is more."

Shuk Wa hesitated, wondering how to best convey the additional anger and contempt, that Wenli was feeling toward him. Shuk Wa took another deep breath and said, "It may be a cliché, but it is true that you were a hero to her. The pride that she felt when she was with you energized her for days, weeks, and maybe even months. She cherished time spent with you and she told me many times that planning future holidays with you always lifted her spirits. It was the combination of honor, patriotism, dedication to the Navy, to your country. She respected what you stood for." Shuk Wa hesitated for a moment and then said, "She resents that you volunteered for an operation that turned you into a person who …," hesitating she continued, "You always told her that clandestine operations were tied to information gathering." Again, she stopped in the middle of the sentence, "To say that you were involved in missions to assassinate foreign citizens seems absurd." Seconds went by and once again Shuk Wa continued, "It was hard for her to accept that you went from being a man of honor to being an assassin." Trailing off in thought, she said in a soft voice, "It hurt her to think of what you had become, to accept that you were being hunted by the CIA, and no longer in a position of honor. She is disappointed and struggling because she wanted to separate the John Gruneburg that she knew from the person that you have become. Do you understand what I am saying, John? Is this making sense to you?"

John sat in silence, sensing that Shuk Wa wanted him to respond. He was trying to gather his thoughts. Finally, John said. "I have spent hours struggling with the memories of certain missions, knowing that I was told that the mission would make our country more secure and would save American lives. Then I found out that I was lied to and people died because I trusted those who were in charge of the operation. I have felt shame and I have been tortured with guilt. I don't know if this is why I lost my memory. I don't truly understand how I got to this place in time, but what I do know is that I have not stopped looking over my shoulder for the last two years."

John stopped talking and sat in silence, looking toward Shuk Wa, yet not facing her, not looking into her eyes. Shuk Wa felt John's remorse and saw the sadness on his face. She wanted to comfort him. Her mind was spinning and she felt a knot in her stomach, knowing that he was in a saddened state and he, too, felt the gloom that they had fallen into.

Shuk Wa moved slightly looking directly into John's face and said, "When you came to my house, I was so honored when you said that it reminded you of who you were and I was blinded by the happiness of the moment. Seeing you alive, I did not comprehend the complexity of this situation. I did not anticipate the impact this would have on Wenli's psyche. I am not a jaded person; I have faith in people. I try to see the good in every situation."

"You have been facing the timeless struggle of good over evil. The yin and yang of your code of honor, the forces that present opposite moral points of view, much deeper than right from wrong, making judgments that hold a person's life in the balance. You have faced the challenge of knowing the root of what is to you, acceptable ethical behavior. You were forced out of duty to your mission to go beyond that point, facing then the dynamic turmoil of your conscience."

"What has been said today needed to be said. Tomorrow will be another day, it will provide a new perspective on this situation. We need to get a good night's sleep and be patient with each other. Tomorrow we will start anew." Shuk Wa got up slowly, walked toward the bedroom and before opening the door said, "Good night, John! Rest well!" Then she opened the door, entered the darkness and quietly closed the door behind her.

John sat in silence thinking about his options. His mind wandered and did not settle on anything specific until he thought about today's interaction with Wenli. It was not the day that he expected when they left Freeport this morning, but what did he expect? Maybe Shuk Wa was right. What was said today needed to be said. Facing Wenli was never going to be easy. He once again thought about his options and it occurred to him that he should check the Internet for updates. John moved to the desk and spent the next few hours searching from sight to sight, and then finally, after shutting down the computer, he went to bed. As he closed his bedroom door behind him, he felt very tired and the bed in front of him was a welcome sight.

John slept soundly, never stirring, never hearing a sound throughout the night. When he finally awakened, he sat silently on the edge of the bed, listening, hearing only distant sounds outside his bedroom window. Approaching the window, he looked at his watch and was surprised to see seven forty-six. Then, once again, he listened for sounds outside his bedroom door. Nothing, it was very quiet. He slowly opened his door glancing across the sitting area to the bedroom door across the room. It was open. He froze and listened intently then decided he must be alone. Moving across the room, John could see suitcases in the bedroom, and clothing strewn on the end of one of the beds. He then noticed a tablet on top of the laptop with what looked like a note. As he got closer he could see, "We went for a morning run. Will be back before nine." and a large script signature, "Shuk Wa and Wenli."

John stood motionless for awhile, then turned and looked out the window at Frenchman's Bay and thought it looked like a nice day. He wasn't sure what he expected this morning, but being alone had not entered his mind. He looked at the kitchenette; saw a kettle on the small range and an electric coffee maker on the counter. There was an assortment of teas so John added water to the kettle and turned the range to high. Seeing packets of coffee, he decided to also brew a pot of what was called Sunrise Light Roast. Searching through the cabinets, John located placemats, mugs, and spoons. As the kettle whistled, he thought at least he'll have hot beverages ready.

John was preparing a mug of English Breakfast Tea when Shuk Wa and Wenli entered the room carrying a number of bags. Wenli cheerfully said, "I smell coffee, you trained him well, Mother" as she walked toward John. When she reached him, she put her arms around him, giving him a firm hug and said, "How are you this morning John? My mother and I had a very good talk on our run, or my mother may say it was a debate. As usual, I think my mother was right about many things. She told me about your conversation after I went to bed last night. I promise to be more civil today."

John stood motionless and speechless as Shuk Wa said, "We stopped at a new place called the Coffee Hound Coffee Bar across from Agamont Park on Main Street. They had these Maine blueberry pies that were baked just hours ago and were providing such an inviting aroma. We had to buy one, plus freshly baked blueberry muffins and these chocolate raspberry macaroons that I could not resist. We ran six miles this morning and we are hungry. How are you this morning, John?"

Without waiting for a response, Wenli started to unpack the bags and said, "We discussed our options, John, and this is what we decided. Number one was to abandon you and we would never do that. You're stuck with us, John. Number two is my mother's analysis of the situation in that we have heard nothing from anyone and she reasons that it is best to continue to keep a low profile and see how events unfold in New York."

Shuk Wa placed on the table three large paper cups that had a picture of a dog and the words Coffee Hound Coffee Bar on the side of the cup. She said, "We certainly have a choice of beverages" as she took a seat at the table and Wenli and John followed her lead. Shuk Wa reached out and held John's hand and then Wenli's, and then Wenli reached out to John who grasped her hand tightly. Shuk Wa started to pray, "Heavenly Father bless this food and this family ..."

As they finished breakfast Shuk Wa turned to John and asked, "Is there additional news on the Internet?"

John responded, "After three days of searching the East River and the surrounding shoreline, the missing CIA Agent or his body have not been found."

Wenli quickly interrupted asking, "What is the likelihood that the CIA is going to stop searching for you if they do not find your body? We discussed one very important point which is that your mailing address has been listed as my mother's house for over two years, long before you got involved with this covert operation. Your payroll statements are mailed to her address, we filed your federal, state, and New York City taxes using that address and even your alumni magazine comes to her house. John, you must understand that my mother and I have had access to your checking account for almost two years, and I have paid your Naval Academy alumni dues, made a contribution to the Academy's foundation, and sent your monthly check to the Saint Ignatius of Loyola Church. By the way, your church envelopes are mailed to my mother's house."

"How likely is it that the United States Navy is going to keep paying you, making direct deposits to your account, without reviewing your current status and processing your next assignment? My point is that we believe that you only have a brief window of opportunity to act. We need to seriously discuss your options. Where are you going? Do you have plans? Yes, we need to discuss your options."

John looked at Wenli, then at Shuk Wa, and then back to Wenli as he said, "I cannot continue to hide in the United States, looking over my back every minute. I will never be at peace. I thought of crossing into Canada, avoiding immigration and secretly living in Quebec City or Montreal. I would speak French, access my Standard Chartered bank accounts in Toronto, possibly make a connection in Toronto for travel to China. I know of a contact in Toronto's Chinatown that can connect me with passage on a container ship to Hong Kong or Shanghai. The contact has Cantonese business associates in Hong Kong who are reliable and their rendezvous point is the Pacific Mall in Markham, one of Toronto's suburbs. There are also Vietnamese contacts who can make Vietnam a possibility. By using maritime shipping routes, I would be avoiding security cameras in airports and railway stations."

Shuk Wa asked, "How will you get to Canada? Do you want me to" John quickly interrupted saying, "I have a big concern about crossing the border; I'm concerned about the New York license plates on Shuk Wa's car. I'm concerned about spending additional time with you and continuing to put you in danger. This may go far beyond harboring a fugitive and your lives may be in serious danger."

Wenli took a deep breath, looked at her Mother and then at John and said, "As we were running, I accessed our bank accounts using my phone and your paychecks for last month were electronically deposited into your account. You must have a commanding officer who is aware of your present assignment, this covert mission. That person or the Navy has not contacted us. You have this window of opportunity to use your passport and relocate to an area that they will not suspect. Take the time to let them vindicate you, to clear your name."

John explained that he was paranoid about using Shuk Wa's computer and Internet connection and about his name being mentioned in text messages or phone conversations. He was concerned about license plates, even the Nova Scotia plates on Wenli's car, about using his passport, traveling on public transportation, even questioning whether he should consider growing a beard.

Wenli once again interrupted, "Your best option is to clear your name."

For a time, everyone sat there quietly thinking. John looked at Shuk Wa and then Wenli. Finally, Wenli asked, "If you traveled discreetly, remaining as you say off-the-grid for a few months, waiting to see if you were exonerated, do you think that would help? John, you said you were following orders and these missions that involved lethal action were supposed to be protecting American lives. You were following the chain of command, and we believe that you will be vindicated. If you disappear somewhere on this planet where no one can find you, what becomes of your life? You said you would never stop looking over your shoulder and you would never have peace. You deserve to have your life back, to be at peace being John Gruneburg."

Wenli took a deep breath and said, "We have an idea, a plan that we think is your best next step. You will come with me to Halifax and I will arrange for us to travel to France and Spain, to take that hiking vacation that we planned two years ago. We will honor your father, remembering James Gruneburg on every step of the El Camino de Santiago, the Way of Saint James, on our pilgrimage to the Cathedral of Santiago de Compostela. John, it was your father's dream."

John looked at Wenli in disbelief and asked, "Are you serious? Do you?"

Wenli interrupted, "It was my mother's idea. This was your father's lifelong dream and he never took the time to make the pilgrimage. He wanted to do the pilgrimage as a family. We can do this in their honor."

Again there was silence and Shuk Wa turned to John and asked, "Have you looked at the financial folder that I gave you yesterday? It has the details on your parent's estate and the rental fees from your parent's brownstone. Furthermore, the Swiss Embassy is interested in an outright purchase of their home instead of continuing to lease it. The accounting firm that our families have always used has continued to manage your investments and they have done a remarkable job. Money will not be a concern for you. Their lawyers are in constant contact with me. They also manage my investments, and they use my address as your legal address. It is just a matter of time until someone comes looking for John Gruneburg and hopefully that person will be from the Navy and not the Central Intelligence Agency. You are an innocent, honorable person, please give this time."

Wenli excitedly said, "We can purchase all our hiking clothing and equipment at L.L. Bean and at the border crossing; I can say that I was on a shopping trip to Freeport. It is a very common thing to do for people from Halifax."

John quickly interrupted, "You do not want to buy hiking or trekking clothing at L.L. Bean because the brand name on the clothing would identify you as an American. There is a trekking store close to the Toulouse airport called Décatholon Blagnac that sells French made clothing. We could purchase all our equipment there."

Shuk Wa immediately said, "Then you will consider it, John? That is wonderful news! I am so relieved. Thank you, John!"

Wenli looked at John and quietly said, "Do you agree, John?"

There was silence. It seemed like minutes went by and John finally said, "The risk will be crossing the border and I agree with you, it is best to do it now while no one is looking for John Gruneburg." Then looking directly at Wenli, "Are you sure? What about your work? This will take weeks."

Wenli quickly responded, "I will give you two months. We should know something by then and hopefully it will be enough time for you to heal."

John looked at her and asked, "To heal?"

Shuk Wa immediately sensed that it would be a good time for closure on this subject and quickly said, "The Holy Redeemer Church has a 4:00 p.m. mass on Saturdays. We can go to Mass and then have a lobster dinner and I'll leave for New York tomorrow morning."

Wenli quickly added, "Sounds like a plan" and then standing said, "I better get a shower." Visibly relieved, she looked at her mother and said, "Thank you, Mom! You are always right." Sure footed, she glided across the room to the bedroom. As she opened the bedroom door, she glanced back at John and her mother before softly closing it behind her.

CHAPTER 11

Oversight of intelligence activities requires a precarious balance of power in the best of times. It is common practice for intelligence agencies to withhold information that is related to national security. The oversight responsibilities of the Congressional Intelligence Committees require that these committees be kept informed by agency officials of classified intelligence operations. But members of Congress seem to always demand access to confidential documents and legal memos that the intelligence community is reluctant to release.

Oversight of the intelligence community is the joint responsibility of the United States Senate Select Committee on Intelligence and the United States House Permanent Select Committee on Intelligence. The power to control the purse strings of the intelligence budget puts teeth into requests for information when Congress is conducting investigations and audits of intelligence activities and programs. Congressional support is always needed to prepare legislation authorizing appropriations to fund the agencies.

Sharing oversight duties is not a strong quality of the legislative branch of government, and when it involves intelligence agencies, the opportunity to be seen on the evening news often overrules the common sense required to hold an agency accountable for its actions. Protecting national security has to be balanced, requiring an understanding of the issues related to policy and the legality of the operation. The public is aware that covert operations and espionage exist. Hollywood makes certain that the imagination of Americans is on the leading edge of what is technically possible and exaggerates agency capabilities to the tenth degree. Classified intelligence requires secrecy, trust, concealment of details, and a level of cooperation that necessitates failing on the side of confidentiality rather than transparency. Listening is more important than voicing an opinion, being supportive overrules being judgmental, and one must always understand that national security is the priority.

Driving down the highway, thoughts of how things should be and how the system should work, kept going through Congressman Spencer's mind. He was troubled by what George Harthmann said earlier in the day and yet he knew it was their close relationship that allowed George to talk so openly about national security activities.

It was only thirty-five miles from Annapolis to downtown Washington and the congressman's Capitol Hill parking garage. Normally at this time of day it would take about an hour to make the trip. With the ongoing afternoon rain, the pace of the traffic was impacted more by the weather than the volume of cars. The congressman had called his office and his staff would be waiting, ready to update him on pressing issues. Maryland's cell phone law prohibited the use of cell phones while driving so it gave the Congressman time to think, as the windshield wipers set a rhythm in the car.

Arriving at his office, Congressman Spencer was greeted with the usual barrage of letters, messages, and legislative issues that required his attention. As the afternoon grew to a close, his Chief of Staff mentioned that George Harthmann had called to say that he sent an e-mail message that contained some of the information that the congressman had requested earlier that day. After his staff left for the day, the congressman sat down at his computer, maneuvered his way through three fire walls and finally got to George Harthmann's e-mail. The leading line immediately troubled him: "Growing CIA scandal over an alleged government assassination program that may have in some cases targeted foreign civilians." The label that was chosen, "Growing CIA scandal" implied more information would be forthcoming and additional personnel would be implicated. Congressman Spencer understood why

George Harthmann was worried that this news story could snowball beyond the CIA's control.

The leading paragraph covered the CIA Director denying involvement in the operation and that he was completely unaware of these missions. The next paragraph dealt with the involvement of two senior officials who supervised a CIA training facility out of their New York City office. The training facility allegedly utilized questionable behavior modification techniques to enhance and condition the performance of the missing CIA Agent. The attached photos identified the two officials as the Deputy Director for Special Operations for the Central Intelligence Agency in New York and a doctor who managed the training operation. The congressman studied the text, mulling over the seriousness of what was implied, glancing back to the photos and then to the text. These were senior CIA officers.

While opening the last attachment about the missing CIA Agent, Congressman Spencer's mind was still troubled with the involvement of high level officials being involved with what was labeled as a scandal. What caught the congressman's eye next was the news headline, "Former CIA Agent Missing" and the implication that he had exposed the operation. Was he called a former agent because he was presumed dead? Concentrating on the story he opened the photo almost as an afterthought then glanced back to the text and the information about the CIA Agent. It was like a light bulb going on, something about the photo caught his attention. He's thinking the person in the photo looked familiar, and he questioned himself out loud, "Is this John Gruneburg?" The congressman's immediate reaction was to stare at the photo and he immediately thought, "Don't overreact." He studied the photo, questioning his memory, totally puzzled by the thought that this could be someone that he knew. He was swept up in his emotions thinking out loud, "It is not possible." Deciding not to jump to conclusions, he would call Senator McDowell in the morning and ask if he had received George Harthmann's message and not mention the photo. Would the Senator raise a question about the photo? It was best to wait.

A few hours had passed and Congressman Spencer was still reading and answering e-mail messages when the phone rang and he noticed that the call was from Senator McDowell. Quickly answering his phone, he said, "Good evening, Senator," and to his surprise, his greeting was followed by a barrage of quick questions from the Senator. "Did you receive the e-mail message from George Harthmann? Did you open the photos? Did you notice anything unusual?" There was silence.

Thinking that it was best for the senator to first identify the photo the congressman hesitated. "Yes, Senator, I looked at the photos", the congressman replied.

Seeming to lose his patience, the senator shot back, "Did you see the photo that looks like John Gruneburg?" Without waiting the senator continued, "Tomorrow morning I will ask my congressional liaison to make a number of inquiries. Her name is Lieutenant Madison Schieffler. She's a Naval Academy graduate. I will tell her that there is a possibility of bringing together all the Naval Academy Midshipmen that have interned in my office. I will ask her to organize their current contact information, where they are living or stationed, e-mail address, and phone number. Let's see what she gets. Are you listening, Spencer?"

The congressman quickly replied, "Yes, Senator, I think that is a good plan."

The senator added, "Do not show that photo to anyone and do not forward Hartmann's message. I will call you tomorrow afternoon." And with that the senator was gone and once again the congressman sat there holding his phone thinking of what had just transpired.

The following afternoon, while meeting in his office with constituents from his home district, a staff member apologized for the interruption saying, "Senator Sam McDowell is on line one." The congressman excused himself and picking up the phone said, "Good afternoon, Senator." As usual, without hesitation the senator got right to the point. "Lieutenant Schieffler is still working on that project I gave her, and tomorrow I am meeting with the CIA Deputy Director for Global Operations that Hartmann said would be contacting the Senate Select Committee on Intelligence. This will be a closed meeting, just two other senior senators and no one else from the Central Intelligence Agency. I will call you after the meeting." With a click the senator was gone and with his constituents looking at him from across the room the congressman quickly added, "Thank you, Senator, I look forward to your update tomorrow. Thank you for the call." The congressman smiled, knowing that when his constituents returned home they would say that the highlight of their visit to the congressman was that he took a call from Senator Sam McDowell while they were in his office.

Lieutenant Madison Schieffler had worked on Capitol Hill as a congressional liaison for almost three months and this was the first time that Senator Sam McDowell entrusted her with an assignment. As a graduate of the Naval Academy it was an honor to call each member of what the senator referred to as his "Wall of Honor." This was certainly a select group and the lieutenant was impressed that when she called an admiral's office on behalf of Senator McDowell she received immediate cooperation. The list was almost complete. Rerouted to a number of offices, the lieutenant was having a difficult time locating John Gruneburg. Not wanting to fail on her first real assignment, she persisted, trying to use all the influence that the senator's office offered. The best that she could do was to track John Gruneburg to the Office of Naval Intelligence where he was assigned to an operation that was still listed as classified. Adding to the lieutenant's frustration was the fact that she could not identify Gruneburg's commanding officer.

She reluctantly left Senator McDowell's office number with the Joint Intelligence Center at the Pentagon accepting their promise that they would have John Gruneburg contact the Senator's office as soon as Gruneburg was available. With reluctance, she reported to Senator McDowell that John Gruneburg was apparently involved with a special mission that was highly classified and she could not get anyone to comment or provide details about any of Gruneburg's missions.

This inquiry became even more interesting when Senator McDowell received a call from the Pentagon asking him to confirm that he had requested what they called an investigation by Lieutenant Madison Schieffler into John Gruneburg's present assignment. After confirming that he requested the inquiry, the senator was surprised with the follow up question, "May we ask why you need this information?" When he explained that he was planning a reunion of all the Naval Academy midshipmen that had interned in his office the response was, "Oh! Thank you for your time, Senator. Good luck with your reunion."

After lunch, Congressman Joseph Spencer was clearly on edge, looking at his watch then his phone, waiting for the senator's call. Finally, late in the afternoon a staff member announced, "Phone call from Senator McDowell." Picking up the phone the congressman quickly exclaimed, "Hello, Senator! Did you have a productive meeting?" Ignoring the congressman's greeting, Senator McDowell's question surprised Congressman Spencer. "Can you trust George Harthmann? I mean to ask him for information in confidence. Responding to our questions and providing answers without divulging that we requested, or he provided the information. Can you trust him with that kind of request?"

Congressman Spencer hesitated, "I'm not sure. I never asked him for anything like that."

The senator continued, "The CIA Deputy Director for Global Operations was very forthright with members of the

Senate Select Committee on Intelligence. She is convinced that the missing agent was framed and her goal is to uncover the truth about the operation and to restore the credibility of the Central Intelligence Agency, ensuring that future agents will act according to CIA principles. One more thing, after three days of searching, the missing CIA Agent has not been found. They have not located the agent or his body. Talk to Harthmann and ask him directly. Will he provide us with information about John Gruneburg without divulging that we requested the information?"

When George Harthmann saw that the call was from Congressman Joseph Spencer he stared at the display wandering what could he want now. Not in his wildest dreams did he expect what was to come. George took a deep breath and answered, "Hello, Congressman. How can I help you this evening?"

Congressman Spencer noted a slight sarcasm in George's voice. The Congressman hesitated, thought for a second and then he got right to the point. "Are you available tomorrow morning? I would like to meet you at the Shrine of the Immaculate Conception. I will be attending the 7:00 a.m. mass. We could have breakfast in the cafeteria at 6:30 a.m. Are you available?"

George took a deep breath and said, "Congressman, you know that I value our friendship, but this is twice in one week and tomorrow is going to be another rainy day."

The congressman quickly responded, "I know the weather is going to be miserable, that is why I chose the shrine. You can take the Metro. The first train leaves Glenmont at 5:46 a.m. and I can meet you at the Brookland Metro Station sometime around six. I'll take the Red Line from the Union Station. That way we can talk as we walk to the shrine. I know it is asking a lot. Please consider it."

George sighed, "You do not have to beg, Joe. What is the purpose of the meeting?"

The congressman quickly responded, "I'm going to have to ask you to be patient until tomorrow."

The morning was cold and windy and the rain blew under George's umbrella as he walked from his car to the Metro station. He arrived before 5:30 a.m. expecting to find a parking space close to the station, but the Glenmont parking lot seemed to be almost filled to capacity leaving George with a walk of over 100 yards from his car to the station. With the blowing rain, it was difficult to leave the warmth of his car. Reaching the shelter of the open train platform, the wind howled and it seemed colder standing still waiting for the train then it was walking in the pouring down rain. In minutes the train arrived and George was on his way to the Brookland Metro Station. Exiting the train, he immediately saw a waving Congressman Joseph Spencer, posted like a lone sentry at the end of the platform. Walking toward the congressman, George yelled, "Can we just meet here? I hate the thought of walking up Michigan Avenue to the shrine in this rain."

The congressman laughed, "Don't worry. There are a number of taxies in the lot waiting for people who are afraid of a little rain."

Reaching his friend, George put out his hand and said, "Don't get me started, Joe. So what is it that you could not discuss in a phone call?"

Holding onto the handshake with two hands the congressman replied, "Remember when we met earlier this week you asked me if the meeting could be off the record? We desperately need your help, George, and I'm not sure how to start. I need to ask you for information. I need to ask you to keep the request confidential. I need to ask questions and for you to provide answers without divulging that we requested the information. Can we trust you with that kind of request?"

Still holding onto the handshake, George shook his head and said, "With that kind of request I'm sure glad that you chose to meet in a church. What are you talking about, Joe? Are you in some kind of trouble?"

Letting go of George's hand the congressman quickly responded, "No! No! It's not me. This might be a case where I am entrusting you with the life of a friend, the most dedicated American imaginable. I need to know if I ask you for information in confidence, that I can trust your integrity, and that you will not disclose this request to anyone."

George hesitated for a moment, his mind racing at the ramifications of what he was being asked to do, and then he said, "Joe, you're the lawyer. I will listen to the question, totally off the record, but I'm not going to promise you anything until I know what you are talking about."

Without hesitation Congressman Spencer started, "You sent Senator McDowell an e-mail message with a number of attached photos. After seeing the photo of the missing CIA Agent, the senator and I agreed that it looks like a Naval Academy graduate who had been an intern in the senator's office and a close colleague of mine when he worked as a congressional liaison for the Department of the Navy. We would like you to investigate the whereabouts of this naval officer."

George Harthmann stood there in silence for what seemed to be a long time. Then he asked, "Why haven't you contacted this naval officer?"

The Congressman immediately replied, "Senator McDowell tried to locate him and hit a dead end. Apparently he is involved with a highly classified special mission. The Senator could not get anyone to comment on his mission, or where he is stationed, or the name of his commanding officer. Senator McDowell is asking for your help." Reaching into his jacket pocket Congressman Spencer pulled out an envelope, "His name is in the envelope."

George Harthmann stepped back. "Joe, I didn't say that I was going to do this."

Congressman Spencer sighed, "I know George. Take the envelope and do not open it now. If it is asking too much of you just burn it."

George waited, looking at the congressman's stretched out arm with the envelope in his hand. Then he snatched the envelope from the congressman's hand and in a flash shoved it into his pocket. "I'll think about it. I'm not promising anything, but I will think about it."

Congressman Spencer sighed again, "Thank you, George! Are you ready to get some breakfast?"

George looked at his watch and then at the congressman. "I need to pass on the breakfast. I'm flying to Fort Gordon this morning and I better get back to Fort Meade and change. I feel like a wet dog."

Congressman Spencer became noticeably nervous. "I apologize George. I didn't know that you had travel plans."

George quickly interrupted, "It is not a problem, Joe. I'm on a military flight out of Tipton. I'll be back this coming Monday. I'll call you Tuesday morning." Just then a train pulled into the platform that was heading to Glenmont. George reached out and shook the congressman's hand and said, "You better get up to the shrine, Joe. You seem to have a lot to pray about." With that, George turned, crossed the platform, and went into the train. As he entered, the door closed and the train moved away from the station.

Congressman Spencer stood there motionless, watching the train disappear in the distance and then for a long moment looked at an empty track. The congressman felt the cold and wind and a shiver hit his body as he pulled his coat collar up on his neck. He silently turned and went down the steps out of the station. Without much thought, he opened his umbrella and started the walk up Michigan Avenue toward the shrine. He needed time to sit and think and reflect on the last fifteen minutes. Staring at the lights of the shrine in the distance he suddenly thought, "It will be alright." He put his trust in George and he somehow knew that George would help him.

For the next four days Congressman Spencer thought about George Harthmann, on and off, questioning himself. Wondering if he had explained the situation well enough and did he convey the seriousness of the situation? Each time, he would rationalize that George was a trusted friend, the ultimate NSA professional, and a man of impeccable integrity. Did he place George in a compromising position? He would find out today. That was the question on the congressman's mind as he started his early morning run heading toward the Washington Monument. He ran on the sidewalk adjacent to Independence Avenue, past the Air and Space Museum, the Smithsonian Castle, turning right at 14th Street, down the slight grade to the American History Museum and then turning right onto Constitution Avenue, past the Natural History Museum, and finally the National Gallery of Art with the Capitol Building straight ahead. This two mile run around the National Mall was a fantastic way to start the day, never ceasing to inspire the congressman and energize him for another day on Capitol Hill.

It was a busy Tuesday morning and most of the congressman's time was spent out of his office. Around noon he received a message that George Harthmann called and said he would call the congressman on his office phone at six. As the afternoon passed the congressman became increasingly nervous. As six o'clock approached he sat poised at his desk with paper, a number of pens, and a cup of freshly brewed green tea. He looked at his watch, checked the three clocks in the room, and looked at the time on his computer and cell phone. At least he had the synchronization of his clocks under control. George Harthmann was always punctual, one of the qualities the congressman valued, and at six he stretched, ready to pick up the phone. The phone didn't ring. Minutes passed and still no call. This was not like George Harthmann. He was never late for anything. When the phone finally rang it startled the congressman and he jumped slightly in his chair. Without looking at the display the congressman quickly picked up the phone and said, "Hello!"

A voice on the other end asked, "Is this Congressman Joseph Spencer's office?"

Recognizing George's voice and feeling a little embarrassed with the way he answered the phone the congressman quickly responded, "Hello, George, this is Joe."

Hesitating for a moment, George asked, "Are you alright, Joe? You sound a little nervous. I apologize for being late with the call. One of the hazards of working late is that your boss may walk by your office and stop for a chat. Once again, I apologize for keeping you waiting. It drives me crazy when I have to sit and wait for a call." The congressman sat there listening, not saying a word. "Are you there, Joe?" George asked the question sensing that this was not the usual talkative Congressman Spencer.

The congressman quickly responded, "Yes, I'm here." Thinking for a moment the congressman finally cleared his throat and said, "I have been a little uptight today, George, waiting for this call, not really sure what I was going to hear from you."

George quickly responded with a little chuckle. "No need to be dramatic, Joe. Let me give you an update on the CIA operation and then we can talk about some other requests that I received from your office. This information about the CIA is not confidential. You may have heard that the doctor in charge of the training facility died of a heart attack before he could be questioned by the Senate Select Committee on Intelligence. After a week of searching there is no sign of the missing CIA Agent. In the report, the Deputy Director for Special Operations for the CIA in New York said he shot the agent as he jumped from the roof of the training facility. Since they haven't found the agent or a body they have not been able to confirm that the agent was shot. Then you have to consider the impact of hitting the water after falling ten stories and the cold temperature of the water. If he survived the fall, at best with some injuries, the possibility of hypothermia setting in was very real. His body would have been immediately exposed to the cold water, his body's core temperature dropping without any way for his body to replenish the heat that was being lost. He would experience uncontrolled shivering and then unconsciousness in a matter of minutes."

"Then, there is the strong tidal current in the East River that must be considered. The East River is a tidal straight with strong, fluctuating currents and when the missing agent jumped into the river, the tide was flowing out toward the Upper New York Bay. Because the Long Island Sound experienced a high tide earlier that evening, it added to the strength of the current as that surge from the Sound flowed through the narrow East River channel and into the Upper New York City Bay, then out to the Lower Bay and into the Atlantic Ocean. The body could have been in the Atlantic before dawn the next morning. Then there is the walkway just down river from the training facility. Hurricane Sandy wiped out the electrical system along the East River Waterfront Esplanade last year leaving that area in darkness. Since it has not been repaired, that entire area is without lights along the river walkway. It also started to rain later that night, and rain and high winds for the next week hindered the search along the East River. Divers searched the area directly below the building and didn't find anything. At this time, the agent has been presumed dead and the CIA concluded their search along the East River."

"The missing agent had passports from seven different countries and each one had a different alias and passport photo. These passports were obtained through CIA channels and are presently being monitored. To our knowledge, none of the passports has been used over the past week. They are not biometric passports that contain a chip that stores a photograph and personal data of the passport holder. The CIA has lost contact and the agent will continue to be identified as missing."

"I also received a request for information about John Gruneburg from your office. These are the preliminary findings and by no means are complete. John Gruneburg has access to three valid passports and they are all biometric passports that were issued after 2007. This is important because each of these passports contains a radio-frequency identification chip that stores the passport photograph, passport data, personal data, and fingerprints. When the passport is scanned by a government agent, the photo and data on the passport document are compared to data on the screen of the passport reader making it impossible to forge the passport documents. When going though immigration, the passport holder presents the passport to the immigration officer who then scans it, compares the data, and then verifies the photo and data through an interchange with the passport holder. John Gruneburg was issued a regular passport with a dark blue cover that he used for travel as a tourist. You can tell it is a biometric passport by the small gold rectangular symbol on the bottom of the front cover called an e-passport symbol. John Gruneburg was also issued an official passport with a brown cover that was used for international travel when he was traveling with members of Congress on official government business. Official passports are only issued to government employees or United States military personnel."

The congressman had been listening intently, taking notes, saying nothing, writing down everything that George said. Suddenly he realized he was being asked a question by George. "Congressman, can you speak German?" "Sprechen Sie Deutsch?"

Surprised the congressman responded, "No! Why would you want to know if I can speak German?"

George laughed, "Let me tell you how little imagination there is in our United States Navy. Grune is German for green and burg is German for castle so when John Gruneburg went on clandestine missions for the Navy he was issued a regular passport with a blue cover identifying him as a businessman by the name of John Greencastle. There is a valid biometric passport with the name of John Greencastle and it has a photo of John Gruneburg dressed in a suit, white shirt and tie. The passport information is linked to the alias John Greencastle and a phony company, bank accounts, and various business transactions. These passports have not been used lately and we are determining when they were used last."

George hesitated for a moment and then said, "I would like to make a few suggestions. Do not make any more inquiries at the Naval Academy or the Pentagon about John Gruneburg. Do not take the risk of connecting the dots for the CIA. Let them close the case. Do not attract attention to the missing agent. I have a scheduled meeting with you and Senator McDowell at the end of this month to present the report that details our strategy and budget to update technology at NSA. Give me until then to close a few gaps and provide the information that you requested."

"In regard to the reported CIA operation, the doctor in charge of the training facility is no longer a factor and the assets that were involved with the operation in Germany have been eliminated. Apparently the missing agent was the first asset through the program who was exposed to torture during his training. This is an embarrassment to the agency." George hesitated, took a deep breath, and then continued. "The bottom line is that Americans do not want terrorist attacks on our soil and they want all potential sources of aggression eliminated. They just do not want to know how we accomplish that, and if it requires questionable operations, they do not want to know our dirty little secrets."

"You have heard the explanation before. This was a rogue operation that was not authorized by Langley. It was disguised as a training exercise. They will not name names and they will find a scapegoat that will not lead to additional scandal. They will create a dead end trail because no one wants details and they will avoid the tragedy of full disclosure at all costs. Denial is easily justified when everything is marked top secret. No one is going to discuss the actions of these assets. It did not occur on their watch and they had no knowledge of the operation."

"You will be told that a few dedicated Americans were the victims. They were duped by foreign operatives. For national security reasons, they need to shut down the investigation and they need to cut public discussion. A financial controller at the CIA buried this loss. There are no budget details. They do not want anyone to dig for details so accept the training mission scenario and accept the argument that evil foreign operatives used CIA agents. Russian operatives were involved with a covert operation that turned into a black op, became a rogue operation, and they now need to bury this mission and move on. It is the responsible thing to do. The CIA wants to close this investigation."

"Congressman, please understand that the National Security Agency does intercept phone messages, track the use of passports, and access surveillance cameras. NSA does not act on the information; we just pass it on to our friends. As a friend, it seems as though the NSA can shed some light on John Gruneburg. Give me some time to do just that. In the meantime, I would ask that you drop your inquiries concerning John Gruneburg. We will need to know if anyone else calls the Naval Academy, the Pentagon, or the Department of the Navy looking for John Gruneburg. We will need to know if anyone responds to the CIA story. What are the dangers of exposing John Gruneburg? It is my understanding that you and Senator McDowell want to know where John Gruneburg is now. Give me some time to answer that question."

Through the phone, the congressman could clearly hear George Harthmann take a deep breath, then George spoke, "Are we in agreement, Joe?"

The congressman struggled for a moment thinking what to say and finally said, "I will update the senator on our conversation and we will follow all of your suggestions. I truly appreciate your cooperation, George. Thank you is not enough, but please accept my sincere thank you for your assistance."

George quickly interrupted, "I am only doing my job, Joe. Stay in touch. Have a good evening. Good bye for now, Joe."

CHAPTER 12

El Camino de Santiago in Spanish, Chemin de Saint Jacques de Compostelle in French, or the Way of Saint James, is one of the pilgrimage routes to the Cathedral of Santiago de Compostela in northwest Spain. The cathedral is the burial site of Saint James, an apostle of Jesus Christ, and it has been a place of pilgrimage since the Middle Ages. This was the chosen route for Wenli Lau and John Gruneburg as they set out as Christian pilgrims on a spiritual adventure, disconnecting from everyday life, in search of a sanctuary of peace. Solitude, walking the entire route, and living in the simplest of accommodations, would be the penance, the atonement for the last two years. Time to separate from the past and renew their lost friendship.

Pilgrims carry a document called a credencial, a pilgrim's passport that is used to record the journey following a sanctioned route to the Cathedral of Santiago de Compostela. The credencial is stamped with a Saint James seal at each stop on the pilgrimage route, confirming that the pilgrim stayed in official overnight accommodations along the way. Official routes in France and Spain are lined with hostels to accommodate pilgrims, called refugios in Spain or gîtes d'étape in France. These pilgrim hostels provide a one-night stay for guests who generally leave by eight the following morning to continue their pilgrimage. At the end of the pilgrimage, the credencial is presented to the Pilgrim's Office in Santiago to verify that the journey followed an official route, and to receive a compostela, a certificate that recognizes the completion of the pilgrimage.

To be awarded the compostela, the pilgrim must walk a minimum of one hundred kilometers or slightly more than sixty-two miles. Wenli and John planned a much more ambitious journey. Starting in Saint-Jean-Pied-de-Port on the French side of the Pyrenees, their pilgrimage would follow the Camino Francés route, a distance of seven hundred and eighty kilometers or approximately four hundred and eighty-four miles to Santiago de Compostela.

Camino Francés translates to the French Way and is the most famous of all the routes to Santiago. Traditionally, the majority of pilgrims came from France, thus the French Way, and the common starting point along the French border was Saint-Jean-Pied-de-Port. The Camino Francés is well marked using scallop shell designs to indicate the route. The shell design is seen on trail markers and sign posts and is often worn by pilgrims to signify that they are travelers on the Camino de Santiago. Scallop shells are commonly found along the Atlantic coast close to Santiago, and the scallop shell has for centuries been the symbol of the Camino de Santiago. Most pilgrims receive a shell when they obtain their credencial, or pilgrim's passport, at the beginning of their journey. Records of medieval pilgrims journeying to the shrine dedicated to Saint James at the Cathedral of Santiago de Compostela date back to the ninth century. It was customary for pilgrims to return with the scallop shell as proof that they completed their pilgrimage. The scallop shell has also been traditionally considered the Christian symbol for Saint James, one of the Apostles of Jesus. Still today, one encounters hikers wearing the scallop shell to identify themselves as pilgrims as they trek through the charming medieval towns and beautiful landscapes.

Since the early Middle Ages, the compostela has been viewed as an act of absolution for pilgrims seeking forgiveness and this belief remains to this day. At noon each day, Mass is celebrated in the Cathedral of Santiago de Compostela, and pilgrims who received their compostela the day before are announced at Mass. For many pilgrims the participation in the sacrament of communion is the spiritual culmination of their journey.

Wenli and John had discussed a pilgrimage to the Cathedral of Santiago de Compostela for what seemed to be decades. Time was always the barrier. Now it would happen. Time was no longer the obstacle, and Wenli believed that this time was needed to begin their healing process.

Wenli and John arrived in Toulouse as planned and stayed at the University Center that houses students from the Study Abroad Program. Wenli was excited to be in France. John, however, was mortified every time someone looked at him and their focus lasted longer than a few seconds. Wenli stayed close to John, walking arm-in-arm, conversing in French, engaging him in conversation to keep his attention on her instead of their surroundings.

John was thankful when they boarded a train from Toulouse to Lourdes the following day. Security cameras and the presence of uniformed police officers kept John on edge; he needed to get to the countryside. They agreed to speak only French from the minute they left the University Center. The goal was not to be identified as Americans when traveling.

Lourdes is a small town at the eastern edge of the Pyrenees Mountains in southwestern France that attracts millions of pilgrims and tourists each year. Famous for the healing waters that flow from the Grotto at the Sanctuary of Our Lady of Lourdes, it becomes a major pilgrimage site each year from March to October. The healing power of the spring water from the Grotto is believed by many to possess healing properties. Wenli argued that a few days in Lourdes would at least cure their jet lag and hopefully start a path back to normalcy. John listened patiently as Wenli stated her case. When he finally agreed to her plan, and told her that he understood that Lourdes was important to her, he saw the smile that he had missed so very much.

They agreed to spend a few days in Lourdes before going on to Bayonne to start their pilgrimage to the Cathedral of Santiago de Compostela. The mid-morning train seemed to be filled with tourists. Taking less than two hours travel time, they left Toulouse at 10:15 a.m. and arrived in Lourdes at 12:12 p.m. The day was sunny and grew warmer with each passing hour and Wenli promised John a quiet lunch before checking into their hotel. As soon as they settled into the Hôtel Saint Etienne, Wenli insisted that they walk the short distance to the Sanctuary of Our Lady of Lourdes. She wanted to walk the Way of the Cross on Mont des Espélugues, or Mountain of Caves, the hillside behind the Basilica of the Immaculate Conception.

Emulating the path to Calvary, the Way of the Cross is a mile-long pathway winding through a steep wooded hillside. It includes over one hundred life size cast iron statues representing the fifteen Stations of the Cross, depicting the journey of Jesus on his way to Calvary.

Following the path, Wenli and John slowly passed groups of pilgrims, some meditating in silence, others in a group that included a reader or someone explaining the Station, and many creating a photo or video journal with cameras focused on the figures at each Station. Everyone's focal point was the Way of the Cross and John was beginning to feel comfortable among these pilgrims. Winding down the hillside, the Basilica of the Immaculate Conception came back into view with its spire rising high above the Sanctuary grounds. Wenli and John avoided the large crowds around the Basilica and Grotto and agreed to walk back to the hotel and return that evening for the procession.

Following a tradition started in 1872, pilgrims are welcomed each evening to the Sanctuary of Our Lady of Lourdes and invited to participate in a procession, carrying a lighted candle as a reminder of their baptism. At the conclusion of the procession pilgrims receive a blessing and are invited to celebrate Mass at the Grotto and give thanks for the graces received that day. Being in solidarity with people of faith from all over the world and celebrating Mass in French with an exchange of the Sign of Peace with fellow pilgrims, presented a special experience for Wenli and John. As they walked in procession with their fellow pilgrims, they each held a candle in one hand, and Wenli linked her other arm around John's free arm. Walking arm-in-arm with John was special for Wenli, the perfect way to end a beautiful day. Wenli was assured that those moments of closeness were restoring in John feelings that they so treasured in the past.

The following day, they visited the Grotto early before the crowds intensified. They spent the rest of the morning in quiet areas, talking and often just sitting in silence, enjoying the serenity of the Sanctuary. Remembering last night's procession, candles flickering in the dark of the night, church bells ringing, voices of a multitude of pilgrims singing in many different languages, they agreed that Lourdes had to be experienced to understand the feeling of faith so alive at the Sanctuary.

As the temperature reached its mid-day high, pilgrims from around the world searched out the water flowing from the spring within the Grotto. Some pilgrims drank the water, rinsed their arms or soaked their heads under the fountains, and others were immersed into bathes, believing in the healing power of the water.

Wenli and John sat across the river from the Grotto in an open field of grass called the meadow, enjoying the sun, watching pilgrims pass through the Grotto. As the pilgrims approached the statue, they touched the rocks that had been polished by the hands of generations of pilgrims before them. Others sat on rows of benches, remaining silent as they prayed and contemplated the beauty of their surroundings.

The mid-day sun was warm and Wenli leaned onto John's arm and softly said, "Do you remember the last time we sat in a field of grass? We were overlooking the tennis courts in Central Park. Do you remember?"

John sat motionless for a moment, and then said, "Yes, I remember. I told you that I missed our honest discussions, and

I remember saying that our time together was very important to me."

Wenli leaned even closer to John and said, "I have been praying that you would remember. I was so afraid that you might have forgotten."

John took a deep breath, turned to Wenli and said, "You have been so patient. I was so driven. If only I would have been more sensitive and included you in the challenges I was facing. I'm sorry. I don't know how I allowed it to go on for almost two years. In the beginning I thought it would be different. I think back and then I am haunted by my memories, of times that I just want to forget."

Wenli softly said, "It is over John. You need to talk about it. I will listen. I will not judge you. I need you to talk to me. To share your fears. Yes, even your nightmares. We need to be close again. Do you understand John? We need to return to those times when you shared your fears and your challenges. I am telling you that I want to share a future with you and you must be open with me John. You must trust me. Is what I am saying, making sense to you?"

John sighed, and said, I understand Wenli. I want that closeness again, but… John hesitated.

Wenli sensed that John did not want to continue and she said, "What is it John? Tell me what you are thinking."

John turned to Wenli and said, "When I told you about my past, that first day in Maine, I saw your look of disbelief, tears flowing down your face. Please understand Wenli, I do not want to repeat…" John hesitated, and then continued, "I put you into a state of sorrow and despair. I do not want to repeat that day."

Wenli looked into John's face and said, "Yes John, you upset me, I hated that moment, knowing what you had done, but do you remember what I said the next morning? I told you that my mother and I discussed our options. We could have abandoned you. I told you that we would never do that. I told you that you're stuck with me, John. Do you remember?" Without waiting for an answer, Wenli continued, "What I did not tell you was how I came to that conclusion. How my opinion changed overnight. It was my wonderful mother, John. She told me to make a choice. If I cared for you the way I had told her, I needed to be strong. To be there for you. Even if you did not understand at that moment that you needed me. To fight for the John Gruneburg that I wanted to spend the rest of my life with. When I said that you're stuck with me, what I was really saying is that I made that choice, I was going to fight to get you back, to keep you, and yes John, to spend the rest of my life with you. I am being honest with you John. There can be no more secrets. I am opening my heart to you. Do you understand?

John sat their trembling, looking into Wenli's eyes, and he softly said, "I understand, and I know how fortunate I am to have you. Are you sure? Do you want to spend the better part of two months…" Hesitating for a moment, then he continued. There are so many uncertainties. Think of your career, your position in Halifax…"

Wenli interrupted John while giving him a hug and said, "John, you must listen. I know there are uncertainties and deep down I am just as concerned as you are, but there cannot be uncertainties between us. Are you getting what I am saying, John?" And once again, without waiting for an answer, Wenli continued, "I must tell you one more thing. My mother challenged me in Maine. I was asking the same questions that you are asking and she told me there was only one way that I would know what was right. I got my answer that morning, right after our run, as soon as I saw you. I walked right to you and put my arms around you and gave you the best hug that I could give you. My mother said that if it felt the same, if the feelings were just as strong, I had my answer. Do you remember what I said to my mother afterwards? I said thank you, mother, you are always right. I felt it then, and I feel it now. Do you feel it John? Do you feel what I feel?"

John pulled Wenli close and said, "Yes Wenli, I feel it. I have always felt it. I am so very fortunate to have you."

Wenli and John talked for hours and this time John said all the right words. They enjoyed a quiet afternoon together, welcoming the realization that they were rekindling the closeness they had both so missed. They reminisced about the wonderful times they had spent together. There were so many memories. Wenli recalled listening to John's father planning a trekking holiday to Santiago de Compostela, remembering the happiness of the moment. In a few days they would begin to hike the Way of Saint James, fulfilling a family dream, and they would do it together.

By late afternoon, they walked to the Crypt church. At the entrance to the Crypt, pilgrims were greeted by a statue of Saint Peter holding the Keys to the Kingdom of Heaven. Mass was being celebrated in French and there was an atmosphere of devotion surrounding the pilgrims. Wenli and John joined them and sat silently, enjoying the serene setting as they recalled the beautiful day. They agreed that they were blessed to have traveled to Lourdes.

After mass the sun was beginning to set and the coolness of the evening engulfed the Sanctuary. Weather changes rapidly at Lourdes with the morning and afternoon sun warming pilgrims, only to face dropping temperatures as the sun disappears and the cool winds flow down from the snowcapped Pyrenees Mountains. It was time to return to the hotel.

Lourdes had provided a feeling of peace for Wenli and John. As pilgrims they were inspired. They agreed they needed this quiet time together, in this setting. It was the gathering of so many nationalities devoted to a common faith, celebrating in many different languages, collectively creating an experience of a lifetime.

Tomorrow they would continue on the next stage of their journey, leaving at 7:23 a.m. on the train from Lourdes to Pau, transferring to the 9:13 a.m. train to Bayonne in time to make the 11:07 a.m. connection to Saint-Jean-Pied-de-Port, arriving at 12:25 p.m. in time for lunch at the Hotel Les Pyrenees. The morning train was filled with pilgrims leaving Lourdes, sharing their experiences, unable to restrain the energy generated by their pilgrimage. Boarding the train in Bayonne it was soon evident that many of the passengers going to Saint-Jean-Pied-de-Port were also preparing to journey on the Camino Francés across northern Spain on the Way of Saint James to the Cathedral of Santiago de Compostela.

They knew the weather in the Pyrenees Mountains changed suddenly and Wenli wanted to enjoy the warm afternoon sunshine exploring this picturesque town. The air was clear and brisk and presented a pleasant day for walking. Wenli wanted to shop for a pilgrim's hat with a wide upturned brim to protect her from the sun and rain that was adorned with a scallop shell to identify her as a pilgrim. John emphasized that they had to limit additions to their backpacks knowing that added weight would not be welcome once they started their journey. Wenli also found scallop shells with leather laces to attach to their backpacks.

It was agreed that they would start their journey walking short distances for the first few days, enjoying the local sites and scenery, agreeing to lengthen the distance as Wenli became more fit. They would obtain their credencials, or pilgrim's passports, from the Augustinian Monastery in Roncesvalles on the third day of their journey. They followed the Camino Francés or French Way, marked so well with scallop shell markers. Some are Council of Europe waymark tiles combined with yellow arrows pointing towards Santiago, painted on tree trunks, walls, road signs, and rocks. Some sections have blue and white metal signs with a picture of a hiking pilgrim, the scallop shell marking, and an arrow pointing toward Santiago.

It was obvious that Spanish was the preferred language along the Camino Francés and Wenli and John decided to speak Spanish when communicating along their journey and revert back to French when talking with each other.

They agreed that they were off to a great start as they stopped at the first granite marker with Saint Jacques de Compostelle 780 kms and the scallop shell marking. John laughed, "Are you sure you want to do this? That is close to 485 miles and we may get some rainy days as we climb into the Pyrenees."

Wenli gave him a light tap on his arm, "Do you remember what your father would say about rainy days? If you can learn to enjoy a day filled with rain the sunny days will be a piece of cake. I remember that your dad once told me that you can learn a lot about a person placed in four situations: a rainy day in Maine, dealing with lost luggage, being stuck in stalled traffic, or untangling Christmas lights. We may have to deal with some rainy days and also deal with untangling our lives at the same time. Are you up for that?"

John was silent for a moment and then looked into Wenli's eyes; the tension he felt earlier was gone. With conviction, he took her hand and led her back onto the trail as he said, "You have always been my closest and dearest friend. I am so fortunate that you are here to help me with this journey. Yes Wenli, I am up for that."

CHAPTER 13

It was another perfect Monday morning, bright sunshine, clear blue skies, and after three days of wind and rain, the air was clear and crisp. Why did it have to rain on the weekend and be so beautiful when it was time to go back to work? George Harthmann checked his watch. It was almost eight. Hearing footsteps coming down the hall, George walked to the door, stepped out into the hall, and from thirty feet away, was greeted by Jennifer Jenkins, Chief of Staff for Senator Sam McDowell, and Sharon Wintres, Legislative Assistant to the Senator. "Did you have a good weekend?" Jennifer asked. Before George could answer, Jennifer continued. "Sharon was just telling me that she saw the movie *The Best Exotic Marigold Hotel* this weekend. Have you seen it? I really enjoyed the Indian take on the English language throughout the movie. Short quips of charm and optimism communicated with a most friendly politeness." Entering the room, Jennifer tossed her purse and attaché case onto the conference room table, and moving toward the coffee, kept on talking without even a slight pause. "We were just laughing at the part when the hotel owner tells a guest… 'In India, there is a saying everything will be alright in the end. So if it is not alright, it is not yet the end!' When there is no door on the room there is a quick response. 'The door is coming soon, most definitely.' Describing the run-down hotel the owner merely says 'The building is of the upmost character, and the photo-shopped brochure offers you a vision of the future. Prepare to be amazed, do not concern yourself with details.' Have you seen the movie?" George just shook his head no.

Taking a sip of coffee and moving toward a chair, Jennifer continued. "That's where we are, George. Sharon agrees that everything will be alright in the end. And just like in the movie, if it is not alright, it is not yet the end."

Sharon turned to George and asked, "I trust that you didn't have a problem getting into the Hart Office Building this morning. I told security that you would be here before 8:00 a.m." Without waiting for a response she continued, "Do you think your budget proposal is ready?"

George laughed, "Hopefully this budget proposal will survive the scrutiny of both the House Intelligence Committee and the Senate Select Committee on Intelligence. I think we have a solid proposal that details our strategy to update technology to meet growing cyber threats. It will be important that Congress understands the need to sustain this initiative at the end of the present budget cycle. I wanted to give the proposal one last critique and wrap it up before eleven because I have a meeting with your boss and Congressman Spencer."

As the clock approached eleven, Jennifer turned over the last page of the proposal and looked across the table at Sharon and George. "I think you covered every question that will be asked. Congress understands that they have the power to control the purse strings of the intelligence budget and this proposal demonstrates that you listened to their requests and that will be recognized when it is time to authorize appropriations to fund this initiative."

Glancing at her watch, Jennifer smiled at Sharon and George. "Thanks for all your hard work. George, you better get down the hall to that next meeting."

Entering the next meeting room, George was greeted immediately by Senator McDowell and Congressman Spencer. "Thanks for coming downtown. I understand you were here before seven thirty this morning."

George laughed, "I'm used to getting an early start to stay ahead of the traffic."

Without responding to George's comment, the senator got right to the point. "Were you able to obtain the information we requested?"

George adjusted his position in his chair and handed a folder to the senator and to the congressman. "Let's start with your first question on page one. The Central Intelligence Agency has a clandestine organization called the Special Operations Group that is responsible for intelligence gathering operations in environments where the United States government does not want to be a known player. Members of this organization do not wear military uniforms or carry any documentation that would associate them with our government. If their activities are discovered by a hostile government, or if they were captured during an act of espionage and they were exposed as a spy, our government would most likely deny all knowledge of their mission. Association with the Special Operations Group is guarded. This is considered to be the most secretive organization in the United States. You do not have a rank or title. You are an operative, selected from the best special operations forces within the United States military."

Congressman Spencer leaned forward on the table and asked, "Is John Gruneburg a member of this Special Operations Group?"

George nervously scratched his ear, "That is a question that will not be answered. If he is, it is classified and I do not have access to that information." George continued, "Keep in mind that covert operations could have major political ramifications, including high risk operations like targeted killings. The consequences of exposing an intelligence driven operation in a hostile high risk environment are enormous. The Special Operations Group is often linked to unconventional warfare, with intentions to create or destroy an insurgency in a foreign country. This is a world where an asset could be an agent that has been planted to drive a covert operation that will effect political change and impact our foreign policy. You are not going to find a list of names."

Senator McDowell leaned in and said, "My contacts confirmed that John Gruneburg did provide translation services for the Naval Special Warfare Development Group, but he was not permanently assigned to the group. Gruneburg was involved with special missions that were all classified and I could not get anyone to comment or provide details on any of the operations. The best guess is that he was involved with high risk counter terrorism activities."

Senator McDowell continued, "As you know, the CIA is authorized to collect intelligence, implementing counterintelligence strategies and conducting covert operations under United States law. The law specifies that covert operations can be of a political or military nature. The law also states that the Department of Defense does not have the authority to conduct covert operations, so all covert operations must fall under the authority of the CIA. Congress has oversight responsibilities of these operations and the task of monitoring CIA programs is delegated to the Senate Select Committee on Intelligence and the House Permanent Select Committee on Intelligence. What is important to remember is that our government has to maintain a position where the United States can deny involvement in covert operations with credible and reasonable arguments. A believable case starts without connection to our government. These operatives are on their own when carrying out their missions, combining their special operations talents and clandestine intelligence capabilities knowing that the United States government will disavow any support for the operation. It is analogous to having oversight of a ghost."

Congressman Spencer took a deep breath and asked, "So where does that leave us? What about the testimony of the CIA's Deputy Director for Global Operations? If John Gruneburg is the agent that they are looking for, this is a ticking time bomb. If he travels using a John Gruneburg passport and the authorities are just checking his passport there will not be a problem, but any police action would put him in immediate danger. If he is identified as the missing agent, he would be identified as a fugitive, and possibly an international terrorist."

Congressman Spencer continued getting more passionate with his argument. "He was used by devious, deceitful, scheming, and cunning scoundrels. They took a man of honor who was in a vulnerable state and exploited his patriotic passion to defend our national security. He was told that he was protecting our national interests by a group of corrupt, rogue agents who used every form of deception to unknowingly involve him in assisting the Russian underworld for their own financial greed and personal gain." Taking another deep breath, the congressman continued. "This is a person of honor who may feel the guilt of his actions; subliminally he may have a need to be accountable for his past behavior. He has lived by a strong code of honor."

George once again adjusted his position in his chair and asked, "So what do we do?"

Congressman Spencer leaned forward and excitedly said, "Hack into INTERPOL and delete DNA data, fingerprints, and facial recognition information."

George leaned back in his chair. "Are you suggesting that the National Security Agency access files controlled by the International Criminal Police Organization and erase data? Do you understand that this data has been distributed internationally to hundreds of member countries? Most of them have an infrastructure and technical support that has been provided mainly by our own government. These are secure communication channels. Can I suggest a plan "B" for your consideration?"

Without waiting for a response George continued, "John Gruneburg is still receiving a paycheck from the Department of the Navy. Did you know that? His checks are deposited into an account using direct deposit information that was provided by John Gruneburg over two years ago. He also gave authorization to access the account and there has been activity; even renewing his membership fee to the Naval Academy Alumni Association and contributing to the Naval Academy Foundation. There are two names that have access to the account, Shuk Wa Lau and Wenli Lau. They have been associated with Gruneburg from his childhood."

Senator McDowell raised his hand and without waiting for a response from George interrupted, "If John Gruneburg is still receiving a paycheck from the Department of the Navy why couldn't my contacts tell me that? If he is being paid, he is active Navy, records have to exist."

George leaned forward in his chair, "Gruneburg was first assigned to the Office of Naval Intelligence and was then transferred to the Defense Intelligence Agency with a group of select personnel. Members of this elite group survived a rigorous qualification screening and were noted for their intellect, cultural knowledge of perceived areas of conflict, and multilingual capabilities. They transitioned into a national intelligence system that evolved into the Pentagon's Joint Intelligence Center whose mission was to develop a joint intelligence doctrine and integrate all intelligence activities and provide consistent support of clandestine national security operations. Recommendations by the Base Realignment & Closure Commission included plans to consolidate intelligence and clandestine operations, aligning them with CIA espionage activities. Middle East and African operations took precedence, but Gruneburg's Russian and Eastern European language skills kept him in the forefront tracking Russian support for Iran and Syria. Gruneburg was assigned to the Naval Postgraduate School in Monterey, California and devoted the next year to the Operations Research Department utilizing the latest technology and mathematical modeling to analyze the intelligence community's hot spots. It is not clear if he was working on an advanced degree or honing his knowledge of international security challenges, but we do know who he reported to at the Naval Postgraduate School. Gruneburg's commanding officer was Admiral Michael J. Lee, an Asian American and Naval Academy graduate who headed up a unit in the Joint Intelligence Center at the Pentagon. Admiral Lee built a close relationship with Gruneburg at the Naval Postgraduate School. They both were interested in expanding their Mandarin and Cantonese language skills and collaborated on a number of Asian intelligence scenarios. While under the command of Admiral Lee, Gruneburg's mother, father, and sister were killed in tragic car accident. His sister was his only sibling and he has no other living relatives. He lost his entire family. Shuk Wa Lau and her daughter Wenli were lifelong family friends and they seemed to have become Gruneburg's surrogate family. A few months later Gruneburg's record goes blank. We have nothing from any of our sources. He has vanished."

Senator McDowell immediately asked, "Have you talked with Admiral Lee? Is he still listed as Gruneburg's commanding officer?"

George dropped his head momentarily and then looking at the senator responded, "Admiral Lee died very suddenly last year of complications associated with stomach cancer. John Gruneburg's records were not in Admiral Lee's files. They must be highly classified. We have no leads."

George took a deep breath, "Please turn to the last page of the report. You will find the contact information for Shuk Wa Lau, her address on 81st Street in New York City and her phone number. May I suggest, Congressman, that you call her and explain that you want to contact your friend, John Gruneburg. If he is alive, she is the best lead that we have. Do not use any of the names associated with the CIA hearings. Never use any of those names in phone conversations, e-mail messages, or any form of communication. You do not want to be the link that connects John Gruneburg to the CIA."

Congressman Spencer smiled at George, "You really exceeded my expectations. Thank you! We can keep this report, is that correct?"

George sat up straight in his chair, "No sir, if you remember our agreement, I am providing this information for your eyes only. As far as I am concerned, this meeting never took place, and at the end of the meeting I will collect the reports and file them back at NSA in the burn box. Please make a note of the information on the last page before passing it back to me."

Senator McDowell quickly added, "Thank you George!" He handed him his copy of the report and gave him a firm, long handshake.

Congressman Spencer handed George the report and said, "I will keep you informed when I make the call." George shook his hand, "Good luck with that."

CHAPTER 14

April in New York City was perfect for outdoor activities and Shuk Wa joined friends from the Junior League for a Saturday morning run in Central Park. A four-mile jog with friends on the first Saturday of the month was a tradition that started many years ago. Meeting at 8:00 a.m. at the East 79th Street entrance, the group ran North on Park Drive behind the Metropolitan Museum of Art, past the Jacqueline Kennedy Onassis Reservoir, up to the Harlem Meer and then looped South on the West side of the park. They stayed on Park Drive around the Lake, crossed to the East side and then turned North once again for the remaining short distance to the Loeb Boathouse Restaurant. Saturday morning brunch was the reward that was the traditional culmination to every run. Mushroom omelets made with egg whites, green tea, croissants, and country potatoes were the customary selections for the group.

Founded in New York City in 1901, the Junior League evolved into an active women's volunteer organization with members in Canada, Mexico, the United Kingdom, and the United States. With the League's New York residence at 130 East 80th Street, the Central Park run was not only convenient, but the setting was a motivational factor to get members out on a Saturday morning. It was a group that enjoyed spending time together.

After a healthy brunch and a morning filled with conversation, Shuk Wa said her goodbyes and walked the short distance back to 81st Street, thinking about her schedule for the rest of the day. Entering her brownstone, Shuk Wa noticed the red light on the phone message indicator and pressed the play button. "Good morning! This is Congressman Joseph Spencer calling from Washington. I believe we have a mutual friend. A number of years ago John Gruneburg was a Legislative Assistant to Congress while at the Naval Academy and after graduation was assigned to the Navy Office of Legislative Affairs. I was trying to contact John and was hoping that you would have a current phone number. Please return my call at 202-225-41."

Shuk Wa reached to the phone and hit the delete button before the message was finished. She had no intention of returning the call. She hesitated, staring at the delete button and thinking, "If only life had a delete button, it would be so wonderful to delete the last two years of John Gruneburg's life." What she didn't know is how persistent Congressman Joseph Spencer could be. He would be calling back. That was a certainty!

Sitting down in her favorite chair, Shuk Wa sat in silence. Praying for a resolution, and yet, she was not certain how it could be achieved. Reaching to her side table, she slid her hand over an opened letter. She did not need to read it; she knew the contents almost verbatim because she had read it so many times over the past few days. Touching the letter was as close as she would get to Wenli and John today. It would have to suffice, at least for now.

Before leaving Maine, Wenli devised a plan, a method to safely communicate with Shuk Wa over the next few months. Wenli understood that e-mail, phone calls, and text messages could be traced. Even direct mail was too risky. John wanted isolation, Wenli and Shuk Wa needed communication. The plan was for Wenli to write using Hanzi, or Chine characters. She would send the letters to Shuk Wa's office at the Metropolitan Museum of Art, and use Shuk Wa's address at Columbia University as the return address. The letters would be brief, without names, and sent weekly for the remainder of their journey. For emergencies, they carried a cell phone with an international calling plan. John repeatedly emphasized that the phone was only for emergencies.

Shuk Wa looked at her watch, it was early afternoon. She decided to change and then walk the few blocks to Saint Ignatius of Loyola Church and spend some time in prayer before attending Saturday evening Mass. She was yearning to be in contact with her daughter, but for today, praying for the safety of Wenli and John would have to provide her only comfort. She reflected again about the answering machine message. The call from Congressman Spencer unsettled her. It made her feel uncomfortable. She thought that possibly she had become too complacent, the quietness of the past few weeks possibly gave her a false sense that everything would be resolved. Was the congressman's message a wakeup call? She needed to be careful.

CHAPTER 15

National Security Agency - - Fort Meade, Maryland

Traffic congestion is one aspect of urban living that no one likes. Annoying, wasteful, stressful, the list of negatives associated with this trend can go on and on. When this nuisance is tied to a government agency, an organization that provides substantial wealth to the local economy, solutions must be found. Whether it is through improved highways, routing traffic more effectively, encouraging employees to carpool or using public transportation, they all help to reduce highway overcrowding. Staggering work schedules, allowing personnel to start and finish work ahead or after peak traffic periods is also effective, especially with large population organizations like the National Security Agency.

Coming in early, starting his workday when traffic was light and the office was still relatively quiet, worked well for George Harthmann. For a proverbial early bird, a staggered work schedule, starting as early as 4:00 in the morning, allowed George to get a jump on what was happening around the globe before being thrust into his never-ending domestic assignments.

Global monitoring of communication and information systems presented an ever-increasing challenge and many organizations relied on NSA's ability to collect and process massive amounts of information and data for intelligence purposes. Adding to the complexity of their mission, NSA's role is also to protect the United States government from someone penetrating our networks, while at the same time having the authority to access everyone else's systems.

Both the Defense Intelligence Agency and the Central Intelligence Agency are authorized to gather foreign intelligence, primarily collected by individuals. Commonly referred to as spying or espionage, human intelligence is one of the specialties of the intelligence community. Our laws prevent the National Security Agency from engaging in this type of activity. NSA is authorized to maintain clandestine operations around the globe to secretly collect information and data by physically tapping into electronic systems: installing listening devices in difficult to reach locations, utilizing surveillance cameras, creating espionage tactics that ensure we gather the needed intelligence. This secret or sensitive information is often encrypted and the interception of communications or "signals" between people is called Signals Intelligence. NSA also coordinates a cryptanalysis network of both military and civilian personnel to decode or decipher the intercepted communications and track the sources of the encrypted messages.

This was the life that George Harthmann was dedicated to, every moment of every working day, proud to work for an organization that he believed kept our country safe. Simply said, he enjoyed the magnitude of responsibility that he faced each day and he admired the men and women who served with him. Their service, both civilian and military personnel, was genuine and he was proud to call them colleagues.

Sitting at his desk, totally absorbed in a report, his mind focused on a specific thought, George Harthmann was startled by the ringing of his phone. No one ever called his land line at 5:18 in the morning. Reaching for the phone he immediately answered, "Harthmann!"

The voice on the phone said, "Good morning, Mr. Harthmann! This is Captain Haistings. I report to the Rear Admiral at the Office of Naval Intelligence. I was told that you start your day early, but I'm a little surprised that you answered the phone at this hour on the first ring."

Avoiding any early morning small talk, George got right to the point and asked, "Good morning, Captain Haistings, how may I assist you?"

Captain Haistings sensed that Harthmann wanted to move onto the purpose of the call so he continued, "The Rear Admiral wants to meet with you this morning at 11:00 a.m. Are you able to adjust your schedule to meet the Rear Admiral's request?"

Surprised by the request, Harthmann responded, "May I ask the purpose of this meeting?"

The response from the Captain was direct. "The Rear Admiral would prefer discussing the details of the meeting in person. Will you meet with her at 11:00 a.m. at the Army Navy Country Club in Arlington? Please dress for a round of golf, but there is no need to bring your clubs. Will that time work for you?"

Harthmann knew there was only one right answer when the request was coming from the Rear Admiral at the Office of Naval Intelligence and he said, "Yes. I will meet you at 11:00 a.m. this morning at the Army Navy Country Club in Arlington."

Captain Haistings immediately responded, "Thank you, Mr. Harthmann, I'll see you at eleven. Thank you for adjusting your schedule to accommodate the Rear Admiral's request. Good bye."

Cradling the phone in his hand, Harthmann wondered, "Why did the Rear Admiral need to meet with him, and why the urgency?"

Capitol Hill - - Washington, DC

Thirty miles south, southwest from the National Security Agency, in the northeast quadrant of the District of Columbia stands the Hart Office Building and Senator Sam McDowell's office. The newest of the three buildings that serve the United States Senate, it is a short distance northeast of the Capitol on a location bordered by Constitution Avenue, C Street, First Street and Second Street NE. This morning the office was abuzz with activity and the Senator was on and off the phone, constantly checking his watch, clearing his calendar for the rest of the day.

Early morning phone calls from the Office of Naval Intelligence caught both Senator Sam McDowell and Congressman Joseph Spencer by surprise. No mention was made of John Gruneburg, but they were told that recent inquiries concerning a Navy officer caught the attention of the Rear Admiral and she wanted to discuss their interest in the officer's welfare. The Rear Admiral asked to meet with them that morning at 11:00 a.m. at the Army Navy Country Club in Arlington. Congressman Spencer was particularly surprised at the request to dress for a comfortable game of golf, but there was no need to bring his clubs. The senator immediately understood. This was to look like an informal social outing to avoid drawing attention to the participants attending the meeting. Thinking out loud, the senator wondered, "Why the need for so much drama?"

The last few days had shed promising light on the location of John Gruneburg. They were kept in the loop by George Harthmann on a daily basis and were relieved to hear that Gruneburg was apparently alive and had crossed the border from Maine into New Brunswick, Canada at the Calais / Saint Stephen border crossing. They had no doubt that it was John Gruneburg because he used a valid biometric passport that contained an identification chip which stored Gruneburg's passport photo and personal data. Harthmann reminded them that you can tell a biometric passport by the small gold rectangular symbol on the bottom of the front cover. When going through immigration Gruneburg's passport was scanned by an agent and the photo and data on the document were then matched to the data on the screen of the passport reader, adding certainty that the passport was not forged.

Staying in touch with the United States Department of Homeland Security Harthmann learned that two days after entering Canada, John Gruneburg departed on a flight from Halifax, Nova Scotia to London Heathrow and then made a connection to Toulouse, France. The flight was booked and the tickets were purchased by Wenli Lau using her American Express credit card.

Still thinking about the Rear Admiral's request, the senator thought out loud "Could this meeting be about John Gruneburg?" Picking up the phone the senator dialed George Harthmann. When the senator explained that he and Congressman Spencer had received early morning calls from the Office of Naval Intelligence, the senator was surprised to learn that Harthmann received a similar call and was apparently invited to the same meeting in Arlington. Looking at his watch the senator thought, "What is this about? Was the Office of Naval Intelligence aware of their meetings with Harthmann?"

Central Intelligence Agency - - Langley, Virginia

That very same day, a meeting was taking place some forty miles south west of the National Security Agency, on a hill west of the Potomac River, just off the George Washington Memorial Parkway, in a secluded and secure complex in Langley, Virginia, the home of the Central Intelligence Agency. Monica Schmidtski arrived early that morning and nervously waited for her meeting with the CIA Deputy Director for Global Operations. Monica was alone in a conference room, arranging her notes and paging through Heinrich Kochmandt's diary.

When the conference room door opened, Monica jumped to her feet. Entering the room, Bethanne Longfield walked directly to Monica and with her outstretched hands, grasped Monica's hands and said, "I'm so very grateful that you had the courage and common sense to contact me when you did.

Thank you for coming to Langley. I apologize, I should have introduced myself. I'm Bethanne Longfield, CIA Deputy Director for Global Operations and I know you are Monica Schmidtski. Thank you for being here."

Still nervously shaken, Monica immediately asked, "Have you heard from John Volkov? I just saw a brief clip on the news when I arrived at Andrews. What happened to Volkov?"

Deputy Director Longfield held Monica's hands a minute longer and then said, "Please sit and relax, would you like a cup of coffee?" as she walked to a coffee pot and without waiting for an answer poured coffee into two cups. Returning to the table she handed Monica a cup of coffee and sat down across from her. "We're not certain about the status of Volkov. I will update you on what I know."

Detailing the events of the last few days, the Deputy Director patiently answered Monica's questions, finally reaching the point of the story that she had avoided up to this time and said, "John Volkov may not have survived jumping from the roof of the ten story CIA building in New York. He may have been shot by the Deputy Director for Special Operations. Considering that the water temperature of the East River would have caused almost instant hyperthermia and with the impact of the fall, down ten stories, the conclusion is that he most likely did not survive. Now the agency wants to close the case."

Monica sat in silence for what seemed to be a long time and then she asked, "Did they find his body? Has the Agency recovered his body?"

Deputy Director Longfield took a deep breath and said, "The strong tidal current of the East River could have washed his body down into the New York City Bay and possibly into the Atlantic Ocean before dawn the next morning. Hurricane Sandy wiped out the electrical system along the East River last year, so there were no lights, and not one surveillance camera along that stretch of the river, plus it was dark. Divers searched the area directly below the building and didn't find anything. At this time, John Volkov is presumed dead and the agency concluded their search along the East River. I'm sorry that I do not have better news."

Feelings of sadness, then outrage, then guilt, gripped Monica. Her emotions were in a state of turmoil as she thought of one more possibility and quickly asked, "Did you check his hotel room?"

Deputy Director Longfield sighed deeply and said, "Volkov was staying at the Hotel Pennsylvania on 7th Avenue. He left a suitcase, clothing and a travel kit in the room. Locked in the room safe were his seven passports that were issued through CIA channels. Just to be certain, we're monitoring the passport numbers to rule out the use of forged copies. None of the passport numbers have been used. The room safe also contained plastic zip-lock bags with a variety of currencies and the amounts are consistent with your explanation that you divided the remaining currencies before leaving Paris. He apparently used the Euro banknotes for traveling and expenses."

Monica quickly interrupted and said, "That makes sense because he was traveling using his French passport."

Deputy Director Longfield took a deep breath and continued, "He never used any of the one hundred dollar bills that were in the $10,000 wrapper and we recovered the remaining Swiss and Euro banknotes. No one has approached the hotel or asked about Volkov's possessions. There have been no inquiries by phone, fax or e-mail. I'm sorry that I do not have news that would lead us to believe that he is still alive."

Monica's emotions were rising with each word and in the end she sat staring at the deputy director trying to gather her thoughts. Finally, with a crackling voice, she said, "I should never have left him. I should have stayed with him and met you in New York. I cannot accept that he is dead. If anyone could survive that jump, it would be John Volkov. I won't accept that he is dead until you find his body. Until you find a body, you need to presume that he is alive and needs your help. He needs to understand that it is safe to come in."

Deputy Director Longfield sat straight up in her chair. She had been talking softly and at a slow pace and now her tone changed as her emotions began to rise. Talking in a firm voice she said, "I suggested that you separate in Paris. It was for your safety. You probably saved his life and your own life with the decisions that you made in Vienna, Zürich and Paris. You took great risks and you made the right decisions. You followed protocol, used your instincts and uncovered information that would have gone undetected. Think of his medical condition. The consensus at the hospital was that Volkov experienced total memory loss, he had been knocked unconscious, was shot and lost a lot of blood. You got him out of Ukraine. You got him to safety. It was with your guidance that he was able to get to New York. He was with me and I asked him to come into my office. He refused. He chose to continue to search for more answers. He told me that he still had one more stop to make. I had no idea that he was going to the CIA training facility. I do understand. I did not want it to end this way. The last thing that Volkov said to me was that if I cared about the agency then I need to do something. That is what we must do."

Taking a deep breath, Deputy Director Longfield continued, "I need to discuss what you found in Heinrich Kochmandt's room in Zürich, Switzerland. I need details about what you found in his safe."

Without hesitation, Monica asked, "Did Volkov give you the document, the *Operation Azov* document that was labeled Top Secret?" Putting her hand on a leather bound book Monica continued, "I have the diary that contains the financial information and records of Swiss bank account transactions. It shows that twenty million dollars was transferred from the Agency to Swiss bank accounts. There are also bank transfers from Russians to the same Swiss accounts. Heinrich documented the corruption in the Berlin office and illegal use of CIA funds by the Head of Operations in Berlin and the Deputy Director for Special Operations."

Monica picked up a cell phone and said, "This is Heinrich's cell phone and when I scrolled through the address book I found your name. That is how we got your cell phone number. Has the Deputy Director for Special Operations been taken into custody? Have you determined who killed Heinrich Kochmandt?"

Hesitating for the first time the Deputy Director said, "Your colleague Heinrich Kochmandt and the Head of Operations in Berlin, Stephen Spearfoot, were definitely murdered and there are leads that implicate a Russian hit man, but this has not been proven. The doctor who was the Training Director for Operation Azov died of a heart attack shortly after he was arrested. The Deputy Director for Special Operations is claiming his innocence, blaming Kochmandt, Spearfoot and the doctor who was the operation's Training Director for masterminding what he calls a black-op saying he was the victim and was not aware of the operation. The agency wants to close the case. They are looking for a scapegoat that will not lead to additional scandal and they are accepting the testimony of the Deputy Director for Special Operations. Kochmandt and Spearfoot cannot defend themselves; they cannot contradict the testimony of the Deputy Director for Special Operations from their graves. Even if we believe that this is a fabricated story, they will take the blame."

Monica was experiencing a feeling of frustration and confusion and expressed her anger to Deputy Director Longfield and then she asked, "Can't you do something? What about this diary?"

Taking another deep breath, Deputy Director Longfield continued, "The Deputy Director for Special Operations was a skillful agent. He didn't become a Deputy Director sitting in an office in New York City. He knows how to play the game;

he is shrewd and we will not be able to prove his involvement. He has said that Kochmandt and Spearfoot were deceitful and this operation occurred on their watch and he did not have knowledge of their black-op. He's telling us that they were clever agents and were experts at avoiding detection."

Monica sat there shaking her head and finally said, "I cannot believe that you are telling me this. I cannot accept that he is innocent. When you read this diary you will understand."

Deputy Director Longfield quietly said, "The Agency wants to close this investigation. It is the responsible thing to do. They cannot afford to risk having details of this operation leaked to the press. They need to bury the operation and move on."

Taking a deep breath, she continued in a firm voice, "If this diary contains what you said it does, I will make certain that the Deputy Director for Special Operations is anchored to a desk in some back office in Langley and he will never see action again. He will be isolated, no phone, no Internet, no mail and no visitors. His career will be over."

Monica listened and then asked, "Can you stop this from ever happening again?"

Deputy Director Longfield smiled at Monica and said, "Always remember that the CIA's mission is to collect secrets, analyze gathered intelligence, and take the necessary covert actions to protect our nation. Policy requires the prior approval of the President for all covert operations. The CIA creates the plan for the covert operation; senior White House officials conduct a policy review and a legal review, with the National Security Team providing the leadership throughout the review process. The CIA does not offer information until we are asked. Depending on the mission, a distinction must be made between what is classified and non-classified. All decisions must support our national security. Decisions must never be political; objectivity must be maintained. The merits of all covert operations are reviewed. Were we right or wrong taking action? Did we conduct the decision-making process professionally? We question our judgment; determine the advantage of moving quickly and moving too slowly.

Speaking with conviction, Deputy Director Longfield continued, "My experience has taught me that CIA employees care deeply about national security, protecting our nation, facing national security issues, and understanding the need for first rate intelligence. They always remember that intelligence is information and what is important is the ability to analyze the information and to understand its significance. We are all aware of the myths that Hollywood creates about the CIA; incredulous plots that portray the CIA as a rogue agency. My experience has been with an agency with incredibly dedicated people who keep this country safe by placing themselves in harm's way, often paying the supreme sacrifice to achieve their mission."

Hesitating for a moment, the deputy director once again continued, "There are times when we lay awake at night; facing the fear that long term radicalization could lead to terrorists dominating a region, overthrowing a government. America remains safe because of our counter terrorism missions. I remain confident about the agency's ability to gather and analyze information, employing our capacity to impact events that undercut terrorism and eliminate long term threats of extremism. I'm talking about the CIA analyst, the operatives that are at the heart of this sophisticated analytical organization, struggling to understand the way that terrorists think. As the Deputy Director for Global Operations, I must be analytic, knowing what is strategically versus tactically correct, staying true to the facts. I cannot tell you that I know what every analyst is thinking. I cannot guarantee that we can stop the possibility of just one person elevating his own corrupt interests above the inspired work of thousands of dedicated men and women like you." Then, with a sigh she said "No, Monica, I cannot guarantee that I can stop this from ever happening again, but I will do my best to make certain that the Deputy Director for Special Operations will never see action again."

Office of Naval Intelligence - - Suitland, Maryland

That same day, another meeting was taking place just thirty-two miles south of the National Security Agency in a complex located within the Suitland Federal Center at the headquarters of the National Maritime Intelligence-Integration Office in Suitland, Maryland. Referred to as NMIO, its mission is to integrate maritime intelligence by partnering with all levels of government to promote a unified effort in protecting the United States and its allies against global maritime threats. NMIO is co-located with the Office of Naval Intelligence, which is the oldest member of the United States Intelligence Community.

What was an embarrassment to the Central Intelligence Agency was a downright irritant for Naval Intelligence. To allow a Navy officer to be subjected to such treatment: hypnosis, behavioral modification, water boarding, isolation, sleep deprivation. The list was endless and it was all criminal behavior. If he had been captured it could have escalated into an international incident. What were they thinking? Now the CIA wanted to brush the entire operation under the carpet, to make certain that it did not get any more public attention, and the Navy wanted to ensure that it never happened again. The collective opinion at the Navy was to move on, to work toward a better day, a day of higher standards, to guarantee that this kind of operation would never again involve one of their officers. It must never be repeated.

A red flag had been raised when Lieutenant Schieffler, Senator Sam McDowel's congressional liaison, called the Office of Naval Intelligence and the Joint Intelligence Center at the Pentagon and asked for John Gruneburg's contact information. Naval Intelligence was concerned that the senator was informed by the Pentagon that Gruneburg was assigned to a special mission that was highly classified. They questioned whether the Senator was really planning a reunion for Naval Academy midshipmen who interned in his office or did he have an alternative motive. Then they were informed that the Navy could not even identify Gruneburg's current commanding officer. This was downright troubling news for Naval Intelligence.

When it was finally learned that Gruneburg's secret identity was protected, sealed as Sensitive Compartmented Information that could only be accessed through the Special Access Programs, the concerns went straight to the Rear Admiral's office. Question after question was raised. How could a Navy officer be assigned to a special branch of the CIA, to an operation that the Department of Defense did not have the authority to conduct? Who authorized the assignment? Was no consideration given to the risks to the officer and to the Navy?

When access was granted and Gruneburg's personnel file was reviewed, the Rear Admiral was outraged by the deception of the CIA's Deputy Director for Special Operations. Gruneburg was promised that he would be saving American lives and instead he was implicated in targeted killings; involved with the assassination of foreign nationals. This should not have happened.

When the connection was finally made between Gruneburg and the missing CIA agent and it was determined that it was really Gruneburg that the CIA was searching for, anger peaked and indignation for the Deputy Director for Special Operations intensified. He was trying to frame Gruneburg. He shot at him. He was trying to kill him, and the motive, without a doubt, was to eliminate everyone who could implicate the Deputy Director for Special Operations with his so called black-op.

And now they had reason to believe that the CIA did not know that John Gruneburg was alive; they did not know that Gruneburg was the missing CIA agent they were searching for. The Rear Admiral reviewed all options with her staff and they finally reached consensus that they needed to throw John Gruneburg a life line. It was clear that Gruneburg had been used by a deceitful and cunning Deputy Director for Special Operations. He took a man of honor who was in a vulnerable state and exploited his patriotic passion and used every form of deception to involve him in a rogue operation, and it was all driven by the Deputy Director's financial greed.

Now it was time to put their plan into action. Captain Haistings had made contact with Senator Sam McDowell, Congressman Joseph Spencer and George Harthmann and this morning's meeting was set for the Army Navy Country Club. Calling the captain into her office the Rear Admiral asked him to close the door and take a seat as she began to speak. "We need to be certain of our next steps and I would like to review what we want to accomplish with today's meeting." The Rear Admiral looked directly into the Captain's face and asked, "Are you comfortable handling this morning's meeting on your own? No need to explain in detail about my conflict, just make sure that you convey my apologies for not being there." Without waiting for an answer the Rear Admiral continued, "These are my priorities. Congressman Spencer must stop calling Shuk Wa Lau and George Harthmann must immediately delete all notes and records concerning John Gruneburg."

Leaning forward on her desk, the Rear Admiral said, "We need our very best to hack into the International Criminal Police Organization and erase John Volkov's data. Make certain that his DNA data, fingerprints, and facial recognition information is deleted from all INTERPOL communication channels."

Relaxing in her chair, the Rear Admiral continued, "Our next step will be to contact John Gruneburg through Shuk Wa Lau. When Gruneburg is safely in the United States we need to secretly admit him into the Walter Reed National Military Medical Center. Because the Base Realignment combined the surgeons from the National Naval Medical Center and Walter

Reed Army Medical Center, we need a trusted Navy surgeon. It is my understanding that there are scars on his back from the gunshot wounds, and they are distinguishing marks that could identify Gruneburg as John Volkov. We need our very best doctor to perform the plastic surgery to remove those scars."

Rubbing her hands together the Rear Admiral continued, "We need to create a position at the Naval Academy, a transition program until Gruneburg stabilizes both physically and mentally. This must be turned into a good situation for Gruneburg, to take what was wrong and make it right." The Rear Admiral took a deep breath, hesitated for a moment, reviewing in her mind the plan that she had just laid out, and then with a firm voice said "Make it happen, Haistings!"

Army Navy Country Club - - Arlington, Virginia

As usual, George Harthmann was early for the 11:00 a.m. meeting at the Army Navy Country Club. Arriving just a few minutes past his planned 10:45 arrival time, George parked his car in the parking lot across from the main clubhouse entrance. He scanned the parking lot for Senator Sam McDowell and Congressman Joseph Spencer and didn't see anyone. He then noticed a person standing in front of two golf carts to the right of the front entrance. Leaving his car, he walked toward the person and as he approached, the person took a few steps forward.

Looking directly at George, the person said, "Good morning, Mr. Harthmann, thank you for adjusting your schedule to meet today. My name is Captain Haistings and I report to the Rear Admiral. Senator McDowell and Congressman Spencer should be arriving shortly. Are you comfortable driving a golf cart?" Before George could answer, a taxi approached and the Captain said, "I believe they're here. I'll introduce myself and then we'll be off."

The taxi stopped right in front of where they were standing and the senator was immediately out of the car with the congressman following close behind him. Glancing toward George Harthmann, the senator then walked toward Captain Haistings who immediately stretched out his hand and said, "Good morning, Senator." Still holding the Senator's hand, the Captain quickly turned toward the congressman and said, "Good morning, Congressman. Thank you both for being here. I'm Captain Haistings and I report to the Rear Admiral's office. She apologizes for not being here to personally meet with you; unfortunately, something urgent came up and she had to attend another meeting this morning at Naval Intelligence. I know you're acquainted with Harthmann, so let's move down the cart path to the 12th tee where we will be sure to have privacy, and we'll get started. I'll drive one of the golf carts and senator you may join me; Congressman, please ride with Harthmann in the other cart."

As soon as they arrived at the 12th tee the Captain circled his cart until he was facing the front of the cart that Hartmann was driving. Stepping out of the cart he faced everyone and said, "The Rear Admiral authorized me to brief you on Lieutenant Commander John Gruneburg, but before we begin, I must state that no one should be recording this conversation and everything that I say is confidential and off the record. Is that understood?"

Both Congressman Spencer and George Harthmann immediately responded with a "Yes" and then the senator asked, "Will you answer our questions? If so, then I'll say yes."

The Captain hesitated for a moment and then said, "You may ask questions, but I cannot promise that I will be able answer all of them. Are we in agreement?"

With an affirmative response from everyone the Captain began. "First of all, the Rear Admiral wants to bury the John Volkov case. Let the CIA close it. She wants no more inquiries. Does everyone understand?" Without waiting for a response the Captain continued, "Then, she wants your cooperation in getting John Gruneburg safely back to the Navy."

Senator McDowell immediately interrupted, "Are you confirming that Gruneburg was the missing CIA Agent?"

The Captain hesitated once again and then said, "We are in agreement with the CIA that John Volkov is dead and the CIA should close their investigation and seal the case. John Gruneburg is a totally different matter that has nothing to do with John Volkov. That is the Rear Admiral's position. Does everyone understand? Are we in agreement so that I can move on?"

Receiving everyone's affirmative response the Captain continued. "The Rear Admiral is insisting that we get to the bottom of this mess. She wants this cleaned up. As far as John Gruneburg is concerned, we need to give him back his life. He was a distinguished Navy officer and the Rear Admiral has authorized me to do whatever it takes to achieve that goal."

The Captain took a deep breath and then said, "We need to know who is aware of your inquiries. The last two years of Gruneburg's life need to be erased and we need to start with you. Do you understand? The Rear Admiral is insisting that we are going to make this right."

Once again, Senator McDowell interrupted the captain, "Are you convinced that the CIA does not know that Gruneburg is their missing CIA Agent? Are you saying they did not know that John Volkov was a Navy officer?"

Shaking his head back and forth, the captain immediately responded, "Senator, I must stress that you must stop this line of questioning. I will repeat, the CIA believes John Volkov is dead and our intelligence confirms that claim. We do not want to provide the CIA with unsubstantiated rumors that may lead to a continued investigation. Do you understand, Senator? Are we all on the same page?"

Congressman Spencer quickly added, "I understand what you are saying. I am starting to understand the situation. I think it would be best that you tell us exactly what you want us to do and right now we will just listen. Do you agree, senator?"

Without waiting for a response the captain continued, "Once again, the Rear Admiral wants your cooperation; we must correct this situation. It will mean pulling out all the stops. You must never contact the CIA about John Gruneburg. They will close this case and the Rear Admiral will arrange that every possible connection to John Volkov will be eliminated. His file and records will mysteriously go blank."

The captain took another deep breath and then continued, "I will tell you this. John Gruneburg's personal information including his real name, social security number, date and place of birth, mother's maiden name, medical, educational, financial, and employment records, driver's license, passports, and civilian and military photo ID's were secured under the Special Access Programs. None of this information was available to the CIA and none of this information is connected to any CIA case file. Does everyone understand what I just said?"

Senator McDowell, Congressman Spencer and George Harthmann looked inquisitively at each other and then the senator said, "Yes! Please continue."

Tapping his right hand into his open left hand, the captain's tone changed and with a serious voice said, "John Gruneburg's biometric records were accidentally transferred to a CIA case file two years ago, and I repeat, this was by accident. These forensic records included Gruneburg's fingerprints, dental records, DNA profile, retinal scan and iris recognition data. It is important to understand that the CIA's forensic information is not tied to the name John Gruneburg. Naval Intelligence is secretly deleting these biometric records from the CIA case file to eliminate the possibility that they could be traced to John Gruneburg."

The Captain took a really deep breath and said, "Does everyone understand that what I just said is confidential? Do you understand the implications for the Navy and for Naval Intelligence? This information must remain classified."

Senator McDowell immediately asked, "Why are you telling us this confidential information?"

Smiling for the first time, the captain said, "Because, Senator, we believe the three of you have already unraveled much of what I have said and we not only need your pledge to keep this information confidential, we also need your assistance in getting John Gruneburg safely back to the Navy."

Growing restless, the senator asked, "I don't understand. Why do you need our help to get Gruneburg back to the Navy?"

Sighing deeply the captain said, "Keeping this information a secret will be a challenge. You already have a vested interest in Gruneburg's welfare and you deal with classified information on a daily basis. The bottom line is that the Rear Admiral believes that she can trust the three of you with Gruneburg's life and it eliminates the need to expand this circle of secrecy to more individuals. Can the Rear Admiral count on your cooperation?"

Senator McDowell, Congressman Spencer and George Harthmann looked back and forth at each other and then the congressman asked, "What exactly do you want us to do that the Office of Naval Intelligence is not capable of doing? I understand the need for confidentiality. What do you want us to do?

Smiling once again, the captain said, "Congressman, you have already contacted Shuk Wa Lau and we know that she has not replied to your calls. We understand that she has an understandable mistrust of anyone trying to contact John Gruneburg, and we also understand that she is our best route to contacting him. We are concerned that continuing your efforts to contact Shuk Wa Lau might cause her to bring up names associated with the CIA hearings. These names could be mentioned in phone conversations, e-mail or text messages. We do not want to be the link that connects John Gruneburg to the CIA. We must avoid all communication that could set off alarms at the CIA. We do not want to take that risk. Do you understand Congressman?

Turning to George Harthmann the captain continued, "Now consider the remarkable efforts of your friend from the National Security Agency. Harthmann complied with your requests and connected the dots to Shuk Wa Lau. We are concerned about your latest contacts with the United States Customs and Border Protection (CBP) Agency and the information they provided from their CBP I-94 forms that recorded the departure information for John Gruneburg and Wenli Lau that was obtained using manifest information from their airline carrier. We are concerned about your continued monitoring of the CBP and Canada's Border Services Agency for the use of John Gruneburg's passport. Tracking the use of his passport and accessing travel records through systems controlled by the Western Hemisphere Travel Initiative may raise a red flag at the CIA, especially if you continue to contact the United States Department of State and United States Department of Homeland Security in order to obtain this information and monitor the use of his passport.

The bottom line is that we need your cooperation now. All conversations about John Volkov must stop immediately. Inquiries about John Gruneburg, Wenli Lau and Shuk Wa Lau must stop until we tell you otherwise. We need your silence, your pledge that everything that was discussed today is classified. We are entrusting you with the life of a Navy officer. Someday, down the road, we will seek your advice and assistance as we transition John Gruneburg back to a normal existence. I know that this is asking a lot, but the Rear Admiral believes that you will do what is right. Do you understand? Does the Rear Admiral have your promise that you will fully cooperate with her requests?

Senator McDowell, Congressman Spencer and George Harthmann looked back and forth at each other and then almost simultaneously said, "Yes!"

Metropolitan Museum of Art - - 1000 5th Avenue, New York, New York

Located on the east side of Central Park with its main entrance at 82nd Street and 5th Avenue, the Metropolitan Museum of Art is simply referred to as the MET by many New Yorkers. Renowned globally, this gem of a museum is found on the upper eastside of Manhattan, one of the five boroughs of New York City.

Captain Haistings planned to meet Shuk Wa Lau without alerting her that he wanted to contact John Gruneburg. Dressed in civilian clothes, the captain would sign up for the noon tour of the MET's collection of five thousand years of Chinese art. Next Tuesday's one-hour *Arts of China* guided tour would be conducted by Dr. Lau and it provided an opportunity to meet Dr. Lau without her knowing his intent.

Finally, it was Tuesday morning. It was time to meet Shuk Wa Lau. Catching a 6:55 a.m. train from the Union Station in Washington, DC, Captain Haistings checked his watch and thought, "I'll be in the heart of New York City in about three hours." Settling into his first class seat on Amtrak's 2154 Acela Express, he was given a copy of the *New York Times* and a cup of coffee. Taking advantage of the complimentary onboard breakfast service, the Captain enjoyed a tomato and mozzarella cheese omelet with diced potatoes and roasted cherry tomatoes. This first class experience was a rarity and Captain Haistings was enjoying every moment.

Arriving at 9:48 a.m. at Penn Station, the Captain walked to the 8th Avenue exit on 31st Street and exiting the station found the queue for taxies going north on 8th Avenue. Once in a cab, the Captain instructed the driver, "I want to go to the

Metropolitan Museum of Art." Rush hour traffic had peaked at nine and they moved up 8th Avenue without delays, continuing through Columbus Circle and north on Central Park West. At the West 86th Street intersection, the taxi turned right and traveled through Central Park, exiting at 5th Avenue and East 84th Street. The driver made a right turn onto 5th Avenue and in just twenty minutes Captain Haistings was standing in front of the Metropolitan Museum of Art.

Entering the museum at the main entrance at 82nd Street, the Captain paid the suggested $25 adult admission fee and walked across the Great Hall to the information desk and registered for the noon *Arts of China* guided tour. Captain Haistings looked at his watch, it was only 10:45 a.m. and he thought, "I got here a lot faster than planned." He looked across the Great Hall and to the right was a sign for the Met Store and he decided to spend the next hour browsing through books on Chinese art. At 11:45 a.m. the Captain walked back into the Great Hall and to the Guided Tour Meeting Point sign that was located in the far right hand corner of the hall. He immediately noticed a well dressed Asian woman with a red Metropolitan Museum of Art badge on the front of her suit jacket. As he got closer he could read "Dr. Shuk Wa Lau" on her badge.

A small group gathered and at 11:55 Dr. Lau announced, "If you are here for the *Arts of China* tour we will start in five minutes. Exactly at noon, Dr. Lau said, "Our group is small enough to take the elevator to the second floor. Please follow me." They walked a short twenty feet or so and followed her into the elevator.

Arriving on the second floor, Dr. Lau started, "The museum's Asian department is the most complete collection of Asian art in the United States. This entire wing is dedicated to the Asian collection and covers 4,000 years of art including rare Chinese jades, bronzes, ceramics, paintings and sculpture. Today we will visit Galleries 217 and 218 and explore one of the highlights of the museum's collection, our Chinese

Courtyard." As they entered Gallery 217 Dr. Lau explained, "This complete Ming Dynasty garden court was modeled after a seventeenth-century courtyard in the *Garden of the Master of the Fishing Nets* in Suzhou, China. This granite terrace was hand-chiseled from a quarry in Suzhou and then assembled by Chinese artisans."

As one o'clock grew near, and the tour was drawing to a close, Dr. Lau encouraged the group to continue to explore the Asian wing of the museum. As the group started to disperse, Captain Haistings approached Dr. Lau and said, "May I please just ask one final question?" Glancing around the room, they were now alone and the Captain said, "I believe I have very good news for you."

Dr. Lau looked startled and said, "I'm sorry sir, you will have to excuse me. I have an appointment."

Captain Haistings quickly interrupted, "Please listen! It is good news about John Gruneburg. Please, is there someplace where we can talk with absolute privacy? It is a beautiful day, possibly a short walk in the park?" Noticing her hesitation, the Captain continued, "It is critical to clear John Gruneburg's name, I cannot say anything more here, please trust me, we need your help. Please!"

Beginning to question if he was too blunt and too quick with his approach, the captain was getting ready to speak again and then Dr. Lau softly said, "I will listen, but not here. We are surrounded by security cameras." And then speaking in a normal voice she said, "Yes, I agree, it is a beautiful day for a walk in the park. We can continue our conversation there."

As they left the museum, they turned right and walked down 5th Avenue and just before reaching 79th Street they turned right into Central Park. Immediately to their right was a children's playground and at its center was a large bronze statue of three bears on a circular stepped pedestal. Surrounding the sculpture was a large circular seating area. Dr. Lau motioned to a park bench in an area that was without other park visitors and said, "Please explain this good news about John Gruneburg."

Still sensing uneasiness, the Captain began "My name is Captain Haistings and I report to the Rear Admiral at the Office of Naval Intelligence."

Immediately Dr. Lau responded, "The Office of Naval Intelligence?"

Feeling uncomfortable about how best to proceed, the captain continued, "Yes! This is delicate, I want to explain and yet I am concerned."

Dr. Lau interrupted, "Please get to the point."

Somewhat surprised with Dr. Lau's frankness, the captain continued, "The Rear Admiral understands that John Gruneburg was in a vulnerable state and exploited and used; she knows that he was involved in a rogue operation. She has authorized me to do whatever it takes to give John Gruneburg back his life."

Once again Dr. Lau interrupted, "You said 'she', is the Rear Admiral a woman? Is she a graduate of the United States Naval Academy?"

Not really sure where this questioning would lead, the Captain once again continued, "Yes, to both questions." He sensed a feeling of acceptance from Dr. Lau and the Captain continued, "We understand that you know about John Volkov. The Office of Naval Intelligence is eliminating, deleting every record, every possible connection that John Gruneburg had to John Volkov. This next part may be hard to understand. I must stress that you and your daughter Wenli must erase from your minds the name John Volkov. He never existed. You must erase in your mind all connections to John's work with the CIA and you must learn to believe that the last two years never happened."

Dr. Lau stared at the Captain, "Are you saying that John will be cleared of all wrong doing; that he will be able to resume his life as John Gruneburg without fear of the past? Is this possible?"

Captain Haistings quickly responded, "Yes! There is much to be done, but yes, it is possible. The Rear Admiral has arranged that every possible connection to John Volkov will be eliminated. His file and records will mysteriously go blank."

Hesitating for a moment, the Captain said, "Dr. Lau, we understand that you may have an understandable mistrust of anyone trying to contact John Gruneburg, but we desperately need your assistance in contacting him." Stopping for a moment, he then continued, "The CIA did not have John Gruneburg's personal information. They do not know of the connection between John Volkov and John Gruneburg. There is no mention of John Gruneburg in the CIA case file. Do you understand what I just said? Please understand that this is confidential and Gruneburg's life is dependent on keeping it classified."

Dr. Lau looked somewhat shaken; she hesitated and then said, "I understand. How can I help you?"

Feeling a sense of relief for the first time, the Captain continued, "We are concerned that misguided efforts to contact John Gruneburg might bring up names in phone conversations or text messages that could be associated with the CIA and we do not want to be the link that connects John Gruneburg to the CIA. We do not want to take that risk. Do you understand?"

Shaking her head up and down Dr. Lau said, "I understand. I have prayed that I could delete the last two years of John Gruneburg's life. What you are telling me is almost too good to be true. I will do whatever you ask."

CHAPTER 16

Six years had passed and Monica Schmidtski was now an important member of a CIA task force that was investigating the use of social media by enemy combatants and terrorist organizations to drive their recruitment campaigns. Living comfortably in a high rise condo located on Clarendon Boulevard just a few blocks from the Rosslyn Metro Station and a short commute on the George Washington Memorial Parkway to CIA Headquarters in Langley, Virginia, Monica had settled into a secure stage in her career. Demanding as her position was, she continued to thrive on challenges, always learning; whether it was languages, new cultures, or constantly changing technology. She enjoyed interacting with her colleagues who were just as driven as she was.

It was the beginning of July. Monica and her friends had spent the weekend celebrating the Fourth of July, picnicking in Arlington Ridge Park, the location of the Marine Corps War Memorial with its famous bronze statue of five Marines and one Navy corpsman raising the American flag over Iwo Jima. Set on a hill just north of Arlington National Cemetery, across the Potomac River from the District of Columbia, the park provided a view across the National Mall, with the Lincoln Memorial, Washington Monument and United States Capitol stretching out in the distance. It was the perfect place to view the fantastic fireworks display that culminated the *Capitol Fourth Concert* that took place on the West Lawn of the United States Capitol. Celebrating America's birthday with the National Symphony Orchestra and the roar of cannons, the concert's finale was Tchaikovsky's *1812 Overture*. The concert was broadcast live on National Public Radio (NPR) as the fireworks lit the sky above the National Mall, with the park's vantage point being the best in Metro-Washington. This was

Monica's favorite time of the year and she looked forward to a fun filled summer. For her, swimming and relaxing outdoors was the perfect way to end each stress filled day.

Monica's outlet for relaxation was her membership at the Army Navy Country Club, her oasis for physical activity located on a hill southwest of the Pentagon, with its first rate aquatics and fitness facilities. Established in 1924, the Army Navy Country Club is a private facility, attracting mainly commissioned United States Military Officers from all five branches of our nation's military. The club also offers membership to certain government officials who live in Metro-Washington, making it possible for Monica to conveniently maintain her workout routine in an environment whose clientele were men and women who she admired and respected. For her, it was a privilege to enter through the club's gate and enjoy the benefits of this premier facility.

Warm summer days with late evening sunsets provided opportunities to swim laps in the fifty-meter pool and to volunteer with the club's aquatics department. Monica continued to hold on to her competitive spirit in and out of the pool, still wearing her favorite t-shirt as a pajama top that had the slogan "Eat Sleep Swim" across the back of the shirt. She was very selective about what she ate, keeping to her morning and evening exercise routines, withstanding the hectic Washington pace by continuing to stay fit, never skipping her morning habit of starting each day with a stop at the bathroom scale, proudly wearing the same size bathing suit that she wore in college.

As a volunteer and certified swim coach, Monica assisted with the instruction of the entry level swim class. The goal was to develop swimmers who would participate at the end of the summer as members of the club's four to six-year-old swim team, competing against other area clubs. These little guys and girls were filled with energy and their laughter and smiles brightened every evening swim class. Monica was especially taken by a blonde haired boy who was the tallest child in the class and very advanced for his young age, but because his fourth birthday did not occur until August 22nd he did not qualify to be enrolled as a member of the four to six-year-old swim team. Recognizing his potential, Monica volunteered to provide him with private swimming lessons to improve his stroke and breathing rhythm.

Meeting with the child's mother, Monica praised the boy's attentiveness and his willingness to listen to her instruction. They agreed on an evening schedule and little James would become Monica's protégé, with the anticipation that he would show great improvement by the end of the summer. Intrigued by the boy's blonde hair and blue eyes and his mother's dark brown hair, brown eyes and Asian features, Monica's curiosity peaked when his mother spoke to him in Chinese. Monica did not want to pry and had to restrain her analyst inquisitiveness, she just wanted to blurt out a question about who was the child's biological mother.

Controlling herself, she engaged in her first real conversation with James' mother. Beginning with a slight laugh, she said, "I must apologize. I focus so much on these young guys and girls I sometimes forget that it is not polite to keep referring to their parents as the mother of or the father of ..." Reaching out her hand she continued, "I'm Monica Schmidtski and I know you are James' mother, but I apologize, I don't remember your name."

Responding with a smile, Wenli reached out and touched Monica's hand, "I'm Wenli Gruneburg and there is no need to apologize. I appreciate that you have been concentrating on remembering the names of all these young swimmers."

Monica laughed, "They're unforgiving if you call them by the wrong name. James is a good swimmer for his age. Did he learn here at the club?"

Wenli pulled James in close and said, "No. His father taught him. We live in Annapolis and his father is on assignment this summer in Washington so we took advantage of our absentee membership at the club and I'm so glad that we did. We have really enjoyed the club's facilities."

Monica smiled, "Yes, I understand, this is like my second home throughout the summer months. So, is James' father in the military?"

Wenli recognized the subtle way that Monica asked the question and laughed, "Yes, my husband, John, is in the Navy. He attended the Naval Academy and joined the club right after graduation when the membership fee was a bargain."

Monica quickly responded, "Wow! He must be very proud of James. He has such beautiful features, especially those blue eyes." Then looking at James she said, "I should be saying you're a handsome little guy."

Wenli quickly responded, "Yes, he gets a lot of compliments and those blue eyes definitely are a testimony to his father's dominant genes. When he was handed to me at birth I could not believe how long he was and when I was feeding him and he looked up at me with those big blue eyes … we just adore this little guy" as she pulled James close.

Monica responded with a big smile and said, "He's so pleasant … and were you speaking in Chinese to James?"

Wenli laughed and said, "He's learning Mandarin Chinese." Looking at James she said "hao yoe-yong (good swimming)" and James immediately responded "she-eh-she-eh muu-cheen (thank you mother)." They all laughed and Wenli added, "He is also learning to speak French."

Monica quickly said, "Bon nage James (Good swimming James)" and James replied, "Merci Coach Schmidtski (Thank you Coach Schmidtski)." Monica responded "Wow! You are an impressive little guy!" and James responded with a smile, a giggle, and, "Merci!" They all then joined in spontaneous laughter.

Wenli then explained, "I teach Mandarin Chinese at the Naval Academy and my husband and I have been teaching James French and Chinese since he was born."

Monica quickly asked, "Do you enjoy teaching at the Naval Academy? Is it a challenge? I'm thinking that it must be more technical then conversational Chinese."

Wenli's voice became more serious, "Faculty members are dedicated, every civilian in the Languages Department has a doctoral degree and each year I've had the opportunity to teach a more advanced course. My colleagues are scholars, striving to be the best possible faculty. I started by teaching Mandarin Chinese to first year midshipmen, developing their ability to understand and speak a basic vocabulary, emphasizing pronunciation, reading and writing, practicing the structure of Chinese characters. My personal goal is to teach advanced courses that expose the midshipmen to higher levels of proficiency in spoken and written Chinese, using reading and writing assignments, studying public speeches, letters, and recorded interviews. That's the kind of challenge I'm working towards, and what makes it unique is that my colleagues and the Midshipmen, everyone is striving to be in a stretch mode. Beyond that, you're building on the knowledge and skills that midshipmen have acquired through previous Chinese courses, enhancing their reading, writing, and verbal skills to deal with problem solving and cause and effect scenarios, presenting positions and opinions on current Chinese activities."

Monica took a deep breath and said, "Wow! You really care deeply about your job. I'm impressed."

Wenli quickly interrupted, "Enough about me, I better get James into the locker room and home to bed. Will we meet at the same time tomorrow?"

Monica responded, "Yes. We'll meet at the Olympic pool. I enjoyed the conversation. Thank you for taking the time."

Wenli quickly said, "Thank you, Monica, you're the one volunteering so much of your personal time to this aquatics program. James and I appreciate your kindness." Popping James onto her lap she said, "Say thank you to Coach Schmidtski."

Waving goodbye, James said, "Thank you!" and then continued to wave as they walked toward the locker rooms.

Wenli and Monica continued to build a strong friendship, enjoying their nightly conversations. They both welcomed the opportunity to just sit and talk and Wenli valued the attention that Monica gave to James and her willingness to tolerate Wenli's long responses to what seemed at times to be Monica's endless questions. Monica treasured the time spent with Wenli, but Monica never forgot the CIA maxim to trust no one and nothing is what it seems, telling Wenli that she was employed by the Department of Defense, offering little detail about what she did. Monica's subtle questions, often simple in nature, were setting the stage for more probing discussions later on; her inquisitiveness was always driven by her analytical background.

And then there was James. Advancing to the Olympic pool was a big step. Swimming in what is called the Teaching and Youth Pool had provided a level of comfort. With its 2½ to 3½ foot depth, James was secure and accustomed to this small rectangular pool. For James, and his mother, the Olympic pool looked really big. The "L" shaped pool was impressive with its 50-meter length and six marked swimming lanes with a depth of 4 feet at the top of the "L" and 5 feet at its base, with the "L" shape providing a 25-meter length with eight lanes that went from the 5-foot depth to a 12-foot depth to accommodate the two diving springboards. This was the pride of the club's aquatics program and James was excited to be swimming in the pool where the swim team practiced and competed.

Wenli and Monica continued their conversations each evening and on one occasion Monica asked about James' father and what he was doing in Washington. Wenli responded,

"My husband is completing his law degree at the Georgetown University Law Center."

"Wow!" was Monica's quick response, "Is he a full-time student?"

Wenli laughed, "No. No. He's a part-time student. He teaches at the United States Naval Academy. As I mentioned before, we live in Annapolis and we're in Washington for the summer. My husband completed his J.D. degree from Georgetown Law this past spring."

Monica interrupted again, "What exactly is a J.D. degree?"

Wenli laughed, "It stands for Juris Doctor, the graduate degree in law that is earned when you complete law school and if you pass the bar exam you can become licensed to practice law in the state that granted you the license. My husband has continued at Georgetown to earn an LL.M. in National Security Law, and before you ask, the LL.M. stands for Master of Laws and if you know a little Latin, Legum Magister means Master of Laws in Latin. Legum is plural and the "LL" is the abbreviation for the plural of law, "laws". The main point is that his coursework in National Security Law provides a multinational perspective and very specialized legal training."

Taking a deep breath, Wenli continued, "Georgetown Law has an exceptional faculty, experts in national security law who held high level positions in the Department of Defense and other government organizations, providing limitless learning opportunities to obtain a legal education that is recognized around the world. My husband ... My husband John has been spending a lot of time writing while he has access to the law library at the Georgetown University Law Center, and the International and Comparative Law Library. While in Washington he has access to so many resources. He has been meeting with experts at the Center on National Security and the Law. They have a network of organizations engaged in all aspects of national security law, especially their contacts with government institutions and agencies and high technology companies. He has completed law courses dealing with bioterrorism, cyber security, and national security investigation and prosecution. He's now dedicating a significant amount of time writing, constructing treaties tied to potential conflicts, creating complex simulations that explore possible resolution to high-level judicial scenarios. It is a great opportunity to engage with experts in this field that goes beyond the course of study."

Laughing, Wenli said, "I must apologize. I sometimes get a little intense. I don't mean to go into a lecture."

Monica quickly interrupted, "I admire your understanding of the importance of your husband's work, and I envy the opportunities that his Georgetown education provides. I'm impressed, Wenli. I am being sincere. I am truly impressed."

Wenli laughed and said, "Enough already, I'm getting embarrassed. If John were here he would scold me for talking too much."

Wenli and Monica had established a true friendship, a bond built around James and his continued improvements in the pool. His freestyle stroke was smooth and strong and he was learning to pace his breathing rhythm with his increasing swiftness through the water. The summer was flying by.

Evenings in July in Washington can be sultry and meeting at the pool was a routine that Monica looked forward to at the end of the day. Wenli and James found solace in the comforts of the club, often spending time together reading his favorite books under the shade of a pool umbrella. James looked forward to his evening swim lessons and with each day's success the bond between Monica and James grew stronger. Wenli encouraged James to listen to Monica's instruction and the positive results built confidence, his style improved, gliding smoothly through the water almost effortlessly, swimming longer distances each week. James practiced without question and was enjoying his new found success in the big pool.

Days turned into weeks and the summer was going by fast. At the end of the evening's session Monica announced, "Next week will be the beginning of August and I think we should plan to time James' 50-meter freestyle. It will be a good benchmark to gauge his future improvements." Then, giving James a hug she said, "Are you ready for that, big guy? I think you are!"

Smiling, James turned to his mother and said, "Please ask Daddy to come. He said he would have time in August to come to the pool."

Wenli hesitated and then with a big smile said, "We'll ask him tonight." Then turning to Monica she asked, "Is it possible to do the timing later in the week?"

Monica laughed, "Whatever is convenient for you." Pulling James even closer, Monica laughed again and said, "You'll be ready, big guy." Monica then asked, "Does your husband ever come to the club?"

Wenli laughed, "Yes, of course. He played golf here with friends last week and he did the same on Tuesday morning. James and I had lunch with them on the Terrace both days. James' favorite is eating on the Terrace because everyone gives him so much attention."

Monica quickly asked, "Who does your husband play golf with? You said he has such a busy summer schedule."

Wenli laughed, "I gave him a hard time about this week's schedule; a golf course has never been my idea of a meeting venue. He's been meeting with two congressmen and the Chief Counsel for the Senate Foreign Relations Committee. He's finishing a paper on national and homeland security issues and has been working with a number of congressional committees including the Senate Select Committee on Intelligence and the House Permanent Select Committee on Intelligence."

Monica immediately responded, "Wow! How does he make those contacts? Maybe I should ask to be his caddy."

Wenli laughed and said, "It's that Georgetown connection again and he has built a solid congressional network that started when he was at the academy." Wenli laughed again "You must get weary listening to me talk about my husband all the time. Stop me if ..."

Monica quickly interrupted, "No. No. I'm interested. It's an area that I am very much interested in. Does he wear a uniform when he's meeting on the Hill?"

Wenli laughed, "You ask the most curious questions. Georgetown Law has an externship program for LL.M. students, and it has set rules; it must be a legal assignment under the direct supervision of a lawyer and students may not be paid by the host organization. Because he's not getting paid he doesn't wear his uniform, but this program has created an exciting spring and summer for John. He was fortunate to be accepted in the Office of the United States Secretary of Defense for Policy and has been assigned to the Deputy Under Secretary of Defense for Policy who is a graduate of the Georgetown University Law Center. It's an opportunity of a lifetime and that is why he's devoted his entire summer to this program. John records the details of his work in a weekly diary, which is then closely monitored for confidential information before it is submitted to the Externship Program Administrator. He has been in meetings discussing matters pertaining to the development and execution of United States national defense policy and strategy."

Monica sat in amazement, "Wow! I would really like to meet John. I think I could learn a lot. He's done things with his career that maybe I should have been doing years ago. So when do we get to meet John?"

Wenli paused for a moment and then said, "I'll talk with John this weekend and I'll let you know what is convenient for him when we meet next Monday."

Monday evening arrived and when James saw Monica he waved his arms in excitement and said, "My Daddy is coming on Wednesday! He's working in the big building at the bottom of the hill. He'll be here on Wednesday."

Wenli laughed and said, "I guess you got that message loud and clear. His Dad is just as excited as he is to see him swim in the big pool."

Wednesday evening arrived. It was a beautiful evening and James was in the pool going through his warm up routine. Looking at her phone, Wenli walked to the side of the pool and told Monica and James, "I just received a text message and James' dad just left the Pentagon and a friend will be dropping him off at the Club. He'll come directly to the Aquatics Center."

When John arrived, he immediately went to the Aquatics Center, moved through the lobby and down the steps to the Dive Inn Snack Bar that overlooked the pool. Scanning the pool, he saw Wenli standing on its edge watching James as he swam toward a young woman who was cheering him on. Focusing on Wenli, then for a long time on James, he didn't pay attention to James' swimming instructor, as she was referred to by Wenli. Then, as James approached his swimming instructor John focused on her face for the first time. He recognized the face, listened closely to the voice as she yelled praises to James, and his initial reaction was to turn and leave. Then he remembered, he was told this day may come. Working in Metro-Washington increased the odds that a chance encounter could occur. This was different. This person just spent the last four weeks coaching his son and apparently building a strong friendship with Wenli. John searched his memory, thinking about conversations with Wenli about James' swimming instructor. "Did she ever mention a name? Could this be Monica Schmidtski?" John took a deep breath and went down the steps to the side of the pool. Dressed in a light gray well tailored suit, white shirt and tie, it was not difficult to notice John as he approached Wenli.

James saw him and instantly yelled, "Hi Daddy! Thank you for coming. I'm ready to swim the length of the pool."

John approached and hugged Wenli as Monica and James swam toward the ladder on the side of the pool. Monica was looking into the evening sun, John was wearing sun glasses, and from her vantage point she saw a smiling couple, hugging and holding hands, walking towards the ladder. James quickly climbed out of the pool and John grabbed him and pulled him up into his arms.

Wenli scolded him, "John, you're getting wet."

John laughed and said, "Don't worry, it's only water." Hugging James tightly he said, "Are you sure you can swim the length of this big pool? You do know that it's 50 meters in length?"

James laughed and said, "You'll see Daddy."

As Monica approached them, John held James firmly with his left arm and removed his sunglasses with his right hand and slipped them into the front pocket of his jacket. Then, reaching out his right hand toward Monica, he said, "I'm John Gruneburg and you must be James' swimming instructor. Thank you for the many hours that you have spent with James. Wenli sings endless praises about your dedication." And then hugging James even tighter, "This big guy has been telling me about your instruction for weeks. Thank you!"

Monica reached out to shake John's hand, smiling from all his praises, finally looking into his face, making eye contact for the first time. Her immediate response was a gasp, rubbing her eyes, "Possibly it was the glare from the sun". She felt as though she had seen a ghost.

Wenli noticed the look on Monica's face and asked, "Monica! Are you alright?"

Monica immediately regained her composure and asked, "You look familiar, have we met before?" She cleared her throat and said, "Please let me start over" and once again reaching out her hand she continued, "I'm Monica Schmidtski and I know you're James' father, or Daddy as James would say. I have enjoyed spending time with him in the pool and your wife, Wenli, has become my very best summertime friend." Reaching out and running her fingers through James' hair, Monica then continued, "This big guy has been a joy. He listens, learns so fast, retains everything. He wants to show you how well he swims the length of this pool."

Monica hesitated. Now under complete control of her emotions, she continued, "You do look familiar. Have we possibly met before?"

John responded, "I'm not sure, possibly in meetings at the Pentagon? Are you a student at the Georgetown University Law Center?"

Monica stared, closely examining John's facial features, listening to his voice, trying to remember. "Is my mind playing tricks on me?" Then shaking her head from side to side, still in deep thought, she answered, "No-ooo".

Sensing that Monica was still searching for a connection, John thought it was best to change the focus of the conversation as he continued, "I spend a lot of time at the Naval Academy. Hesitating for a moment, John asked, "What exactly do you do? Where are you currently assigned? Are you in the military?"

Monica immediately felt uncomfortable about John's questions and did not want to discuss her position at the CIA. She quickly changed the subject saying, "Sometimes I ask too many questions. Will you be getting into the pool, joining James in his warm up swim?"

John laughed and said, "Today, I'm just a spectator, here to see this big guy make some waves."

Monica smiled and said, "Well James, we better get back in the pool and finish our warm up routine." As John placed James down on the pool deck Monica continued, "It is a pool rule that young guys like James must be accompanied and closely monitored by an adult swimmer while they are in this pool. So I'll be swimming the side stroke in the lane next to James, staying close to him for the entire length of the pool. Will you and Wenli do the timing? I have two stop watches."

John responded with a clap of his hands and said to James, "Are you ready big guy? We're going to time you." John was very impressed as James glided through the water, his stroke had improved so much over these few short weeks, and his breathing rhythm was perfect. Monica's instruction certainly achieved more than he ever expected. He noticed how she watched his every move while they were in the pool and how comfortable James was with her instruction and praises, happily returning her hugs when she praised him.

After the timing was completed and endless congratulations were given to James for his extraordinary 50-meter swim and to Monica for her superb instruction, the question was once again asked by Monica, "Are the two of you going to join us in the pool?"

John responded laughing, "Not today, but I will come to the pool tomorrow afternoon and I will race this big guy. I understand that Wenli invited you to dinner this evening. It's a perfect night to sit on the Grille's terrace and enjoy a beautiful sunset as we refuel this big guy. Does that sound like a plan, James?"

After quick showers and changing into casual clothing, Monica, Wenli and James joined John in the lobby of the Aquatics Center and they walked the short distance across the parking lot to the main Clubhouse. The food was enjoyable and the early conversation continued to focus on James and his improved swimming and endless appreciation for Monica's successful instruction.

When there was a break in the conversation, Wenli asked John, "Since you will be joining us at the pool tomorrow afternoon, will you come for lunch?"

John quickly responded, "Yes, I have good news. I finished up at the Pentagon today. They signed off on everything."

Wenli clapped her hands and said, "That is not good news, that is great news! Did you hear that James? Your Daddy will no longer have to spend his days, nights and weekends at the law library? We get your Daddy back, James. Everyone clapped and laughed and then John continued, "I meet with the Externship Program Administrator tomorrow morning at the Georgetown University Law Center and I'll complete my summer coursework Friday morning. I'm on schedule to graduate at the end of the fall semester."

Monica had grown close to Wenli and James and being part of this evening's celebration was special. Throughout the evening she found herself staring at John, searching her memory, listening to his voice, trying to confirm her suspicion that the person sitting across from her was John Volkov. "Was her mind playing tricks on her? Was it just a strong resemblance and her imagination was getting the best of her? Were her emotions overriding her analytical skills?" Then, she knew the answer to her mystery. Tomorrow afternoon will provide the answer; she will look for the scars on the back of his right shoulder.

That evening after James finally got to bed, John asked Wenli to come sit with him. They were away from James' bedroom and John started talking in a whisper.

Wenli immediately asked, "Why are you whispering?"

John put his forefinger in front of his lips as a sign of silence and whispered, "Please just listen."

Wenli became silent and John continued, "I know Monica from my time with the CIA. She was the woman who got me out of Ukraine, probably saved my life with her quick actions in Vienna and Paris. She definitely thought that she recognized me. We need to be careful. Have you ever talked with her about my past?"

Wenli hesitated, "Oh my, she has asked so many questions, but no, we never talked about your past or even where we met. We have talked about law school and your present assignment; what I do at the Academy."

John asked, "Did she ever say where she is assigned?"

Wenli hesitated and then said, "At the Department of Defense. She gave very little detail about her work or where she works, James always seemed to be her focus. What do we do?"

John sighed, "We go on as before. We must be careful not to show any emotion. Continue your friendship and conversations. Be careful if she starts asking questions about my past, our past ... stay current, keep James as the focus. There was always the possibility ... this was eventually going to happen, I just never expected it to be like this."

As soon as Monica walked into her condo she went straight to her laptop, googled John Gruneburg, searching for clues. She found nothing. Thinking, she regretted that she always followed CIA policy. She did not have personal photos of John Volkov. She searched her files with no results, finally going to bed, thinking that her question would be answered tomorrow.

The next day at the pool, as soon as Wenli saw Monica she laughed and said, "I told John that he better use a lot of sun screen. This is the first time that he has been swimming this summer and with his fair skin and this strong evening sun it might present the right combination for sunburn." Continuing to laugh she joked, "John, your pale body is certainly a testimony to the many hours you spent in the library this summer."

Sitting at pool side, Monica waited in anticipation for John to remove his shirt, expecting to see, wanting to see, scars on the back of his right shoulder. The scars that she would never forget. The scars would confirm her suspicions that this was indeed John Volkov. The waiting was beginning to antagonize her, when almost unexpectedly John stood up, removed his shirt and walked to the edge of the pool. Monica stared. She was astonished. She was certain that she would see a scarred back, and yet there was nothing, not even a sign of a scratch, just smooth skin on a muscular back. "How can this be?" was her immediate thought.

Later that evening, once again enjoying dinner at the Grille's terrace, Wenli and Monica reminisced about the summer. John mostly sat in silence, thinking, knowing deep down that this day would eventually come. He thought, "It was inevitable that someday they would meet, but he never expected it to be under these circumstances. This was certainly a surprise."

James reached over to Wenli and whispered something to her. Wenli cleared her throat and said, "Please excuse us for a short time, James and I will be back shortly."

John laughed and said, "Do you want me to take him?" and then looking at James said, "Daddy is proud of you big guy!"

Wenli quickly responded, "We've been using the child care center so everything is the appropriate height. Please continue your conversation, we'll be back soon. I know exactly where to go."

As Wenli and James walked away, Monica leaned forward to talk to John. She so much wanted to talk with him about her experiences over the past few days, how he resembled someone she knew, but the moment never seemed to present itself. Finally, alone at the table, she started by saying how she cherished her friendship with Wenli and James, how she so much enjoyed their nightly conversations, then she hesitated. Monica was remembering, never forget the CIA maxim to trust no one and nothing is what it seems. Should she continue? Then she said to John, "Do you recall when we met yesterday and I asked if we had met before? I told you that you looked familiar. You very much resemble someone I knew. I once had a colleague who was a true friend, someone I admired. Our work required a certain level of discretion. It was sometimes dangerous. We were on a mission and I faced a situation where I thought it would be safer … I thought if we stayed together it would be dangerous for both of us, more dangerous than if we separated. It was even suggested by a Director … that doesn't matter … the bottom line is that I am here today and he is not. He didn't make it. At least that's the way it was reported. I have asked myself many times, did I abandon him? Did I put my own safety ahead of my responsibility to bring him in safely? I have felt guilt, real heart breaking guilt, would he be alive today? Did I put him at risk, was my main concern ... was it for my own safety, or did I follow protocol and make the right decision? I have had to live with that decision and possibly ... no probably, someone else suffered the consequences for the decision I made."

Monica hesitated for a moment. John was sitting in silence, listening intently, and then she continued, "I have helped others work through flashbacks and nightmares, common symptoms of post traumatic stress disorder, individuals who suffered from emotional anxiety. I can recognize the symptoms immediately. A few years ago," She stopped in mid sentence, hesitated and then continued, "It was a rainy weekend and in the evening I turned on the television, checked out a number of channels and finally settled on a James Taylor concert that was a fund raising event on the local Public Broadcasting Station. It was funny. I remembered seeing James Taylor on *Sesame Street* as a child. I listened, just relaxing, and then he sang this song. It was somewhat familiar, but not something I had heard on a regular basis, and then I heard the line, "But I always thought that I'd see you again." He sang a few more lines and again it was repeated. Then it hit me, I was feeling survivor's guilt. I expected to see my colleague again, but it never happened. Then the words came ... "Thought I'd see you, thought I'd see you" ... and then they were repeated. I was not hearing any other lyric, just those words. I sat almost in a trance, blocking everything out, and I realized that my perception was that I had done something wrong by surviving when he did not. I had a classic case of survivor's guilt. My self-diagnosis was correct and I got professional help. I needed help to talk this through. It was necessary for my psychological health." Monica hesitated and then she said, "Do you understand? You look like that person. When I saw your face for the first time

I had a flashback. I thought I was seeing him. You must think that I'm crazy."

John quickly interrupted and said, "It's alright Monica, I understand." John waited. There was a long silence. He was weighing his options and for the moment silence seemed to be his only option. Monica sat looking at John and he knew she expected a response. Finally, he took a deep breath and she immediately sat up, as if she was waiting to listen. Another deep breath and then he said, "I recently read an article about "The Road Not Taken," the famous poem by Robert Frost. I think the article was in the *New York Post*. It explained how many readers believe the poem encourages us to follow our individual dreams, to promote independent thinking, but that is not the point of the poem. The basis for understanding the meaning of the poem is to read the entire last five lines and not to concentrate on just the last three lines. It is important to listen to the words ... "telling this with a sigh, somewhere ages hence" ... it is looking back on life's choices, remembering with a "sigh," second guessing what might have been. Reflecting on our choices, using hindsight to look back, recognizing the reality that we must live with the choices that we have made, and the key is to read the entire last five lines and not to concentrate on just the last three lines."

John stopped for a moment and then he recited the last five lines of the poem.

> *I shall be telling this with a sigh*
> *Somewhere ages and ages hence:*
> *Two roads diverged in a wood, and I –*
> *I took the one less traveled by,*
> *And that has made all the difference.*

John paused for a moment and then said, "It is easy to be a *Monday Morning Quarterback*, when all the tough decisions were already made in the heat of the moment. It is so tempting to pass judgment after the fact, to point out alternatives. We make choices in life, we do our best, and we must have the courage to live with those choices, and learn; learn from our successes as well as our mistakes."

John hesitated for a moment and then said, "If you would not have made the decision that you made, maybe you wouldn't be here today. Monica, you made the right decision."

As John was finishing his sentence Wenli and James were approaching the table and seeing them John said, "Is the big guy getting ready to say good night?"

As they left, Monica thought out loud, "He seemed to understand. When he said I made the right decision, he said it with such certainty, he really seemed to understand."

That evening and throughout the next day John thought about his conversation with Monica and he knew that somehow he needed to tell her more. Thinking about what he should do, it suddenly came to him and with a smile he thought, "It's the right thing to do."

Just four miles west of Rosslyn on the Lee Highway is a little piece of transplanted Germany called the Heidelberg Pastry Shoppe. Opened in 1975, it was the dream of Wolfgang Büchler to establish a European style bakery in the Washington area. Recreating the delicacies of Heidelberg, Germany, Wolfgang's specialties included Sacher torte, a dense chocolate cake with almonds, apricot jam and marzipan filling, and covered with dark chocolate truffle. Another favorite was the apple raisin strudel with its paper thin pastry.

Wenli told John that the Heidelberg Pastry Shoppe was Monica's regular Saturday morning stop for what she referred to as her old world indulgence. Allowing for one morning of excessive calorie intake was a tradition that dated back to her first assignment in Europe.

Arriving just before eight, John parked on Culpeper Street just off the Lee Highway and waited for Monica's arrival. Just a few minutes later a two door black Jeep Wrangler pulled into Heidelberg's parking lot and John watched as Monica walked to the bakery and entered through the front door. John's plan was simple, but it relied on Monica's professionalism, her discipline and control, regardless of the situation. Entering the shoppe, John took a number and moved forward stopping just behind Monica as she scanned the assortment of pastries in the display case. Leaning forward John softly said, "I understand that this is your Saturday morning tradition. Is the quality comparable to Europe? Possibly even Vienna. If so, I would recommend the apple strudel or the Sacher torte and if it is too difficult to choose it is best to take both. Do you remember having to make such a decision?"

Monica turned and saw John moving away from her and before she could speak he was out the door. She smiled. Shaking her head back and forth, softly saying, "If anyone could have survived I knew it would be him." And then she remembered, he once said, "Remember, Monica, you are the only person that I know so who else can I trust?"

Monica knew that she would never see John Volkov again and she had learned a secret about John Gruneburg that she must take to her grave. It was just the way it was, but she would miss John Volkov just the same.